RED CITY REAPER

Book 0 - Dead in Red City*
Book 1 - A Shot For Death - March 26, 2024
Book 1.5 - Death Uncaged - March 21, 2024
Book 2 - Death Orders a Double* - June 25, 2024
Book 3 - Death on the Rocks*
Book 4 - Death with a Twist*

*Forthcoming
Titles and release dates may be subject to change.

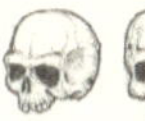

A SHOT FOR DEATH

AN EXILED GRIM REAPER URBAN FANTASY
NOVEL

RED CITY REAPER
BOOK 1

C. THOMAS LAFOLLETTE

A SHOT FOR DEATH
C. Thomas Lafollette

A Broken World Publication
13820 NE Airport Way
Suite #K395495
Portland, OR 97251-1158
A Shot For Death
Copyright © 2024 by C. Thomas Lafollette
ISBN 978-1-960766-08-3 (ebook);
ISBN 978-1-960766-09-0 (paperback)

Cover Design: Ravven
Edited by: Suzanne Lahna
Copy Editing & Proofreading: Amy Cissell

CONTENTS

Author's Note	ix
Chapter 1	1
Chapter 2	7
Chapter 3	13
Chapter 4	19
Chapter 5	23
Chapter 6	29
Chapter 7	37
Chapter 8	45
Chapter 9	53
Chapter 10	57
Chapter 11	65
Chapter 12	71
Chapter 13	75
Chapter 14	83
Chapter 15	93
Chapter 16	101
Chapter 17	109
Chapter 18	117
Chapter 19	125
Chapter 20	127
Chapter 21	133
Chapter 22	137
Chapter 23	143
Chapter 24	149
Chapter 25	153
Chapter 26	157
Chapter 27	161
Chapter 28	165
Chapter 29	179
Chapter 30	191
Chapter 31	197
Chapter 32	205
Chapter 33	209
Chapter 34	215

Chapter 35   221
Chapter 36   223
Chapter 37   229
Chapter 38   235
Chapter 39   239
Chapter 40   245
Epilogue   249
The Red City Reaper Rides Again in   253
Contents   261
Glossary   263

Newsletter   265
Acknowledgments   267
About the Author   269
Also by C. Thomas Lafollette   271

To My FAKA Friends
The best writing group ever!

AUTHOR'S NOTE

This story contains words and phrases in Louisiana Creole and Haitian Kreyòl. They are spelled according to Creole and Kreyòl standards.

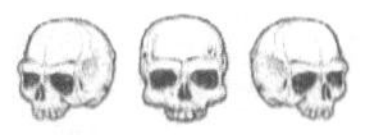

ONE

DAX

Dax leaned against the scarred wooden bar top, looking over the sparse mid-morning crowd. Each time the front door opened, the knots between his shoulder blades clenched tighter. Until he'd become a human, he'd never known the annoyance and discomfort of physical responses to emotions. Something had felt off since he'd parked his motorcycle, something that was all too familiar. Something dark.

Death was present everywhere all the time, especially in a place like Red City. But today, something about the constant undercurrent niggled at the back of his mind. Every time someone came or went, a whiff of a frayed life thread entered, teasing him, taunting him.

He checked his watch. Tomi was late, which was unlike him. His bar manager and friend was one of the most reliable people he knew. Dax swallowed nervously and pulled in a deep breath through his nose, breathing slowly so as not to make noise. Even concentrating on every detail, he couldn't sort it out, he couldn't identify where the thread came from, went, or to whom it belonged. He figured that if it belonged to someone he knew well, it would be easier to find the owner. At least, that's what he hoped. He stopped a frustrated grunt from escaping his lips. Still nothing.

With a quick scan down the bar to distract himself, he pushed off and strolled to the balding white patron at the end of the bar. "Can I get you another round, Bill?"

"Yeah. I got one more in me," Bill replied, slugging down the last swallow before sliding the glass the short distance toward Dax.

Setting the glass by the sink, he grabbed a clean pint glass and filled it with Pabst before setting it in front of Bill. Four dollars were already waiting on the bar. Dax grabbed them, dropped one in the tip bucket, and deposited the other three into the till.

A gust of cold, moist air and another hit of impending darkness blasted through the freshly opened door. He whipped his head around to the front. Still no Tomi. Ginger, one of his morning regulars, shivered for a second then proceeded into the bar. He liked Ginger as much as any of his regulars, but the disappointment of not seeing his friend added to his discomfort.

Dax's worry compounded. His manager was never late. Well… rarely. But never forty-five minutes late, and certainly not without calling.

"I didn't expect to see you in today, Ginger," Dax said. "What can I get you?"

Ginger ran a hand through his shaggy, wet red hair, flinging away some of the accumulated rain. "Hadn't planned on it, but got home after work, and the heat's out in the fucking building. The super has no idea when it'll be back on." Ginger hung his coat up on the hook under the bar.

Dax pushed off the bar and turned toward the glassware. "That's unfortunate. The usual?"

"Yeah, the usual." Ginger turned toward Bill, running a hand through his damp hair again. "Hey, Bill."

Bill chucked his chin toward Ginger. "Yo, Ginger."

Dax grabbed a bucket glass and poured in a heavy shot of Jim Beam then filled a half pint for the beer back. After he set it down, he refilled his coffee from the carafe on the counter, cradling the cup in both hands to warm them as he leaned up against the back bar. After he felt it had cooled enough, he took a sip and made a face.

"Gack," he tossed the coffee into the sink then followed it with the rest from the carafe. He couldn't tell if it was just bad coffee or the increasingly bad mood he found himself in as he tried to home in on the sense of death. He couldn't even tell if it had happened or was only the potential of future events. He used to be so much more in tune with the threads of life and death—before his exile. Before being forced to live as a human.

Bill laughed. "You've got to get better coffee."

Dax scowled. "It's fine when it's fresh."

"Do your taste buds work, bro?" Ginger asked. "Even fresh, it tastes like shit."

Shaking his head, Dax shrugged. "If you want good hot beverages, I'll make you tea. Coffee is just wake up juice."

"You can keep your hot leaf juice," Ginger replied, with a coarse laugh.

Bill chuckled along, nodding at his friend down at the other end of the bar. "It's cold as fuck out there. Get some better coffee. I might want a Spanish coffee sometime."

Dax narrowed his eyes and looked between the two men. Coffee cocktails would be an up charge compared to their usual PBRs. He'd have to talk it over with Tomi, if he ever showed up. Looking up at the clock, the ball of tension in his gut tightened further. An hour late.

Movement out of the corner of his eye drew his attention. A tall, fat black man stepped out of the hall leading from the back of the bar. He'd shucked his coat in the office already, but the black beanie he wore glistened with rain. Dax sighed in relief, his shoulders dropping but only fractionally.

"Sorry, boss. Had to help my mama with something this morning, and she insisted on making me breakfast." He shrugged. "You know you can't say no to her when she insists on offering food."

Dax nodded. "No worries. How is your mama?"

"The same. But when does she ever change?" Tomi washed his hands in the sink before drying them off. "Looks like I missed the morning rush."

"You didn't. This is it. If you can handle this unruly crowd, I'm going to head to the bank." He'd hoped Tomi's arrival would alleviate his sense of dread, but not only did it linger, it had intensified. Even with Tomi's presence, he couldn't discount him as a possibility. He still couldn't figure out why his sense of death was vibrating his awareness nor where it was intersecting his own life thread.

"Have fun. It's nasty out there."

Dax grunted and stepped into the hall and down to the office, pulling his keys from his pocket. After he threw on his black leather coat and a scarf, he opened the safe and pulled out the deposits from yesterday. His brow furrowed. The envelope was much thinner than he'd have preferred. Though this bar had never made a robust revenue in the years since he and Tomi opened it, he'd hoped things would pick up some. At least they kept enough money coming in to keep the employees paid, the bank off their backs, and enough left over to keep a roof over his head, barely. Stuffing the deposits into the custom zipper pocket inside his coat, he padlocked the pocket closed. He grabbed his helmet and pulled it over his shoulder-length black hair.

He pushed through the back door, shoving it closed, and paused under the awning in the alley. The rain had picked up since he'd opened this morning. It poured off the awning in rivers. Sticking his pale white hand out, he let the cold, late winter rain wash over it. An involuntarily shiver ran through him. At least it washed some of the stink of the alley away.

He sighed. "I need to get a car."

Inhaling deeply, he narrowed his eyes. The hint of death lingered. He shook his head, frustrated with his inability to track it. Being a human definitely hampered his former strength. About to close the visor of his helmet, he stopped when he thought he heard something. Looking down and to the left, he almost missed the movement in the shadows.

"Mew." A tiny kitten stepped out of a half-soaked box—the awning provided protection to part of it—but the rain was quickly winning the battle as it seeped into the rest of the cardboard.

In the dark gloom of the rainy day, the black kitten looked like a smudge. Pursing his lips, Dax squatted down. The kitten looked curious but stayed back. Holding out his hand, he left it hanging until the kitten approached and sniffed his fingers. He gave it a scratch under the chin. The kitten gave a half-hearted purr then shuffled back toward his box, looking over his shoulder before disappearing into its shadows. Was it the kitten's life thread?

Shrugging, he flipped down his visor and walked to the end of the long awning and mounted the big, custom chopper motorcycle. Kicking it to life, it rumbled loudly, adding its sound to the rain and the few cars moving down the street. He joined traffic and headed toward Redemption City First National Bank. Fortunately, they had a parking garage nearby, so he didn't have to park in the rain.

After he made his deposits, he slipped into a nearby coffee shop, picked up a proper cup, and sat down to warm up. Bill and Red were right. The coffee he served was shit. He'd have to get something better. When he finished, he tugged his helmet on and darted outside to run toward the parking garage. He really needed to get a car if he was going to make it another winter in Red City.

TWO

DAX

Dax hoped Tomi had the inventory finished before he returned to the bar so he could call in his order to his beer distributor and the liquor store. If the bar was still dead, he wanted to get his tasks finished and head home. Tomi could have the bar for the day.

After parking under the awning, he glanced toward the box. The kitten raised its head then returned it to its paws as it curled into a ball. He narrowed his eyes, wondering and worrying about where the kitten's mother was. Sighing, Dax headed into the bar and shucked his coat, shaking the excess water off it before hanging it in the office along with his helmet.

When he popped his head into the bar, the same handful of people were exactly where he'd left them. Without a word, Tomi handed him the clipboard. Nodding, he returned to the office and closed the door, turning on the small space heater. He tossed the clipboard onto the desk and sat down. As he ran his eyes over the pages, he realized he hadn't assimilated any of the information.

He looked toward the door and sighed. Standing, he slipped out of the back and propped it open with a brick. He squatted down next to the box and folded the flap back, revealing the kitten within. It lifted its head and gave a weak "mew." He gently laid his hand on the kitten's back, closed his eyes, and reached out.

Tracing the thin tendrils backwards, he felt only severed connections and death. Even the largest of the threads led back to nothingness. Pulling back his awareness, he pushed forward this time but only found a short, fraying thread that ended abruptly… If he did nothing.

He shook his head and scooped up the kitten. It felt like nothing but skin and bones. Wrapping his awareness around the kitten, he found a few fleas eking out a meager existence on the poor kitten. As he homed in on them, he clipped the threads tying them to life. Once the last tiny life winked out, he pulled the brick out of the door and stepped in, letting it close behind him as he returned to the office. Holding the kitten, he stared around the office, wondering what to do. His eyes settled on the stack of sixteen-ounce cans he kept for back stock.

With one hand, he took out the four six-packs of tallboys from their cardboard flat and tossed the shallow cardboard tray onto the floor. Then he grabbed a package of bar towels, peeled off the wrapper, and wadded up the towels into the bottom of the flat. Once he had what looked like a good nest built, he grabbed another bar towel, carefully dried the kitten off, and set it in the box, covering it with a towel. Finally, his eyes settled on the space heater, so he turned it to face the box.

While the kitten snuggled into its box, he pulled up a browser on the computer and looked for the nearest pet store. When he found one between the bar and his apartment, he sent the address to his phone, then called in his orders to his vendors. He'd never had a pet before. He wasn't sure if he'd keep the sad ball of fluff, but he couldn't let it die on his stoop. It felt too soon to send the little orphan on to join his mother and siblings who'd already crossed the veil.

When he finished the few last pieces of paperwork for the day, he pulled on his leather coat then scooped up the kitten in a towel, stuffing him into the same pocked he'd stashed his bank deposit in, though he didn't zip it all the way. The kitten didn't seem interested in fighting. It wiggled around for a few seconds then settled into a ball. A faint purr vibrated just under Dax's chest as he walked out front.

"Tomi, I'm heading home. Call me if the things get busy." The speech had disturbed the kitten who wiggled around before resettling.

"You…uh…got an alien about to burst through your chest there, boss?" Tomi smirked, gesturing toward Dax with his head.

Dax pursed his lips and shrugged. "Don't worry about it. Office is locked." Then he pointed at Bill and Ginger. "And I'll get some better coffee."

" 'Bout time," Ginger mumbled before throwing back the rest of his Jim Beam.

Dax turned and raised his middle finger before disappearing down the hall. He grabbed his helmet and scarf, putting them on quickly before stepping back into the frigid pissing rain. When he sat on his bike, he checked the alley's exit to see if it was clear, noting a sedan parked in front of the convenience store across the street. He patted his pockets looking for his keys but came up empty. As he dismounted, a shot cracked out from across the street, spraying cinder block shards from the wall.

A second shot sounded, and pain exploded in his chest near his right shoulder. The shot knocked him off balance as he tottered backwards, slipping on the wet concrete of the alley. A third shot whizzed over his head, grazing his helmet before it smacked into the ground. Stars exploded across his visor like an IMAX astronomy show except with far greater detail and clarity.

Through the fog of his ringing ears, he heard tires spin out, rubber screeching against wet pavement. Behind him, the back door squealed open. He needed to remember to get some silicon lubricant for it. The mundane thought made him laugh.

"Ow! Knock it off, you little shit," he mumbled as the kitten growled and dug in his claws.

"You OK, boss?" Tomi said quietly.

Groaning, he lifted his visor and pushed himself to sitting then patted his chest over the kitten. "Calm."

The hand seemed to steady the puny kitten as he settled back into a still lump on his chest. He jolted up as Tomi scooped him up under the shoulders, sending blinding agony radiating from the gunshot wound.

"Fuck!"

"Shit, did they hit you?" Tomi asked, nearly dropping him in the hurry to stop causing his boss pain. "Man, I'm sorry. Fuck."

He knew his friend would feel bad for hurting him—Tomi was a pretty gentle guy—but right now, all he could focus on was the pain. Dax staggered to the other side of the alley, propping his good, left arm against the wall to stabilize himself. He wasn't in danger of falling over, but the rain cascaded over him, seeking out any dryness he had left.

Bill poked his head out the door. "Should we call the cops or an ambulance?"

Pushing off the wall, Dax waved him off with his left hand. "No. I just landed funny on my shoulder. Let's leave the fucking authorities out of this. They cause more problems than they solve."

Bill snorted. "Need a belt of whiskey, then? I'll go grab one for ya."

Tomi pointed aggressively at the bald white man. "Hey. You stay away from my side of the bar, you hear me?"

Raising his hands in the air and backing away, Bill winked. "I'll be good. I'm just going to go back and nurse my Pabst."

Once the door shut, Dax sagged back into the wall, letting it prop him up. "You better go make sure they don't decide to serve themselves while we're out here."

"You sure, boss? You don't look too steady."

Not wanting to worry Tomi too much, Dax pushed off the wall and stumbled before righting himself. The kitten, apparently not liking being tossed around in his secret hideaway, squirmed before letting off a weak growl.

"What the hell's moving around inside your coat, Dax?" Tomi crossed his arms and stared at the lump moving around inside the leather coat.

Leaving his right arm dangling, he carefully unzipped his coat, then dropped the pocket's zipper a couple inches. The kitten shoved his head out of the gap and hissed.

"Hush, you." Dax tapped it gently on its nose.

With a final grumpy growl, the kitten pulled its head back in and settled down again.

"What are you doing with a kitten?"

Dax shrugged, hissing and wincing at the pain in his right shoulder. He reached across his body and touched his shoulder, drawing back a bloody hand running thin from the rain.

"Shit, you did get shot," Tomi said.

"It didn't hit anything vital. I'll be fine. You know that." He'd been shot before, but he found he was still annoyed by it, bordering on pissed off. Perhaps the reason he couldn't find the source of the thread flirting with death was because it was his. He'd been distracted by the kitten, thinking it might have been the tiny creature's line intersecting with his. He'd think about it later.

Tomi furrowed his brows, his lips drawing into a thin line across his face. "Whatever you say—"

They perked up at the distant sound of sirens.

Dax shook his head, wincing. "Looks like someone around here still has hope Johnny Lawless will do something." He sighed. "I'd better get out of here before they arrive. You know the drill if they come in."

"Yeah. You know the regulars do, too. Nobody heard or saw anything." Tomi scowled briefly before fishing his keys out of his pocket.

"Tomi," Dax called to halt his manager. "Can you grab my keys off the desk and hand them out to me?"

The Black man nodded, ducked inside, then reappeared a couple moments later and handed the keys to his boss. "You better hurry up."

He nodded and took his first steps carefully as water sluiced down the alley toward the gutters running nearly bank full alongside the sidewalk. He straddled the motorcycle and kicked it to life, cursing as the vibrations rattled his bones and jarred the wound. For the third time that day, he wished he drove a car. A nice, easy automatic that he wouldn't have to shift.

Flipping down his visor, he reached out with his right arm and wrapped his fingers around the grip on the handlebar. The movement brought tears to his eyes as he gritted his teeth through the pain. The ride home was going to be hell.

THREE

DAX

By the time Dax made it home through the cold wet streets of Redemption City, he was exhausted and on the verge of passing out from the pain of gripping a handlebar and navigating through traffic. After he stashed the chopper in the secured parking garage, he staggered over to the elevator. A handwritten "Out of Service" note stared back at him like a giant middle finger.

Growling, he pushed the button, willing to risk a plummet on the odd chance it worked. Nothing. He stifled a string of profanities and made his way to the stairs. It was only a four-story building, but after being shot, each step felt like Everest.

He groaned when he opened the door to the fourth floor and stumbled out, bouncing off the opposite wall. Keeping his left hand out, he trailed it along the wall in case he needed to catch himself. Once he arrived at his door, he fished his keys out and fumbled with them before finally getting his less coordinated hand to slide the key home.

He slipped in the door and awkwardly removed his helmet one-handed just in time to avoid whichever busybody had opened their door to see what the staggering noise was. They probably just thought he was drunk. He dropped the helmet with a heavy plastic thud.

The bathroom. He needed to get to the bathroom and its easy-to-clean tile floor. After he shut the door behind him, he pulled a dry towel from the rack and made a little wad in the tub on the opposite side of the drain. Unzipping his coat and the inner pocket, he waited for the kitten to pop its head out then snagged it with his left hand, prying it out of the warm pocket.

The kitten didn't protest too much when he set it down in the towel, but instead of making a nest, it investigated the tub. It was safe for now. Even as small as it was, it was too big to slide under the door, even if it climbed out of the tub.

Groaning, Dax turned around and nearly fell into the mirror above the long vanity. He propped his left hand against the mirror and stared at his own pale white sweaty face, a drop of perspiration dangling from the end of his prominent eagle-like beak nose. He let it fall into the sink, unable to wipe it with the right hand and unwilling to risk face-planting into the mirror if he relinquished his stability against it.

He needed to shift. He tried to pull in his other form, but it didn't come. It was almost tangible, but something tethered him to his corporeal body. Closing his eyes, he concentrated and tried to separate his other self from his façade.

The sweat on his face intensified as he grimaced through the pain. Focusing inward, he followed the tendrils of the deeper agony of being unable to transform. They followed parallel with the thrumming of the wound. As he stretched and tried to peel this body away from his flesh, he found the source.

The bullet.

The tether was thin, tenuous. It wouldn't take much to snap it. Taking a deep breath, he grunted and slid his awareness next to the bullet, then gripped the tendril tying him to the flesh of his body and pushed outward, anchoring himself between the bullet and his grip on the tendril.

Straining, he nearly gave up. But as the thread frayed, he poured more strength in until it snapped. The sudden release nearly floored him. The only thing keeping him upright was the vanity locking his knees upright and the friction of his hand stuck to the mirror. He breathed through the jolt of red-hot agony the snap caused.

When the corners of his vision returned from the nearly faded out blackness, he reached for his other self and found it unencumbered. The flesh of his body disappeared into the aether where he stored it when it wasn't in use.

Without flesh to hold it in place, the bullet dropped, bouncing off his ribs but staying contained within the confines of his clothing, though his pants threatened to slide down without an ass and hips to hold them in place. Each time the bullet touched his bones, it sent a searing flash of pain through him. When it scraped down his femur then bounced off his tibia into his fibula, he almost fell backwards. Finally, it came to a stop inside his motorcycle boots, resting against the bones of his heel.

Stumbling backwards, he sat awkwardly on the edge of the tub and nearly slipped backward into it but halted himself with a bony-fingered grip on the porcelain-covered cast iron. Once he stabilized, he reached down and pulled the boot off, turning it upside down. The bullet plinked to the floor and rolled in a semi-circle. It left an arc of blood where it'd rolled.

The relief of removing the bullet from his body was instant, like a cold beer on a summer day. His fleshless ribs expanded and contracted more out of habit than any need to fill lungs that weren't there. He straightened, his vertebrae popping as he rolled his back straight. His bare skull and empty eye sockets stared back at him from the mirror.

"Mew."

He startled. During his struggle with his body and the bullet, he'd forgotten the kitten. Behind him, the kitten stretched up, swatting at the chain connecting his wallet to his belt. Reaching down, he scratched the scrawny kitten's neck with the tip of his finger bones. The kitten leaned into it, purring.

You are lucky I found you or you would be a dead kitten —Mortuus Catulus, Dax thought, projecting it into the kitten's brain. He laughed, the sound raspy and breathless. *Morty.*

Standing, he pulled off his leather coat and found the hole, sticking his finger through it. He set it aside and stripped off the rest of his sopping clothes, throwing them into the shower so the blood wouldn't stain the floor. When he was fully naked, nothing but bones, he put his flesh back on, wincing in pain.

He turned to look in the mirror. The wound was still there, though it looked like it had mostly closed up. It should be gone. Looking down, he stared at the bullet. He'd been shot before, but never like this. All he'd had to do was shed his flesh and let the bullet drop, and he'd been nearly good as new. It had never been a struggle to slip out of his mortal face before.

Squatting, he inspected the bullet. Scratches drew his eye. They didn't look like the normal striated action marks on a fired bullet. Taking a deep breath, he reached out, hovering over it before grasping it between his forefinger and thumb. Even through his flesh, he could feel the tug of the bullet, though it was only a dull, tingling sensation seeking to find a way through his defenses.

He stood and rinsed it off in the sink. Holding it in the light, he turned it slowly. There were marks engraved on it. They appeared to be runes, but he wasn't an expert. It looked like the striations had scratched through some of the marks. He'd need to find someone to tell him what the marks meant.

"Mew!"

He set the bullet down beside the sink and turned around, placing his hands on his hips. "What am I going to do with you?"

The kitten tried to jump up to the ledge of the tub but slipped on the smooth porcelain, sliding down the edge to land in a heap. It was hard to see through the grime, but it looked like he had a white chin and chest. As scrawny as he was, food would need to be a priority. He grumbled and pulled out his first aid kit and cleaned and dressed his wound.

"I guess I'm going to have to go back outside, my little fuzzy friend." He shut the shower door and pulled the bathroom door closed behind him. The kitten couldn't get up to much mischief locked in the bathroom.

He pulled on some dry clothes and grabbed a bullet hole free coat from the closet. Before he closed the door, he grabbed an umbrella and a large backpack. He'd brave the bus. It'd be drier and easier to bring home supplies than on his motorcycle. Patting his pockets and finding them empty, he returned to the bathroom and grabbed his wallet and cellphone. He had a message alert.

Tomi had sent a text containing a single question mark.

Dax sent back a thumbs up emoji. They'd touch base in person instead of leaving anything anyone official could subpoena. With the backpack over his left shoulder, he ventured out the door and into the rain to acquire kitten supplies.

FOUR
DAX

Knock. Knock.

Dax jolted awake. The kitten startled, digging his needlelike claws into his leg.

"Damn it," he grunted, peeling the kitten off his leg. He held the kitten's torso so he couldn't get any claws into his skin and stood up, unlocking the door. "It's unlocked."

He flopped back onto the couch, groaning as he bumped his right shoulder. The kitten wiggled out of his hand and pounced on something invisible on his lap. Once Morty'd stuffed his belly to near bursting and taken a nap, he seemed to have some energy to burn.

"Hey, boss. How ya doing?" Tomi shut the door behind him and held up a six-pack of bottles. "Beer? Grabbed a sixer of pales ales from the cooler."

Dax nodded, absentmindedly moving his fingers for the kitten to chase.

Tomi set the beer down on the end table and pulled off his damp, faded black denim jacket covered in patches and hung it in the closet. He wore a black T-shirt and black jeans with a few rips in them. Before he stepped further than the door, he took off his beat-up Docs. He grabbed a pair of bottles from the holder.

"What the hell is that?" Tomi pointed with the bottle before prying the cap off and handing it to Dax.

"It's a kitten."

"I can see that. He looks less pathetic after a bath. Since when did you want a pet?" Tomi sank into a worn-out recliner opposite of Dax and took a deep drink of his bottle.

"I'm not sure I want one, but I couldn't leave him there to die."

Tomi nodded and grunted, taking another drink.

"Ow." Dax pulled his finger out of the kitten's mouth, then shed the flesh of his hand, leaving only bones. He ran his fingers down the kitten's back.

"No matter how many times I see that, it still makes my skin crawl." Tomi feigned a shiver then took another drink of beer. "The cops were disappointed they missed you. Your old friend Detective Ryan in particular."

Dax snorted. "I'm sure he was annoyed one of the bullets didn't find a home between my eyes."

"He intimated as much."

"What's the story?"

"The usual. Music was too loud. Didn't hear anything. You'd already left. Had no idea where you'd gone." Tomi covered his mouth and belched.

"The usual." Dax raised his beer and tipped it toward his friend and bar manager.

"Oddly enough, none of the neighbors saw you leave on your bike." He chuckled, finishing his beer before grabbing another.

The kitten pounced on Dax's hand and bit into the finger bone before bouncing away, hissing. Instead of reengaging, the kitten decided to curl up into a ball on the opposite side of the couch.

"So, what the hell happened?" Tomi asked, popping his socked feet up on the coffee table. One of them had a hole in the heel.

"I don't know. Not really. I climbed onto my bike and realized I didn't have my keys. If I hadn't stepped off at that moment, the first shot would have probably taken my head off. As is, the second hit me"—he reached over and pulled the collar of his t-shirt down to reveal the bandage. A bit of blood had seeped through, leaving a pink rosette in the middle — "right here. That shot knocked me to the ground and probably saved me from being hit by the third shot. After that, they skedaddled out of there."

"Shit. You're bleedin' still?"

Dax nodded, stood up, and walked into the kitchen. When he returned, he dropped a plastic baggy in Tomi's lap. "That's the culprit right there."

Tomi held up the bullet, pulling the plastic tight around it so he could inspect it more closely. "What's this etching? Looks like some Viking shit."

"I don't know either. There's something…extra to it. It tingles to the touch. At least mine." Dax grabbed his beer from the end table and took a drink.

"Do you mind?"

"I didn't wash it in soap, just rinsed it."

Tomi nodded, setting his beer down, and pulled the bullet from the bag. Leaning closer to the lamp, he turned it in his fingers as he stared at it.

"Do you feel anything?" Dax asked.

"I don't think so. It's hard to tell if it's just the squick factor of it having been in your body, or something." He shrugged. "But then again, I'm just a human. What do I know? What do you pick up?" He dropped the bullet back into the bag and headed into the kitchen, turning on the water in the sink.

Dax waited until Tomi returned, wiping his damp hands on his pants. "Now, it just tingles. Kind of like electricity, just on the edge of being a burning sensation. I tell you what, it hurt like a son of a bitch all the way home."

Tomi chuckled. "I bet it wasn't easy to navigate that big *choppa* of yours." He always added the Arnie inflection.

"It wasn't."

"So, the big question is who?" Tomi asked.

"I don't know. I haven't rubbed anyone wrong in a while. Assuming it was even meant for me." He gave a half shrug with his left shoulder.

Tomi snorted. "They set up aiming for your bike at your bar. Did you get a look at them?"

"No. I saw a sedan parked in front of Thuc's, but I wasn't paying much attention."

At some point, Tomi had picked up the baggie with the bullet and was mindlessly fidgeting with it. "We need to figure out who's taking potshots at you. I don't feel like picking my teeth with a stray bullet meant for you. I don't have your…uh…special abilities."

"I don't suppose you know anyone who can look at that bullet and tell us what those markings might be." He tipped the neck of his beer bottle toward the baggy in Tomi's hand.

"I realize there were Black Vikings, but I ain't one of them." He narrowed his eyes, staring closely at Dax, then exhaled slowly. "I'll ask Mama if the manbo will speak to you."

Dax raised an eyebrow. "Manbo?"

"Voodoo priestess. She fled New Orleans after Katrina. When we did."

He nodded. "Thanks."

Tomi checked his watch for the time. "I have to go. I have a date."

"Catch ya later." Dax gave a single wave as Tomi slid his jacket on.

"And don't name the cat. If you name the cat, you'll never get rid of him."

"Morty," he mumbled.

"What?"

"I named him Morty." He spoke the words a bit louder and clearer but looked away from Tomi.

"Morty?" Tomi shook his head and laughed. "Congratulations. You're now a cat owner." He continued laughing as he shut the door.

The sound of the heavy door hitting the jamb woke Morty, who stretched then made a running pounce at Dax's hand. He rolled the kitten over onto its back and let the little fluff ball play with his skeletal fingers before it fell back to sleep, its four legs akimbo.

FIVE

JAMIE

Mr. Carter droned on endlessly about supply and demand as he pointed to simple graphs projected onto the room's wall. She knew it would be a mistake to take the senior economics class, but Cory wanted to because he liked the teacher. Unfortunately, the class was mostly filled with douche bros who always talked over her. Despite the low demand, there definitely was a surplus of assholes packed into this small classroom. It was just another day at Augustus "Gus" Atlas High School.

When the bell went off, Mr. Carter waved to get everyone's attention. "Don't forget your essays are due on Monday!"

With that, the class dissolved into chaos as everyone scrambled to be first out of the door.

"Finally!" Cory said, slamming his textbook shut.

"Yeah," Jamie said. Her reply lacked Cory's enthusiasm for the end of the school day, even though she was glad to be done with econ.

"Come on. I'll drop you off at home."

She nodded, tossing her books into her backpack. "Thanks."

"Hey, if you want to work on the essay this weekend, just come over if you need a little quiet." His brown eyes filled with sympathy.

"Let's get out of here before the lot is jammed up." Jamie slung the bag over her shoulder and followed Cory through the door and to the parking lot.

The tall, athletic young man carved a swath through the crowds of students making their way to the exits to begin their weekend. Cory waved at friends as they worked their way through the halls. Jamie nodded to her friends, though far fewer than Cory.

She and Cory had been friends since they were kids. When Cory hit puberty, he grew tall and good looking, but he'd never abandoned Jamie, who was smart but awkward. Once they made it out to the parking lot, they climbed into Cory's old beat-up Kia. It had a fender that didn't match the original color and more scratches than she could count, but it ran and got them where they wanted to go…most of the time.

"Do you want to go to my house?" Cory asked.

She wanted to. Cory's mom always made her feel welcome. "No. If I don't go home, Dad will pitch a fit. Maybe I can come over later."

"Sounds good. We'll find something to stream and veg out." He stopped the Kia in front of her apartment building. "Good luck."

"Thanks. Talk to you later." She shut the door and trudged toward the entrance to the building.

The closer she got to her apartment, the slower she moved. When she finally hit the last step up to her floor, she paused and took a deep breath before opening the door that led to her hallway. Gathering her resolve, she crossed the threshold into the hall and almost ran into the tall, blond, white man with his hair pulled back in a ponytail. He was dressed in a black leather jacket and dirty jeans. A scraggly beard completed his look. He held his hands in front of him, blocking her door.

"Watch where you're going, girlie," he grumbled.

"Sorry," she mumbled, adrenaline dripping into her veins. Wondering what her dad had done now, she slouched a bit, the knot in her gut tightening. "This is my apartment."

"Let her in," a voice yelled from inside.

The man stepped aside, grabbed her shoulder, and shoved her

through the door. Catching her balance, she paused by the couch and dropped her backpack next to it.

"Now we've got a little audience here for you," the same voice said.

"No… Let her go," her dad said, though he sounded strained.

She closed her eyes, deflating more.

Someone snorted. "And deprive her of a chance to see what kind of man her father is?"

She had no delusions about the kind of man her father was. She didn't need to see his latest failure firsthand. But she was smart enough to know that she didn't have much of a choice, so she followed the sound of the voices into the kitchen. The first thing she saw was her father strapped into one of the kitchen chairs, his face bloody and swollen. His messy brown and gray hair looked sweaty, drops of perspiration glistened on the ever-expanding bald patch and dripped down his graying brown hair. He slumped in the chair, one of his hands resting on the table, his fingers splayed out in directions they shouldn't be able to naturally. Seeing her walk into the room, he started sobbing.

"Oh, now, be a man." Leaning forward, the man directing things came into view. He was tall and broad with greasy gray hair. The top was mostly gone, the rest was pulled back into a lank ponytail that fell between his shoulders. He wore a black leather vest over a flannel shirt. "You want to set a good example for your…daughter, I'm guessing? You can at least serve as a good object lesson about paying your debts and not making wagers you can't meet." The man leaned back in his chair. "If people don't pay their debts, then what of the families and children of the people to whom you owe money? What about the employees your debt holders support?" He nodded at someone standing out of sight.

Another tall man stepped into view and punched her father in the face. She winced at the sound of fist on flesh. Her father rocked back in the chair, but the man grabbed his shoulder and slammed him back onto all four chair legs. Broken sobs slipped from her father's bleeding, swollen lips.

She tried to back away but stopped when she ran into a mountain of muscular flesh. Whoever it was grabbed her shoulders and roughly shoved her back into the kitchen.

"You can't learn if you don't observe," the leader said, turning back toward her father. "Now, what am I going to do with you, Toby? Judging by this shithole, I can't squeeze much more blood from the turnip that is your life. Unless..." He turned his head and looked Jamie over. "I might have some tasks your lovely daughter can perform."

"No!" Her father tried to surge from the chair, but the restraints held him. The muscle laid a lazy backhand across his cheek with a crack, calming him down as he whimpered.

"She'll do what I tell her, or I'll find other ways for her to pay back your debt." The boss stood up. His shirt was unbuttoned too far, revealing a thatch of gray and brown chest hair. A Hammer of Thor hung from a large gold chain around his neck. Grabbing her jaw with a meaty hand, he leaned close. His rank breath smelled of the whiskey. "We'll be sending you a messenger who will give you a little job to perform. You refuse, and we'll return to escalate the situation. And you don't want to see me again. Understand?"

She nodded weakly. "If I do this one job, will my dad's debt be cleared?"

The boss snorted. Flecks of spittle hit her face as she cringed away. The goon behind her grabbed her head and held it steady.

The leader twisted his thick neck to address her dad. "She's got more spine than you do, Toby." Returning his gaze to her, he squeezed her jaw. She winced. "Depends on the job, girlie." He released her face, then turned, but before he finished the turn, he slapped her cheek. Stars exploded in her vision, and her neck wrenched as the goon behind her held her head still. "Just so you know I'm serious."

The goon let go of her shoulders, and she sagged against the wall, tears burning in her eyes. She sat dazed as the bikers turned and left while her dad blubbered.

"Wh...what's going on? What are you doing in my house?" the voice of her mom called from the entrance to their apartment.

"Honey... I'm sorry," her dad mumbled. "I'm so sorry."

"Oh my god, what happened?" Her mom stood at the entrance into the kitchen, her hands covering her mouth as she stared on in horror. "Jamie?"

Shoving her way to her feet, Jamie pushed past her mother and stumbled out of the apartment. The tears finally fell, burning tracks down her cheeks.

"Jamie! Get back here," her mom called.

Ignoring her, Jamie bolted toward the emergency exit, blasting through the heavy door, and ran down the stairs, barely keeping her balance. When she hit ground level, she shoved the door open and ran behind the building, hoping to avoid the bikers. The sound of noisy motorcycles fired up from the front of the building then disappeared into the distance.

With the threat of the bikers receding, the tears turned into racking sobs as she staggered away from her apartment building, picking up speed as she tried to run away from her life.

SIX

JAMIE

Jamie, her feet pumping and her lungs burning, ran through the rundown park and into the neighborhood next to hers. By the time she reached Cory's house, her clothes were drenched on the outside from the rain and the inside from sweat. She pounded on the door. A minute later, Cory's mom opened the door, letting her in.

"Oh, sweetie, what happened to you? You're positively soaked. Oh my… What happened to your face? Did your father do that?"

Jamie shook her head.

"Wait here, dear. I'll get you a towel."

"Mom?" Cory called, rumbling down the stairs. "Is Jamie here?" He stopped at the bottom of the stairs. "Damn. What the heck happened? I would have picked you up…"

She opened her mouth to speak but couldn't force the words from her lips. Her tears, which had slowed to a trickle on the harsh run over, started again. Cory's mom, Linda, reemerged with a towel and a pair of jeans.

"Here's a towel and some dry jeans and socks for you. They should work well enough. Cory, grab her a t-shirt and let her change in your room," Linda said.

They both responded to her kind but firm voice. Cory led her to his room and dug out a black t-shirt and a hoodie, setting them on his bed.

"I'll wait outside for you."

Jamie nodded and sniffed, wiping her nose on her sleeve. Cory squeezed her shoulder on the way by, shutting the door behind him.

"Let's get out of here so Mom doesn't interrogate you. She means well." He paused for a moment. "Tell ya what, I'll treat you to burgers and shakes. Meet me downstairs. I'm going to see if Mom will give me a twenty," Cory said through the door.

While he talked, she stripped down to her underwear and bra. Using her wet t-shirt, she swiped it over her face to sop up the mix of sweat, rain, and tears. Once she had on her baggy mix of borrowed clothes, she slipped out to the bathroom to give her face a proper wash and finger comb her hair. When she felt put together enough to head downstairs, she took a deep breath and fixed her best attempt at a neutral expression on her face—anything beyond that wouldn't have been possible.

Cory and Linda were waiting for her in the living room when she emerged. As Linda stepped closer to Jaime and pulled her into a hug, Cory gave her an eyeroll. Wrapping her arms around Cory's mom, Jamie welcomed the warm embrace and the affection of her best friend's mother.

"You don't have to say anything, but if you ever need to talk, I'm here for you." Linda rubbed her back soothingly.

Jamie sniffed, trying to keep the tears from returning. "I know. Thank you, Linda."

Linda released her with a final squeeze. "You two get out of here and try to enjoy your Friday. Call me if you need anything."

"I will." Jaime stared down, not wanting to make eye contact with Linda in case her eyes held pity.

"You ready, Jaime?" Cory asked.

She nodded and followed Cory to the door.

"Have fun and be safe."

"We will, Mom." Cory smiled at his mother and held the door for Jaime.

They didn't say anything until they were buckled into Cory's Kia. Turning on the engine, Cory twisted to face her, patting her knee. "Do you want to go for a run first? I heard about a place that sounds great. It's mostly stopped raining, but I have some towels in the trunk."

She thought about it. The dash over hadn't relieved her stress, only adding to the desperation that had driven her to sprint all the way to Cory's in the pouring rain. Runs with Cory, though, allowed her to forget about her daily life for a while.

"Do you want to pick some road music? Or do you want me to handle it?" Cory asked.

"You do it," she replied, turning to stare out the window at the front of Cory's house.

The sight of the green door always brought a sense of peace and diminished anxiety as she neared the sanctuary. Since first grade, she'd been fleeing to his house whenever things got bad at home, which seemed too often, especially the last few years as her dad's gambling addiction worsened. When his boss fired him, it should have served as a wake-up call. Instead, he ran through the meager money Mom had stashed aside for emergencies.

She sighed and gazed out the rain-spattered window, letting her eyes go unfocused at the passing lights sparkling through the drops. As she tried to empty her mind, she found her head bobbing to the music. The lights grew thinner, eventually disappearing as they left the limits of Redemption City behind them. After a few turns, Cory pulled off the road and stashed the car behind a small stand of trees.

Cory unbuckled his seatbelt and peeled off his hoodie and t-shirt. "This is it. Just on the other side of the hills, there is a nice forest we can run through."

Jamie kicked off her shoes and socks then stepped out of the car and stripped the rest of the way, throwing her clothes into the passenger seat and closing the door. Before the cold could eat all her body heat, she made the shift. Falling onto all fours, she shook out her silvery-gray fur and jogged around the Kia, meeting Cory on the other side just as he shifted.

He sneezed and shook out his mostly black fur. Stepping closer to Jamie, his tongue lolled out as he darted forward and licked her wolfy face before turning and loping off toward the hills. He stopped after fifteen feet to make sure she was following. She dashed after him. For the first time since she'd gotten home, she felt a bit better.

The rain-damp air felt pure and cleansing outside the city. The smell of decaying leaves and rich soil added to the heady aroma. But mostly, she reveled in the feel of her muscular lupine body stretching and bunching as her nails dug into the soil to propel her forward. She wanted to raise her muzzle to the sky and howl her joy but restrained herself.

Once they disappeared into the woods, a mix of firs and denuded deciduous trees, they played a game they'd been playing since they were old enough to disappear and shift, which resembled a mix of hide and seek and tag.

The simple focus of hiding or finding her target centered her and allowed her to push the last of the anger and humiliation away. Both of them huffing and puffing, they decided they were finished and flopped down on the dry needle-strewn ground beneath a particularly large fir tree.

Cory rolled onto his side, letting Jamie rest her head on his thick barrel of a chest. They lay there, listening to the sounds of the night as they mingled with the wolves' breaths and the beating of their hearts. When the gurgling of Cory's hunger injected itself into the quiet symphony, Jamie stood up and let her tongue loll out in a wolfy laugh and gestured in the direction of their parked car with her head.

Cory launched to his feet and jumped up on his hind paws, gamboling around to amuse her, then dashed off at a speed that was a bit foolhardy for as tightly packed as the trees were. Instead of following at her own pace, she took off after him, enjoying the recklessness of sprinting through the trees. When she caught up to him, he slowed to a more respectable pace. Once they broke free of the trees, he reduced his speed even further to allow them time to cool down before they arrived at the car.

Jamie's stomach was growling, too, now that she'd worked off the worst of her emotions. Her normal low-level anxiety returned as she neared the point where she'd have to shift back to her human body, but the run and play had left her feeling content and drained. The gurgling in her stomach was just hunger, which was a nice feeling after everything that had happened that day.

She looked forward to wherever Cory had planned for dinner. He always knew the best places to get burgers and delighted in finding new burger joints to try out. He no doubt had found one out this way and then found the place to go running so they could stop there after.

The already cold night had dipped down close to freezing. Her breath fogged in front of her as she scrambled to dive into her clothes as fast as she could before flopping into the passenger seat and slamming the door shut.

"Careful with my baby, she's not as spry as she used to be," Cory complained.

She stuck her tongue out at him. "Take me to the burger joint, driver. And make it snappy."

Cory laughed. "I'm glad you're feeling better."

He fired up the car and pulled back onto the road. Winding through the countryside, he led them to a small town and what looked like a hopping local burger joint.

"Do you want to go in or drive through?" Cory asked.

"I don't feel like peopling in a strange new town."

"Drive through it is." He pulled into the line.

When he rolled down his window to place the order with a person in a window, the smells rolling out of the restaurant intensified the growl in her stomach as she salivated in anticipation. After they collected their burgers, fries, milkshakes, and sodas, Cory pulled back onto the road and headed back toward Red City. They nibbled on their fries while he drove to their next destination. Fortunately, it wasn't too far away. They pulled onto the road that led up to the bluff that overlooked the city.

They were the only ones in the parking lot, so they found a great spot that allowed them to overlook the city below them. The lights twinkled while flashes of shifting neon in various neighborhoods spilled their garish light pollution into the night sky.

"From up here, you can forget the city is an utter shithole," Cory said around bites of his burger.

"Almost." Even up here, it was a bit harder to forget when she lived in the household that she did. She dipped a few fries into her chocolate shake before popping them into her mouth.

Cory gave her a long look before returning to staring out the window at the city and focused on his food. When they'd finished everything and stuffed all the wrappers and boxes back into the bag, they sipped on their sodas as the music played.

After he sucked down the last of his soda, he turned to her. "So. Are you going to tell me what happened? I mean, it's OK if you don't want to, but I'm here if you need to talk."

She sighed and paused before launching into what she'd been subjected to after he'd dropped her off that afternoon. "It's my dad…"

Cory listened raptly, only interrupting a couple times to ask clarifying questions. After the last words tumbled from her lips, they sat silently. Reaching over, Cory grabbed her hand and squeezed it. The warmth of his hand fought off a bit of the cold the retelling had filled her with.

"And so you have to do something for a gang of dirtbag bikers to pay off your dad's debt? That's fucked up. I'm so sorry." Cory ran his hands through his shaggy brown hair.

"Yeah. I can't wait to graduate and get out."

"Jamie, you don't have to do this alone. I'll help you."

The earnestness in his eyes nearly broke her heart. "You can't get involved. Not with these guys. They're bad, bad people."

"We've been best friends since we were six. I'm not going to abandon you when you need me most. The two of us together will do better than just you by yourself."

"Look, Cory. It's not going to be something like fetch a rare herb from a far-off mountain. This isn't a video game. It's going to be something illegal. I can't drag you into that. Your mom would kill me. I'm probably going to get killed in the process." She sagged forward, resting her head on the dash.

Cory rubbed her back. "I don't care." Cory injected steel into her voice. "You're not getting rid of me that easily. We've been getting in and out of trouble for twelve years. We work better as a team. You know it. We'll do this together."

Sitting back, Jamie stared at Cory, tears brimming in her eyes, before lunging across the car to hug him. "Thank you."

"We're in this together, right?"

She nodded into his shoulder.

"Pinky swear you won't hide anything from me?"

Jamie sat back and clasped Cory's pinky with hers. "I promise."

SEVEN

DAX

Dax held the umbrella over Mama Adele as Tomi trailed along. She'd insisted on filling Tomi's and Dax's bellies with fresh gumbo before she took them to visit the manbo. Tomi could never say no to his mama, and she'd never take a no from Dax when it came to her attempts to put more meat on his, in her opinion, underfed bones. The fifty-something Black woman wore her Sunday best—a long, dark blue dress and a silver cardigan under her coat, along with a set of pearls, and a brown flapper cap with a knit flower on the right side over her ear.

When they arrived at the nondescript shop on the first floor of a four-story brick building, Dax held the door for Adele as she transitioned from the protection of his umbrella to the shop. The scent of incense, herbs, and spices washed over him on the warm air escaping from the door. Tomi slid in quickly while Dax closed his umbrella. The only thing marking the store was a wooden sign that said, "Madame Thibodeaux's," and a neon open sign.

The inside of the shop was a sensory riot of colors and smells. New Orleans jazz played quietly over the store's speaker system. Wooden masks and figurines hung around the walls and sat on shelves next to a huge variety of beads. Various voodoo practitioner materials sat in bins near and behind the glass case counter. Behind the counter stood a tall, Black, trans woman wearing a long, colorful patterned dress. Her hair was hidden in a bright turban that, despite the riot of colors, coordinated with her dress. Large gold hoops dangled from her ears, and a necklace of wood beads graced her neck.

"Bonswa, Manman Delphine." Adele set the bag she'd carried in with her on the counter.

"Adele Chenevert, bonswa! What is that delicious smell?"

Tomi's mother pulled out a container full of the fresh gumbo they'd eaten earlier, as well as warm cornbread wrapped in aluminum foil. "It's fresh and warm."

"Ah, Adele, you're too much, but I thank you. What can I do for you and your fr…" Her eyes swept over Tomi but paused on Dax and went wide before she cleared her throat and continued. "Your friends?"

Adele switched to Creole, talking animatedly while gesturing toward Tomi and Dax, and Delphine replied in kind. Uncomfortable being the center of their discussion, Dax looked over the shelf next to him. Stacks of tarot decks, most of them—according to the tags in front of them—created by Black artists, lined the shelf along with other items that looked less specific to voodoo. He didn't know if tarot was a part of voodoo, but it made sense to carry a variety of items to cater to practitioners of other traditions. Businesses in Red City couldn't be too picky about who wanted to spend money if they wanted to keep their doors open and lights on.

He picked up a scruffy-looking deck that had been handled too many times by the customers and cut the deck, flipping it over to see what card it was. He pursed his lips and grumbled nearly inaudibly. The death card. He returned the deck to the shelf and turned around, clasping his hands behind his back to keep his curious fingers occupied.

"Dax, honey, show Manman Delphine what you've brought." Adele stepped out of the way.

He reached into his coat and pulled out the baggy with the bullet from an inner pocket, setting it on the counter. He returned his hands to behind his back.

"May I?" Delphine gestured toward the baggy.

He nodded once. Bending over, she stared at it for a moment then peeled the bag open and dumped the bullet onto the glass. The plink of metal on glass resounded far more than it should for such a small piece. She held her hand over the bullet and hovered above it, not touching it. Then she paused for a moment before laying a finger on it. Eyes narrowing, she picked it up and stepped toward an O lamp with a magnifying lens in the middle. She flipped it on and held the bullet under it, rotating it so she could see every part of it.

As Delphine leaned closer to the lens, Dax leaned over, staring at the bullet. Despite his proximity, he couldn't understand the words she mumbled. When she straightened her back, she stepped away from the counter and set the bullet in the middle of the glass.

"And someone removed that from you?" Delphine asked, pointing at him.

"I removed it myself." He pulled down the collar of his t-shirt. "From there."

She turned and waved him after her. "Let's take a look in my office. No need to strip down in the middle of my store." She stepped through a beaded curtain and stopped in the middle of a comfortable office with a desk, office chair, recliner, and an old cathode ray tube TV on a tray. A few shelves carried excess stock. "Shirt."

He took off his coat, grunting when he had to move his shoulder then repeated it with the T-shirt.

"Bandage." She picked up a garbage can and held it out to him.

He peeled off the bandage covering the still unclosed bullet wound but folded it in half and shoved it in his pocket.

"Smart boy." She set the garbage can down, then stepped closer, looking at the wound. She sniffed then ran her hand over it without touching him.

"It should have healed already," Dax said.

"When were you shot?"

"The day before last." He grew increasingly uncomfortable as she stared at his wound, her nose only a couple inches away from his chest.

"Then what are you worrying about?"

"It should be healed by now," he insisted, looking down his long nose at her with a firm gaze.

She straightened up and stretched backwards, then looked at him with a well-manicured eyebrow arched. Silence hung heavy between them as she stared at him until she shrugged, turned around, and stepped out into the store. Rustling through jars and drawers, she dumped measuring spoons full of herbs and other unrecognizable items into a mortar. With her pestle held above the bowl of the mortar, she turned around looked at him. "Are you allergic to anything?"

"Just bullets," Dax replied.

She chuckled and shoved the pestle into the mortar and started grinding her concoction together.

"What are you making?" he asked.

"Just a simple poultice with a bit of something-something extra. It should help you finish healing."

"Any thoughts on what created the necessity for the poultice?" He crossed his arms, the lack of shirt and coat raising goosebumps.

"I can't read runes."

He snorted.

"But...I can feel the power on it, and it isn't a blessing for a bountiful harvest."

"Do you know who might be able to tell me what the runes mean?"

"Someone who can read runes." She grinned and winked at him.

Tomi snickered.

Dax rolled his eyes.

"Don't worry. I'll reach out to someone on your behalf and see if they'd be willing to meet with you." She turned back to her work. "Now let me be for a few seconds so I can finish this poultice."

Her grinding took up a more steady rhythm as she muttered low over her mortar. Extending his senses out, he could feel the power moving through her. When she finished grinding the ingredients together, she divided out a small portion then put the rest in a baggy with a precut sheet of paper with instructions on it. With the remaining portion, she dribbled in a bit of water and mixed it into a paste. After she finished, she washed her hands and wet a paper towel, holding it up and gesturing toward his wound. He nodded and unfolded his arms. Leaning forward, she cleaned carefully around the wound. After she handed him the damp paper towel, she prepared a large bandage.

"Step over here so I don't dribble all over the floor," Delphine instructed.

Dax stepped forward and stood still, presenting the wound to her. With one hand, she scooped up the paste. Normally, he erred on the side of caution, but after being ambushed and shot, his normal reticence spiked to new levels. Before Delphine could slather on the poultice, he caught her wrist in his hand with a gentle but firm grasp. He lowered his nose to her fingers and drew in a long sniff—herbs and other things he couldn't identify. But under it all, he picked up an undercurrent of power.

Opening his mind, he let the undercurrent seep through his senses. Though there was strength in it, he couldn't detect anything malicious. And he trusted Tomi and Mama Adele. He let out the breath he was holding and relaxed, releasing Delphine's wrist. She raised an inquisitive eyebrow.

Tomi smirked. "A little paranoid?"

Dax ignored his friend. "Proceed...please."

She nodded and piled the paste over his wound then grabbed the bandage and covered the small mound, careful not to disturb the poultice.

"There. I'm sending you home with enough for five more poultices. Change it tomorrow and put on a fresh one. And again on the day after. If it's not healed over, give it a couple day's rest with a clean bandage. Then do another three-day cycle. If it's still not healed by then, it may be beyond my limited abilities. Instructions for the mix are in the baggy." She bowed by graciously nodding her head and stepping back.

While she'd explained the instructions, he'd thrown on his shirt and jacket. He guessed she was being humble. The power she'd laced through the poultice hinted at a deep well she could probably draw from. "Thank you, Manman Delphine. I appreciate your expertise." He reached back to pull out his wallet.

She laid a hand on his forearm, stopping him. "No money for the trade we've done today."

"Trade implies a two-way transaction," he replied, raising an eyebrow.

"Call it an offer of respectful friendship, then." This time, she curtsied elegantly, grabbing the sides of her dress as she dipped down.

He nodded. "That I can accept." He extended his hand, and she shook it.

"Once I hear from my contact, I'll send the information along."

"I appreciate it."

Tomi, who'd stood in the background while Delphine dealt with Dax, raised his arm in the air and pointed to his watch. "Boss, we need to get to that thing…"

"Right, Tomi." He turned to Delphine. "We'll leave you to enjoy Mama Adele's gumbo and cornbread while they're still warm."

A genuine smile swept across Delphine's face.

"Thank you, Manman Delphine," Adele said.

"Of course, cher. Will I see you for Bourré tomorrow?"

"You think you're going to win back your money?" Adele cackled. "You're welcome to try. I'm sure I can find room in my billfold for more of your cash."

Delphine threw her head back and laughed. When the last chuckle stopped, she waved. "Please turn off the open sign on the way by."

"Adyeu." Dax gave her a half a wave and wove his way around the counter and through the cluttered store with Adele and Tomi in tow. He stepped out and opened his umbrella, waiting for Adele to join him. Tomi pulled the string on the neon sign before he stepped outside. As soon as the door met the jamb, the door lock engaged with a click despite no one being there to have turned it. Nobody broke the silence until after they were sitting in Tomi's car.

"Thank you for introducing me to Manman Delphine," Dax said from the back seat.

"You're welcome, honey. Just keep your head down and make sure to keep Tomi safe," she said, her New Orleans accent thicker after speaking with Delphine.

"Mama!" Tomi protested. "I can take care of myself."

"Sure you can, baby," Adele said, patting him placatingly on his forearm.

Tomi shook his head and pulled into traffic. Dax did his best to keep the smirk off his face in case Tomi looked back and saw it. Adele loved her oldest child, but she was incredibly protective of her entire brood. Hurricane Katrina had expelled them from New Orleans, along with dozens of others who washed up in Redemption City.

As Tomi and his mother talked on their way to drop her off at her home, he stared out the rainy window. Where the poultice sat, his wound felt cool and slightly numb, the constant hot ache since he'd removed the bullet gone.

He'd hoped they'd be a little closer to finding who might be trying to kill him, but at least they had another potential lead to follow up on. That, and he'd made the acquaintance of a powerful manbo. Though that could be a double-edged sword…

EIGHT

DAX

After they dropped Adele off at her apartment, they headed back toward the north side of Red City and the bar. He wasn't in the mood to talk; he rarely was. He stared out the window as Tomi worked his way over the surface streets. The residential neighborhood Adele lived in was quieter, though it still had its mix of boarded-up houses and sketchy apartments. Once they pulled onto one of the larger through streets, various businesses lined the avenue. Adult video stores, convenience stores, bars, pawnshops, laundry mats, massage parlors, etc. Some were open, a lot were boarded up. Nearly all had at least some graffiti covering their walls and windows.

Occasionally, the headlights and brake lights would be broken up with flashing red and blue lights. Tomi kept his speed at the limit and followed all the rules of the road. Red City cops loved pulling people over to fish for reasons to write tickets or mess with citizens.

"Sure you don't want me to drop you at your place? You should probably rest up after being shot," Tomi asked.

"No. I want to see if any of the neighbors saw anything."

Tomi snorted. "Good luck. They told the cops they didn't see anything, but that doesn't mean they'll tell you anything. Seeing and hearing things is a good way to wind up something someone else didn't see or hear."

Dax nodded, returning his gaze out the window. Tomi was right. His chances of getting any useful information from the neighbors was next to nil. Getting involved was either a way to get on the radar of the cops, which no one wanted, or a way to find out who the less trustworthy neighbors were. Suspicion bred suspicion. It was the only thing prospering in Red City, besides the corrupt and the crooked...

But who knew? Maybe he'd get lucky and someone would feel talkative.

When they arrived at the bar, they parked in the neighborhood behind the building and walked the block and a half back. Tomi stepped into the bar to send home the bartender after their shift. Dax waited for the bus to pass by then walked across the street, stopping in the middle as a taxi flew past, and entered the convenience store.

"Hello," an older Vietnamese man called from behind the counter.

Dax walked to the cooler and grabbed two of the store's house made instant pho kits and dropped them off on the counter, pulling his wallet from his pocket.

"Oh, Dax. I didn't see it was you. Need anything else?" the man asked.

"Hey, Thuc. No. Just the pho, and a few answers if you're willing to give them."

Thuc narrowed his eyes. "Depends."

Dax leaned against the counter, resting an elbow on it. "Were you working in the afternoon of the day before yesterday?"

Thuc nodded. "Yeah?"

"Did you hear the shots?"

He nodded again.

"Did you see the shooter?"

Thuc shook his head. "I only heard it."

A bit of movement out of the corner of his eye drew his attention to a black and white security monitor showing an image of the sidewalk and street just outside the store's door. He couldn't remember where the car had been parked; it had all happened so fast after the bullets started flying.

"What about your camera?" He pointed toward the monitor.

Thuc shrugged. "Sometimes it works. Sometimes it doesn't." Behind them, the electronic bell sounded, announcing someone entering the store. Thuc's eyes flicked toward the new shopper, his eyes going wide, fear seeping into them.

"The camera wasn't working that day. Do you need anything else?"

"If you could check your tapes, I'd appreciate it." Dax pulled a twenty out of his wallet and set it on the counter.

"The recording doesn't work. I haven't fixed it," Thuc replied quickly, his eyes tracking the other person.

Dax wasn't going to get anything out of the old man, not right now. He scooped up his change, grabbed the pho, and nodded at Thuc, giving him a half-assed attempt at a friendly smile. As he turned toward the door, he stopped when he spied the uniformed cop doing a poor job of not staring at him, then continued on.

After he entered the bar, he nodded at Tomi and held up the pho containers. "Got some dinner for you. I'll cover you after I'm done."

"Thanks, boss." Tomi grabbed the tap handle and poured a Pabst.

Heading down the hall past the office and restrooms, he slid open the door to his tearoom. A compact corner bar stood to the left of the entrance of the rectangular room. Along the walls sat a half dozen two-top tables. A long communal table with cloth-covered benches on two of the sides formed the centerpiece of the room.

Dax set the pho on the bar top, stepped behind it, and turned on the kettle. Putting one of the pho in the undercounter cooler, he grabbed a bowl from the stack he kept under the bar for just this occasion. He turned and leaned against the bar, staring at his wall of tea and teapots. Green. His eyes settled on a tin of Vietnamese Trà Xanh green tea.

Once the kettle hit the appropriate temperature, he made a pot of the tea in a porcelain teapot, then set the kettle back on to bring it to a boil for the pho. While he waited, he played a bamboo flute playlist through the room's speakers.

After his pho was ready, he grabbed his chopsticks and spoon and leaned over the bowl, inhaling deeply. Thuc may not want to talk about the shooting, but he did make a nice pho kit. The ritual of tea and sitting down in one of his favorite spaces helped to center his mind as the bamboo flute calmed him and the hot, flavorful soup filled his belly.

He was nearly finished when the door slid open. "I'm almost done, Tomi."

"Oh, did I interrupt your dinner?" an oily voice replied.

All the efforts to center himself evaporated like a drop of water in a too hot pan.

"Detective Ryan." Ignoring the cop, he wound rice noodles on his chopsticks and scooped broth into his spoon.

Detective Randall Ryan, a white man of average height, slid onto the bench opposite Dax. The cop had a five o'clock shadow from two days ago and the greasy, unwashed brown hair to match it. His gray suit looked wrinkled. A darker spot hinted at a stain. "Are you going to offer me a cup…" He leaned forward, looking into Dax's teacup. "Tea? I don't suppose you have some whiskey back here."

"It doesn't matter what I have back here. If you want a drink, you can pay for it up front like all the other customers. The tearoom is closed right now."

"Oh, I'm not here to spend money. I seem to have missed you a few times. Rumor about the neighborhood is you were shot." Detective Ryan rested his elbows on the table, leaning forward. He stared at Dax through the top of his eyelashes.

Dax took a sip of his tea then went in for another spoon of pho. "You know you shouldn't put much stock in rumors."

"Rumors… Maybe a witness might be a much more appropriate word."

"If you didn't mince words, you'd get to the conclusion much faster." He spoke through a mouthful of food.

"Don't you know it's rude to talk with your mouth full?" Detective Ryan asked.

Dax shrugged. "You interrupted my meal. It's too good to let it go cold." He picked up the bowl and slurped down the rest of the broth, setting the bowl out of the way. "As you can see, I sit here unshot." He stuck his arms out to display his body, holding in the twinge of pain and maintaining his mask. "I think your witness is yanking your crank."

Ryan leaned a little closer. "Why don't you take off your jacket and t-shirt? Let me confirm that there aren't any wounds."

Dax picked up his teapot and refilled his cup. "It's kind of chilly, and I don't feel like it. So, unless you have a warrant, I think you know where the exit is."

"What? You're not enjoying our little discussion?" Detective Ryan straightened up and leaned to the side, his elbow sliding along the edge of the table as he tried to look relaxed.

Taking a sip, Dax snorted quietly into his cup. "You're not that interesting of a conversationalist."

Detective Ryan's eyes narrowed. "Why didn't you file a police report?"

"I wasn't here. Based on what my bar manager said, I'd just left when it happened. Sorry, I can't be more helpful." He shrugged, swirling his cup and inhaling the vegetal aromas of the green tea.

The detective leaned forward again. "You know it's usually a good idea to cooperate with the police, right? For your own safety…" He spoke lowly, adding an ominous edge to his words.

Setting down his teacup, Dax leaned forward, holding the cop's gaze. He let a bit of his true self slip into his eyes. "I have given you all the cooperation the Red City cops deserve. If you want to see if I'm wounded, you can get a warrant. Now if you don't have anything else for me, I need to get to work." He'd let a little too much loose and his voice had filled with a baleful hollowness.

Detective Ryan swallowed and his jaw trembled, releasing a bit of tooth chatter. Clenching his jaw, he shivered and sat up, breaking eye contact. "I…" He cleared his throat. "I'll be back if I have more questions."

Dax pulled down his mask, returning to his mortal façade. "If you're thirsty, you can have a PBR. Only three dollars. Police discount."

"I'm on duty," Detective Ryan mumbled. Before standing, he straightened up, apparently stiffening his spine. As he turned to slide off the bench, he swept his elbow over the table, catching Dax's teapot and knocking it to the floor.

The porcelain teapot shattered, splashing the last third of the tea over the floor. Dax held in the annoyed sigh and didn't look at the mess, not wanting to give the cop the satisfaction.

"Oopsie. Sorry about that. I can be such a klutz sometimes." Randall Ryan slid the door open and stalked through, leaving it open.

Dax picked up his teacup and took another sip. Sighing, he set it down. "Cold."

A moment later, Tomi poked his head in. "The pig is gone." His eyes drifted down to the mess on the floor. "Shit. I thought I heard a crash. I'll go get the broom and mop."

He held up his hand. "Don't bother. I'll take care of it. He already ruined my dinner. He doesn't need to ruin yours, too. When I'm done, you can take your break."

"Alright, boss. Holler if you need me."

"Thanks, Tomi. I do appreciate it."

Tomi nodded and disappeared.

Detective Randall Ryan had been a pain in Dax's ass since he'd bought the bar. Ryan had just been a beat cop then, shaking down the neighborhood businesses for his protection racket. The sad thing was, Rand Ryan wasn't even the worst of the lot. Corruption was endemic from top to bottom. Though as he'd been promoted, his grift had increased accordingly.

Bending over, he picked up the larger shards then fetched the broom and mop. He'd liked that teapot. The floral pattern of green vines and colorful flowers was pleasing. It had been a good thrift shop find. He dumped the pieces into the garbage bin, some of the pieces breaking as they hit each other at the bottom of the can.

At least it wasn't one of his Yixing clay teapots. Most of them had years of patina and would have been a tremendous loss, especially the old ones that were manufactured with clay from the mines that were no longer used. If Ryan had broken one of those, he might not have walked out of the bar alive.

NINE

JAMIE

The week after finding the bikers in her apartment was hell. Each day, Jamie waited for someone to approach her. But by the end of the day when no one showed, she felt no relief. The lack of inaction only added to her growing anxiety. She still hadn't spoken to her parents, either immediately disappearing into her room or heading straight to Cory's after school. When she finally fell asleep late at night, she slept poorly.

She had always been quiet, keeping her head down at school while doing what she needed to earn the grades to escape her situation. As time passed, she grew more irritable.

"Hey, I'm your friend. I'm on your side," Cory said, some uncharacteristic heat in his voice.

Jamie huffed. "I'm sorry. I just wish something would happen. I want the waiting to be over."

Cory reached out and pulled her into a one-armed hug. "Maybe that's what their torture is. Waiting."

She loved Cory. He was her best friend, but he was being naïve. He hadn't grown up like she had. His mom took good care of him and kept him safe. Too much of her life had been tainted by her dad's gambling. It seemed like all her mom did was work her fingers to the bone to keep them off the streets while her dad did his best to ensure that's where they'd wind up. Her role in their catastrophe was to get out as soon as she could. She'd appreciated Cory's gesture to help, but he had no idea what his promise meant. But to be fair, she had no idea what the bikers would want from her.

"I wish. People like that don't make empty threats to torment people. They expect payment. And I'm it."

A stern-looking teacher in a dress stalked toward them. "Hey, you two. Get to class before you're tardy."

"Yes, Mrs. Lee," Cory replied. He gestured with his head to follow him.

They didn't have class this period, so they headed to the library for study hall. They found a small table buried in the back of the library and pulled out their books to study for the test next period. Despite the approach of the test, Jamie had trouble concentrating, often asking Cory to repeat himself. Even the usually mild-mannered Cory was becoming frustrated.

Grumbling, he shut his book. "Is it even worth attempting this?"

Jamie rolled her eyes. "Fine, Mr. Grumpy. I'll pay attention."

"Look, Jamie. It could be a while before you hear from them. You're going to have to navigate that and still participate in school. You've worked too hard to get the grades you need so you can escape."

She sighed, exasperated. "It's one test. I'll be fine."

"OK, OK." He looked around the library to make sure no one was eavesdropping. "Do you want to go for another run tonight? Burn off some energy?"

That did sound like a good idea. "Let me guess, found another awesome burger joint to check out?"

Looking offended, he held his hand to his chest. "You wound me, madam. But yeah, totally."

"Yeah. Let's do it." She felt a little of her anxiety recede at the thought of a run and burgers. Opening her book, she sighed. "I guess we can try to get some more studying in. I promise I'll pay attention."

He looked at her warily as he slowly opened his book. They managed to get a good twenty minutes of review in before they decided to pack up and head to class so they wouldn't get stuck in the crappy desks.

"Hey, nerds."

She looked up. Travis Becker stood over them in his beat-up leather jacket. He always had a smug smirk spread across his face, though she wasn't sure what he had to be smug about. While he waited for one of them to address him, he ran his hand through the longer blond hair on the top of his head.

"What do you want, Travis?" Cory asked.

"Just delivering a message." He flicked his fingers, and a folded piece of paper flew from his hand and landed in the middle of the table, sliding to a halt before falling from the edge. He turned and walked toward the exit of the library.

After he walked out the door, Jamie turned her attention to the note he'd dropped. It sat where it had stopped. In the center, a Thor's Hammer surrounded by a black sun marred the surface of the white paper envelope. Her mouth went dry, and her stomach flopped as she stared at it.

"Want me to open it?" Cory asked.

She shook her head and reached for it with a trembling hand. Flipping it over, she ran her eyes over it, finding the flap. She picked up her pen and slipped it into the corner of the fold and ran it down the length of the envelope. With the letter finally in her hand, she hesitated before closing her eyes and unfolding it. When she opened them, it took a second for her vision to clear as she held her breath.

"What's it say?" Cory whispered harshly.

It took her a second to get some moisture into her mouth, but she eventually found her voice. "It's just a date, time, and address."

"And?"

"Tonight, ten p.m. I don't recognize the address." She looked up at him, showing him the letter.

His blank stare told her he didn't recognize it either. He snorted. "At least the waiting is over."

She grimaced. Indeed. The ball of anxiety that had been living rent free in her stomach exploded into a fiery explosion of terror. Waiting might have been better…

TEN

The rest of the day passed in a blur of worry. Her earlier anxiety about hearing nothing was replaced by the fear of what awaited them at ten. Although, the run had helped some, it didn't return her to a place of calm like it usually did. She'd barely touched her burger. Cory, who was an eighteen-year-old boy, had no trouble finding room in his stomach for her burger, promising a replacement after their meeting if she was hungry.

After they'd mapped the location and had an ETA, they found a quiet place to park and listen to music. Jamie said little while Cory, a nervous talker, said too much of nothing. He was probably regretting his decision to help her out, but he never said anything to indicate he would back out. Despite probably wishing he hadn't become involved, she was glad he was with her.

When the alarm on his phone sounded, he pulled out and navigated toward their meeting. Her heel beat out a rapid staccato pattern on the floor of the car as her nervous energy spilled out. About halfway to their destination, her hands joined her foot as she wrung them together while her eyes darted around nervously.

Cory had decided to approach their destination by winding through the neighborhood and parking several blocks away from it.

When they parked, he quickly pulled his license plates from their holders and stashed them in the trunk, per her instructions. They'd both seen enough cop shows to know that it was often the license plates that gave someone away. Fortunately, he didn't have any bumper stickers that might identify the car, though the off-color fender was a dead giveaway.

"Too bad you haven't painted your fender," Jaime said, more to spend her energy than to make a valid comment.

Cory shrugged. "Red City is full of shitty cars. Ready?"

"Do I have a choice?" The question even sounded whiny to her own ears.

"You always have choices. You just have to decide which consequences you want to deal with." Cory had a good brain under his pretty face, even if he liked to downplay it most of the time.

She scowled at him.

He gave her a lopsided smile. "It's true."

"Be quiet." She inhaled then exhaled noisily. "Let's get this over with."

She took off, walking purposefully. Cory caught up with her, shoving his hands into his pockets as he strode beside her. Trying to keep her mind from focusing on her doom, she scanned the neighborhood. It looked even more run down than hers. Broken windows and boarded-up buildings seemed more prevalent than occupied houses. Not a single inhabited house had a window with curtains drawn—in a neighborhood like this, being a busybody could be dangerous.

When they arrived at a wider crossroad with a mercy lane in the middle, Cory stuck out his hand and stopped her before she stepped across. "That's it there."

She focused on the neon lights of a bar. Lines of motorcycles were parked out front. The large neon sign at the top of the building declared Valhalla as the bar's name. As motorcycles approached and left, their loud motors preventing quiet from settling over the street, the bar resembled a beehive.

They waited for a pair of bikes to pull off the street before darting across. As they dodged the activity in the lot, they made their way to the front of the bar but were stopped by a giant of a man. He looked to be nearly six and a half feet tall. His bald tattooed head and long beard added to his mean biker façade. He unwound his arms from across his chest to raise a hand to stop them.

"Go home, kiddies. This place isn't for you." His deep voice rumbled nearly as deeply as one of the noisy Harley's moving in and out of the lot.

Jamie opened her mouth to speak, but nothing came out. The biker's placid face didn't shift, though he kept his hand up. Cory reached into her hoodie pocket and pulled out the envelope, showing it to the doorman. He took the envelope and inspected it, focusing on the logo. He handed it back and lowered his hand, nodding toward the door.

"Go to the bar, ask for Ivar." He returned his gaze to the parking lot and the street.

Cory stepped forward and held the door open for Jamie. Cigarette smoke and loud rock music poured from the open door. Once the door closed behind them, they stopped. Jamie tried to orient herself with the sensory overload.

Leaning over, he blocked his mouth with his hand. "Isn't it illegal to smoke in bars?"

She turned her head and blinked slowly at him.

"Right."

Cory's silly question helped break her free from her inertia. "Come on."

She cut her way through the tables and bikers and their dates, making her way to the bar. Reclaiming the envelope from Cory, she showed it to the bartender when he swung his disinterested eyes her way. "I was told to ask for Ivar."

He gestured toward the back corner to the right of the bar with his head. "Back there."

"Thanks," Cory mumbled as they headed toward Ivar.

They found a set of double doors left open and raucous laughter coming from inside. Jamie stepped through the threshold and knocked gently on the doorjamb.

"What the fuck do you want?" someone asked.

She held up the envelope, pointing it toward a table full of men in leather and flannel. Playing cards and poker chips were strewn about the wooden surface.

"I was told to ask for Ivar," she mumbled.

"Speak up," said a man sitting in the back of the room. Though his voice wasn't loud, it carried across the room, propelled on a menacing baritone rumble. He had light brown hair, long on top and shaved on the sides. He wore a black leather vest over a red and black flannel shirt, along with a tightly cropped beard and a large, black iron Thor's Hammer dangling from a gold chain around his neck.

Jamie cleared her throat and stiffened her spine. "I'm here to speak with Ivar."

"I'm Ivar. You must be the errand girl the boss mentioned." He looked around the table. "Clear the room and shut the doors behind you." His eyes narrowed as he looked behind Jamie. "Your little friend can wait outside. He wasn't mentioned."

Jamie caught Cory's eye. He lifted an eyebrow in question. She nodded slightly. Stepping back, he posted up against the wall near the door into the restrooms. She moved out of the way as the rest of the bikers cleared the room, most of them heading toward the bar. Once the doors closed behind her, she stood in the middle of the room, holding her hands in front of her and fidgeting.

"Sit down." Ivar pointed to the chair opposite him.

Nodding, she pulled out the chair and sat down, setting her hands on the edge of the table, one on top of the other.

"So, you're Toby's daughter."

She nodded again, fixing her gaze on the center of the table.

"I see you're a stunning conversationalist like your father. Well, if you're not going to be interesting, I have better things to do tonight." He pulled on a set of gloves then twisted in his chair and grabbed something from behind him. With a casual toss, a manila envelope settled onto the center of the table. Then, with a loud thunk, he set a handgun on top of the envelope.

She starred at it—its wooden handle, scuffed black finish, and the glint of a bullet staring at her from the cylinder seemed more deadly than a venomous snake. She swallowed, unable to take her eyes off it.

"It's a gun," he said, a trace of humor in his otherwise even voice.

She nodded. "What am I supposed to do with it?"

He snorted. "It's not for tickling. I hear you're a smart girl. The information you need is in the envelope. I'll leave it to you to assemble the errand."

She swallowed and licked her dry lips. "And if I do this… My dad's debt will be paid?"

He nodded. "If you succeed. But, if you manage it, you remind your father he's banned from all our establishments. He comes sniffing around one of our gaming tables, and you'll never see him again."

She nodded weakly.

"Look me in the eyes," Ivar commanded.

Slowly raising her head, she stopped at his cold, steely blue eyes.

"Do you understand everything I've said?"

She nodded and mumbled, "Yes."

"What did you say?"

"Yes, sir," she said a bit louder.

He chucked his chin toward the door. "Now get out of here."

She reached out and grabbed the gun, stashing it in her pocket. The envelope, she tucked under her arm. Standing, she walked briskly toward the doors.

Before she touched the knob, Ivar spoke up. "Don't waste those bullets. They're not replaceable. And just so we're clear. You were never here, and you've never heard any of this. Correct?"

"Yes, sir."

"Good."

She grabbed the doorknob and pulled it open, darting out before he could stop her again. Nearly breaking into a jog, she walked past Cory, catching his eye as she made her way to the exit. He followed in line. Once they felt the cold, fresh breeze of the night on her face, she broke into a jog across the parking lot. When her feet hit the pavement of the street, she ran across it and into the neighborhood.

She didn't look back to make sure Cory was behind her, but the slapping of his feet told her he was.

The farther from Valhalla they got, the faster her feet carried her toward Cory's car. Once she made it to the Kia, she yanked the door open and jumped inside, buckling her belt. A moment later, Cory joined her, breathing heavily.

"What's going on, Jamie?" he panted.

"Just drive."

"What?"

"Put your key in the ignition, start the car, and get. Us. Out of here. Now!" she said through clenched teeth.

"Right. Right. I guess I'll put the plates on later..." His keys jingled as he fumbled them. It took him a second, but he started the car and pulled away from the curb.

Clenching her jaw, she teetered between anger and abject despair. She settled on rage. Rage at her father. He'd brought her to this point. He'd subjected her to a poverty filled childhood with two absent parents—one who was too busy losing their family's money and one who spent all her time working to keep them fed and housed.

The entire ride home, Jamie ground her teeth as she stared out the window. Cory tried to engage her in conversation to break the ice, but when she didn't respond, he gave up, probably hoping she'd tell him when she was ready. Wrapped up in her fuming, she had no idea how long the actual drive back to his house took.

"We're here," Cory said, shutting off the car.

"What?" She blinked her eyes a few times and realized the house they were parked in front of was Cory's.

"Let's go."

They piled out of the Kia and made their way up the sidewalk. After Cory let them in, he looked around for his mom but only found a note saying she'd gone to bed early. He heaved a sigh of relief, his shoulders sinking to lower levels.

"Let's go downstairs. We can play some video games to unwind." He headed through the kitchen, stopping at the fridge to grab a couple cans of seltzer water, and headed down to the basement family room.

Grabbing the remote and a controller, Cory flopped down on the chaise lounge but stared off into the space between them and the entertainment center.

Finally, Jamie took a deep breath and pinched the metal tines holding the envelope closed. Inside, she felt two textures, smooth paper and the slick grip of what might be a photograph.

She decided to pull the paper out first. In the center of the page in large type, she found an address to someplace on the north side of Red City. She rarely went up north. Shaking her head, she snorted. Cory probably knew a burger joint or two up there. She set the page down next to her and pulled out the photo.

A tall, skinny white man in a leather jacket stood in front of a what looked like a bar. He had medium length black hair and a prominent nose and sharp cheekbones that made him look like a bird of prey…or maybe a vulture. He also wore jeans and biker boots. As she stared at the picture, a hollow pit in her stomach, Cory leaned over, crowding in on her space to see what she was looking at.

"Who's that? Is that your…uh…mission?"

She nodded and handed him the picture.

"He doesn't look that tough. What do we have to do? Collect a debt or deliver a message or something?" Cory set the photograph on the couch between them.

She swallowed and stared at the floor. Reaching into her pocket, she pulled the revolver out and set it on the photo. "I…I think I have to kill him."

ELEVEN

DAX

With nothing better to do and wanting to keep an eye on the bar after his shift, Dax bellied up to the bar in the corner next to the wall. The evening crowd was filtering in, and the small bar was getting noisy as the drinks flowed and the punk and metal blared from the jukebox.

"What can I get you, Dax?" Jason asked. The tall, slender bartender usually worked the evening shift.

"I'll take a can of Rainier."

Jason nodded and reached down into the undercounter cooler and pulled out a sixteen-ounce tallboy and cracked it open with a crunch of the aluminum tab followed by the hiss of the CO_2 releasing. After he set the can on a coaster, he scooped out a bowl of the bar peanuts from a large plastic jar and set them in front of his boss.

Taking a sip from his beer, he grabbed a copy of the Red City Review, the local alt weekly, and flipped to the first page. Somewhere halfway through the paper, his phone vibrated. It had been a week since they'd met with Adele's friend, Delphine, and he still hadn't heard from her. He rarely received texts, so he hoped this was an update.

I'm an acquaintance of Delphine's. She said you need to consult on a translation. -G

Dax replied, *Correct. Name the time and place, and I'll be there.*

I can meet you tomorrow at twelve, but I'd prefer to meet at your place of business.

That is acceptable.

Where is it? G asked.

House of the Rising Sun Pub and Tearoom.

He sent his next message to Tomi. *Can you come in tomorrow at noon?*

Tomi sent back a thumbs up emoji. Maybe they'd find out something valuable. It had taken the remainder of the poultice to clear up the wound, and the shoulder was still tender. So far, no one had tried to make another attempt on his life, but he couldn't help but be wary every time he stepped outside.

After finishing his single can of beer, he tossed a dollar onto the bar for Jason then slid off the barstool. The spot at the bar would be more productive if it was occupied by a paying customer. Besides, considering the mood he was in, it was growing too noisy for his tastes as people downed their drinks and let their inhibitions down.

"Later, Dax," Jason called out.

Grabbing his jacket and his helmet from the office, he pushed the side door open but stopped part way out, nearly stumbling forward after trying to halt his momentum mid step. His stomach tightened. After licking his lips and taking a quick fortifying breath, he peeked out into the alley, looking down toward the road in front of the bar. Other than someone walking down the sidewalk, the street was empty. He waited until they passed then stepped out. Apparently, being ambushed and shot made a person a bit jumpy.

He tugged his helmet on and climbed on to his bike. As soon as the bike fired up, he rolled down the alley and made sure it was clear before he gunned it out into the street and headed toward home. Today had been the first rain free day in a while, and with his shoulder feeling well, he'd decided to skip the bus and take the bike out today. But his luck had run its course as the first sprinkles fell from the sky, marring the clarity of his visor.

"Oh, well," he mumbled to himself. It wasn't that far to his apartment.

As he reached for the turn signal with his thumb, he paused. He was about to turn onto the road that led to his place when something felt wrong, sending crawling chills up his spine. Going on alert, he checked in front of him to ensure there were no obstacles or dangers waiting. When he judged the way clear, he checked the small round mirror sticking up on the left side of his handlebars. A car followed.

It shouldn't be a problem. Cars had the right to drive behind him. Normally, he'd just ignore it, save for his growing awareness of something not quite right. He couldn't tell if it was a cop car with the blare of their headlights in his mirror. The growing coating of rain didn't help, scattering the light to further obscure his view.

Instead of making the turn, he depressed the accelerator and danced around the speed limit. He kept on a straight course, thinking about the road ahead and how he could use the various neighborhoods, periodically checking the mirror. After about a dozen blocks, he took a left and used the opportunity to look over his shoulder.

The car was a nondescript, dark, late-model sedan. He thought he saw two silhouettes in the front. He took his time getting back up to speed, waiting. Sure enough, the car took a left. It could be a coincidence, but then again it might not be. His mouth went dry, and he licked his lips. He waited for another half dozen blocks then took a right onto a broad street with two lanes in both directions. A few moments after he straightened out, the dark car fell in line behind him.

With a quick check of the speedometer and the nearest posted sign, he quickly pulled into the left lane and sped up to move around a car in front of him. When he was clear enough, he whipped back into the right lane and slowed to match the car, not leaving enough room for a car to pull in between them.

With a quick flick of his eyes to the mirror, he waited. Then he checked again. So far, the car hadn't pulled into the other lane to get closer. They could just be people heading in this direction or people experienced with tailing a mark. He wanted the first to be the case, but a twinge in his right shoulder whispered into his ear that he was delusional if he thought that was the case.

Soon, he was going to have to make a definitive determination. He checked the oncoming side to look for traffic, spying a smaller road that took off to the left. Gunning it, he took a hard left turn from the right lane and cut across the road in front of a pair of oncoming cars. He chuckled. If it was a cop, that'd get him a good ticket, no doubt.

Behind him, brakes screeched, cars honked, and headlights wobbled as cars swerved. Once again, the dark car pulled in behind him. He *was* being followed. He waited for the inevitable flashing red and blue lights, peeking into his rearview mirror regularly, but they never came. If it was a cop, they were keeping it on the down low.

"Hmm." He narrowed his eyes in thought. If they were cops, they didn't want it to be known, which was never a good sign in Red City. He was far enough away from his home that he had plenty of room to maneuver and little incentive to follow the rules of the road if the cops didn't want to pretend to be on the job.

He pressed the accelerator, the big engine of his chopper roaring to life as he cruised five, ten, twenty miles past the residential speed limit. With little traffic, he took advantage of it, heading toward a busier road where he could lose them in the thickness of traffic.

When he approached a stop sign, he looked for the telltale signs of oncoming cars and blasted through the intersection when he saw none. He grinned at the car cruising up to the intersection on his right. He put on more speed and waited for it. Cars screamed as they swerved to miss each other.

He cursed as the dark car narrowly survived when the other car slammed into the stop sign. He felt bad, but he reminded himself he wasn't the impetus for this little car chase. Now, he needed to think about his next series of moves.

As he approached the next major road, he wished he was coming at it from the other side. It didn't run perpendicular but cut across the road at an angle. A right was a hard acute turn. A left turn would be a sweeping soft angle across two lanes of traffic and the mercy lane before he was able to nestle into the other side's lanes. The only factor on his side was the time of night. They were a few hours past the evening rush hour.

He eased up on the speed as he approached the avenue then mashed on the accelerator as soon as he saw a window between passing cars. Earning himself brakes, horns, and no doubt obscene gestures, he swerved through the crossing cars with only the need for a few deft adjustments. With cars occupying the other lane, he took advantage of the mercy lane, roaring down the middle of it until he found a place to pull into traffic.

The car pursuing him had already committed acts of vehicular mayhem, another wasn't going to stop them. Horns shrieked and tires squealed. With the slam of car on car, he hoped that was the end, so he pulled into the right lane and settled into the speed limit, hoping to hide in plain sight.

However, a quick check in his mirror told him that was a wasted hope. Whoever was after him had thrown caution to the wind and was weaving in and out of traffic, swerving into the mercy lane, risking life and limb to themselves and every other driver in the area. So far, he'd not felt any life threads snap, but with the adrenaline pumping through his veins, it was hard to be aware of everything going on around him. No doubt if they kept this up, lives would end, and others would be injured. He just didn't want to count himself in either category by the time the night was done. He had no desire to test how much damage his fragile human shell could handle before it became too much.

Speeding up, he wove between gaps that left him cringing as he narrowly missed mirrors and startled drivers. He collected enough middle fingers to form a healthy flock of fuck yous.

Checking the mirror, he needed to make a decision and fast at the rate his uninvited friends were moving through traffic. Ahead, he found a tractor-trailer riding the center lane, leaving a gap against the curb. With the flick of a finger, he turned his lights off and zoomed forward, nestling into the dangerous embrace of the big rig.

He hoped the driver didn't see him and panic. His helmet wasn't that good. Locked in a life and death situation, he fell back on death and shifted into his skeletal form. His helmet settled onto his skull and his robe fluttered out behind, snapping in the wind and the slip-stream of the truck.

Without the distractions of a human body, he could feel the threads around him, the pursuing car fraying threads like dull scissors. He drew in the darkness, weaving it around him like a second cloak. Stop light ahead.

Dax slowed, keeping pace with the truck. Taking a chance, he dropped back and pulled a quick right onto the side street before the stop light. Ahead was a clear road with few streetlights illuminating it. He pressed his speed, the echo of his engine sounding startling loud as it bounced back at him as he rode.

After a few blocks, he grabbed another right to head in the opposite direction. With a quick check to his rearview mirror, he grunted in frustration. The cloak of darkness he'd woven around himself blocked his view, though it appeared to be thinning as he zipped down the street. He thought he saw a set of headlights somewhere behind him, but he couldn't be sure.

As soon as he hit his next turn, he jettisoned the cloak and sound returned to normal. Block by block, he turned, zigging through the neighborhood, looking for an opportunity.

There. He slowed and pulled into a neighborhood lined with poorly trimmed hedges and the occasional fence. When he saw a garage door, he rolled up next to it and stopped, standing to look into it. There was space.

He didn't like using power, didn't want to draw the wrong kind of attention. Since his exile, he'd rarely used any power and hadn't explored what powers were left to him or what he might be able to do after the limitations he'd been forced to accept. The cloak had worked. He hoped this idea would as well. He was quickly running out of choices.

TWELVE

DAX

Shoving the kickstand down, Dax settled the bike and took a deep breath, letting it out as a long sigh. He returned to his human form then pushed his essence out, trying to leave his flesh behind. Trapped.

He couldn't move. He felt constricted and squished with no place to go. Before panic could settle in, he forced himself back into his flesh body and lurched up, breathing heavily and fogging up his visor. He snorted and calmed down. His visor. He flipped it up and pushed his essence out again, though slower this time.

With the helmet open and the visor no long obstructing his exit, he slipped entirely from his body. But when a breeze tugged at him, he lurched away from the haven of his corporeal form then dove back into himself.

The third attempt worked better. He left a small tether in place so he could find his way back. Floating around the garage door, he found a gap between the door and wall and slipped through it. The door of the detached garage was attached to an automatic opening mechanism. The garage was full of stacked boxes. If he was careful, there was enough space to fit his bike.

Drifting along the wall, he looked for the switch. He found the button near a door leading in from the yard; he hoped he could manipulate it in this form. He tried to form a point to press it but slipped through. He wasn't sure what happened, but something around him sparked and the door ground to life.

With a hard tug on his tether, he zipped back to his body and slammed into it. Before he could regain control of his muscles, he tipped over and fell off the bike. He stood up, his cheeks burning, and looked around. No one had seen him fall.

He switched off the bike and climbed on. Putting it in neutral, he walked it back into the garage, knocking over a stack of boxes he wasn't paying attention to as he checked to make sure the front wheel cleared where the door would come down.

He didn't hear any breakage, but he'd look later. He slid off the bike and shimmied down the wall, then slapped the door mechanism when he got within reach. It started its noisy descent.

Heaving a sigh of relief when the door stopped, pressed firmly to the concrete of its pad, he slumped, taking a moment to catch his breath. Except for the rear wheel, his bike was effectively hidden from anyone looking in from this angle. The bike was close enough to the garage door that it should be out of the field of view of anyone looking in from the alley.

When he didn't hear anything stirring, he worked his way along the wall and picked up the fallen boxes, stacking them next to his rear wheel to block the view. With order restored, he slipped up to the window and peered out into the alley. Nothing.

The door handle jiggled. He dove to the ground, tucking in between his bike and the garage door. Looking down, he pulled in his feet to make sure he was completely hidden. A moment later, the door opened, and a light flicked on.

Slowly and carefully, he reached up and lowered the visor to muffle the sound of his breathing. He restrained a frustrated sigh. Of all the indignities, he now lay crunched up on the floor of a dirty garage, hiding from a mystery pursuer and now some poor schlub who'd heard something in his garage.

He who used to be feared by the mighty and mightless equally. He who reigned supreme over the most dreaded force in the world.

Now, he cringed in the dirt, afraid someone would put another glob of rune-scratched metal into his body.

When the light went out, he stayed motionless until he was sure the coast was clear. As he unwound his body, he halted when the dim flicker of red and blue filtered through the dingy windows of the garage. He rolled toward the garage door and snugged up against it. Judging by the lights, they might be at the end of the alley on the street that it intersected with.

His muscles grew tight from the odd angle he'd crunched himself into, so he stretched his legs out slowly to avoid knocking anything over by accident. He wasn't sure how long he laid there, waiting, but when the lights grew brighter, he hoped nothing on the outside looked out of the ordinary. Or worse, that the home-owner had called the cops because of the noise they'd heard… Though, this would be the fastest response time ever from a Red City cop.

They seemed to be in no hurry. As he wiggled to get more comfortable, he eventually found a position that wasn't too bad on the hard concrete. At least the helmet cradled his head.

He wasn't sure at what point he fell asleep, but he was very sure at what point he woke up.

"What the fuck? Who are you, and why are you in my garage?"

Dax's eyes flashed open. The lights were on in the garage, but the sun also poured through the garage door's windows. He'd slept the night away. As he tried to get his mind working again, he lay still, waiting.

"I've got a shotgun!" the person yelled.

Clenching his jaw, he lurched up. He was tired of being threatened, and this was a bridge too far. He spun to find the speaker and flipped his visor up. The blood drained from the man's face and his jaw dropped, his eyes going wide. He tried to speak but only managed to stutter.

"P-p-please… D-d-don't hurt me…" the man, wearing a bathrobe, walked backward, his empty hands in front of him to ward off his supposed attacker. Not paying attention to his surroundings, he tumbled backwards over a stack of boxes and crashed to floor, groaning. At that point, he panicked and leapt up, stumbling and staggering out the garage's side door.

Shaking his head, Dax repositioned the helmet that had ridden low at some point and peered out the garage door's window to make sure the coast was clear. He started, then chuckled, the dry raspy sound filling the garage. His skull stared back at him in the window's reflection. He'd scared the poor man nearly out of his skin. He slid around his bike, worked his way to the garage door opener, hit it, then slid back along the wall to his motorcycle as the door opened.

He put the bike in neutral and walked it out of the garage. With a quick downward jerk of his neck, his visor flipped closed. He kicked the engine to life, the loud rumbling of his chopper shattering the morning silence of the quiet residential neighborhood.

He rolled his way out of the alley and onto the street toward home. His kitten was probably hungry. He knew he was.

THIRTEEN

DAX

"Hey, boss," Tomi said as he walked through the door. He shook off the rain from his coat and hood and pulled it off.

"Tomi!" the handful of barflies called.

"Yeah, yeah. Go back to your drinks, you reprobates." Tomi passed the bar and disappeared into the office to stash his stuff. When he reemerged, he waited out of the way to allow Dax to pass by.

"I'm going to go set up in the tearoom. Send back Delphine's friend when they show up," Dax said.

"Sure thing." Tomi slid behind the bar.

"Tomi, pour me another Peeber," Red said from his seat at the bar.

Dax passed the office and pulled the sliding door to the tearoom open and stepped in, closing the door but leaving it a couple inches open. The room was dark, but he could navigate it with his eyes closed. Once he was behind the bar, he turned the lights on and filled the kettle with purified water, setting it for a hundred and fifty degrees. He'd finish the heat up depending on what tea his guest selected.

Standing before a shelf of tea trays made from various types of wood, he settled on a beautifully carved dark wood tray and grabbed a light blue table runner on his way to the table. After laying out the runner so it bisected the long central table down its length, he set the tea tray on top of the runner, so it was just off center.

With the water heating and the tray set up, he stepped behind the bar and turned on the sound system, opting for a playlist blending a mix of traditional Chinese instruments. Now all he had to do was wait.

Fortunately, his guest showed up on time. "Hello?"

"Come in, please."

The guest slid the door open and stepped in, stopping just past the threshold. He was tall, over six feet, and broad at the shoulders, with only a slight swelling of a belly. His graying blond hair was swept back, just touching his shoulders. He wore a neatly trimmed beard. Going for cozy, he wore a thick, collared green cardigan. He held a coat over his arm.

"If you wouldn't mind closing the door and locking it. I'd like to ensure our conversation remains uninterrupted. You can hang your coat on one of the pegs on the wall behind you," Dax said. The tall man nodded, closing and locking the door. When he was finished, Dax stepped forward, extending a hand. "I'm Dax. You must be Manman Delphine's friend."

The man nodded, taking Dax's hand. "I am. You can call me Gunnar."

"Would you care for some tea?" Dax asked, gesturing toward the back wall covered in tea pots and canisters of tea.

Gunnar chuckled. "I wondered. Not many pubs and tearooms. I thought it was some sort of hipster joke."

"I like tea, though we don't use the room much yet. I'm hoping to grow the business."

"Interesting. I'd love some tea. It's nasty out there."

Dax walked behind the bar and waved Gunnar forward. "What's your preference? White, green, black?"

"Black, please."

Dax nodded and turned to the wall of teas. Reaching out, he

grabbed a disk of Pu-erh about the size of a dinner plate and peeled back the wrapper. He took a sniff, savoring the rich, funky, earthy aromas then held it out for Gunnar to smell. He took a tentative whiff, and his face scrunched up.

"Not Pu-erh then." Dax replaced the disk of tea back onto the stand and pulled down a tin of an old tree variety from Fujian. He removed the lid and inhaled the delicate fruity aromas before sticking it out for Gunnar.

"I like that."

Since this wasn't a full ceremony, Dax didn't need to find the perfect match for Gunnar. He took down the Yixing purple clay teapot he used for this variety of black teas with a couple of tiny clay teacups. Setting them on the tea tray, he grabbed a small glass pot that looked similar to the teapot.

"Please, sit." Dax gestured to the other side of the table.

Gunnar nodded and slid onto the bench, stopping in the middle. Behind the bar, Dax weighed out the loose-leaf tea into a bamboo tea scoop. Once the kettle dinged, he grabbed the scoop and water and took them to the table. First, he poured hot water over and into the empty teapot, glass pot, and the teacups to warm them. Dumping the tea into the teapot, he added water and let it steep for a few seconds, then he poured the tea into the clear pot and returned the teapot to the tray.

"This is a pretty fancy setup you have here. Usually, I just dunk a teabag into a cup of hot water," Gunnar said, his eyes fixed on Dax's hands as he moved through the motions of the tea ceremony. "Do you do this a lot for customers?"

Dax chuckled. "No. Most people who want tea here just want a quick cup of something hot. Few are into the intricacies of a gong fu tea service."

Aiming carefully, he poured the first tea over the clay pot and teacup. The liquid cascaded over the clay, bringing a shine to it, and disappeared into the slits of the tea tray. He grabbed a set of bamboo tongs and used them to drain the cups, then refilled the teapot and counted to six in his head. At seven, he poured the tea into the glass pot, shaking the last drops out so the tea would be evenly blended.

He carefully poured the tea into the two teacups. With the tongs, he picked up one of the cups and wiped the bottom on a towel, then set it on a small pad that sat in front of Gunnar.

Dax lifted his own cup in both hands and held it up, nodding toward Gunnar. "Thank you for joining me today."

Gunnar lifted his cup and nodded, the corners of his mouth twitching up slightly. Dax sniffed the tea, enjoying the elegant aroma, and took a sip. Once he finished his small cup, he set it back on the train and poured more water into the teapot for another steeping.

After another cup, Gunnar cleared his throat and sat a bit straighter. "Thank you for the tea. What can I do for you, Dax?"

"The tea has plenty more steepings. When you're done, just turn your cup upside down. We can discuss the matter while we sip." He stood up and grabbed a small wooden tray from behind the bar.

He set the small tray down just to the right of Gunnar. On it, the bullet sat nestled on a small piece of cloth next to a set of forceps. "Delphine said you might be able to read the runes on this bullet."

Gunnar leaned over the bullet, squinting at it. "It looks like it's been fired into something."

"It has. Unfortunately, I was that something. That's why I put the forceps there for you." He lifted the lid of the teapot to add more water.

"You're lucky this is a full metal jacket bullet and not a hollow point." Gunnar narrowed his eyes as he stared at the bullet.

"Yeah. That would have hurt a lot more."

Gunnar snorted. "Definitely. Also, it might have destroyed most of the runes. That's probably why they didn't use a hollow point. Otherwise, the runes would have been ruined."

Dax grunted to acknowledge the point.

Gunnar, still staring at the bullet, set his cup on the tray for a refill. Taking the forceps, he flipped the bullet over to look at the other side. "Hmm, I recognize the runes. On their own, there's nothing unique about them. In combination, they tell a troubling tale." He picked up the bullet again, looking at the base. "What's this…"

Dax hadn't thought much of the scratches on the base of the bullet. He'd just assumed it was from the violence of being fired.

"These scratches are obscured by the damage, but they look too organized. I can't quite tell what it is…"

"Can you venture a guess?" Dax asked.

Gunnar fixed his eyes on Dax. "How familiar are you with Norse beliefs?"

Dax held up his hand and wobbled it back and forth. "Once upon a time, I knew far more than my current limits."

Staring at him, Gunnar raised an eyebrow then flicked his eyes away when Dax didn't elaborate. "Norse paganism never really died out, not entirely. It survived in small communities far from the Christian urban centers. But in recent decades, it's undergone a revival. Though, like a lot of things, there are those who warp it for their own darker purposes."

"And that's what you think is going on here?"

Gunnar nodded. "I think so. In the 1930s and 40s, the Nazis appropriated a lot of pagan symbols, repurposing them for their own needs. Unfortunately, that didn't die when the Third Reich fell. A lot of white supremacist groups still use the symbols, some even professing to be Norse pagans."

"And you're sure it's one of those groups who are involved?"

"At least as far as making this bullet." Pushing the tray away from himself, he sat straighter. "I obviously can't speak to the fact they were involved in its use, but it would take a powerful hofgothi to produce an ensorcelled bullet like that."

"And now the big question. What exactly is the enchantment on it?" Dax leaned closer, his gaze firm and steely.

Gunnar swallowed nervously. "You have to understand that a lot of things like this lie in the intent. The runes function as shorthand and guides for the intent. The reason I'm guessing it's a strong hofgothi is that I can still feel around the edges of his power. Enough of the shielding has faded to let me see past their barrier to the remnants of the original enchantment. The pieces I can read have to do with binding, shifting, forms, and death."

Dax exhaled noisily, trying to keep it from turning into a hiss.

He'd suspected as much based on the effects and his trouble shifting out of his human façade. It must be designed to keep his flesh pinned to the bones of his truer form. He could be attacked in the flesh. Damaged. Hurt. Though, he had no idea how much damage his form could take before it suffered the fate of all mortal beings. He'd never tested the boundaries, nor did he feel like it.

Gunnar cleared his throat, breaking Dax from his thoughts. He didn't know how long he'd disappeared into his mind.

"Do you know who I am?" When Gunnar narrowed his eyes in confusion, Dax clarified. "Beyond a man who owns a bar and tearoom and who sought information about some runes."

Gunnar shook his head slowly. "Only that you had a question I could answer and that Manman Delphine told me to treat you with the utmost respect. Beyond that, I know nothing. And to be frank with you, I don't want to know any more than that. I'm a simple man. I enjoy my studies and community of fellow Norse pagans."

"Fairly spoken. Two questions and then you're free to go if you have no more need of me. Is there anyone in your community who could make something like this?" He gestured toward the bullet.

Gunnar moved his head side to side. "I mean, maybe? Though I doubt anyone would do it. This is dark and powerful stuff. Creating tools of this sort leave a mark on you. A mark that can be felt by those who know what to look for. I'd have seen it. And even if they managed to keep it hidden, I know what the feel is like now and will be able to recognize it immediately."

"Unless they were more powerful than you…"

"There is that, but power is not everything in such matters. There are always leaks and cracks, no matter how powerful the shield or the disguise, if you know where to look."

Dax nodded along. "I see."

"And your last question?"

"If I may, an elaboration on my previous question before we proceed to my ultimate question." Dax raised an eyebrow in question, tipping his head slightly to the side.

Gunnar nodded and gestured with his hand to proceed.

"Who outside your community might be capable of creating something like this?"

"I don't know specifically. I find it best to not go looking for trouble, especially in these kinds of circles."

"Even on a less specific level? You've bound to have heard rumors of people or groups who might not be on the up and up. Do you know of any groups who are dabbling in the darker side of Norse paganism?"

Gunnar gave a slight, one-shouldered shrug. "There are a couple biker gangs, maybe a few other groups who might drift toward the darker side, but I don't know where you'd look for them. I've never tried to find them or investigate them. It's a good way to be noticed, and being noticed by such people is how you get disappeared in Red City."

Dax held Gunnar's gaze for a moment, then nodded briefly. "What do I owe you for your time and expertise?"

Gunnar narrowed his eyes then smiled. "I consider us even after the excellent tea service. This was mostly a favor repaid to Delphine. That, and my own curiosity."

Though the smile felt genuine, there was still a nervous undercurrent running through Gunnar's eyes.

Dax nodded slowly. "And you don't want any lingering attachments to me beyond repaying a favor to Manman Delphine."

"I hope you don't feel it's rude to say, but yes, that's correct. Whoever put that bullet into you isn't a friendly sort. Nor is the person who created it. This is a dangerous city, and I'd like to keep my head down so I can look out for my community."

"Then for the price of a tea service, I consider our transaction complete." Dax stood, extending a hand. "It was a pleasure meeting you, Gunnar. And thank you for helping me track down some of the missing pieces to my little mystery here."

"You're welcome. If I'm in need of a beer or a cup of tea, I may see you again, but let's keep our relationship strictly on the professional level of beverage purveyor and consumer."

Dax chuckled. "Fair enough. I appreciate you even being willing to go this far. I'll show you out."

He unlocked the door and slid it back. Gunnar grabbed his coat and slipped it on before striding out of the room. Not wanting to waste the good leaves, he heated the water again and grabbed a clean cup in case Tomi popped his head in to see how the meeting went.

He'd just picked up his cup for the first sip when Tomi slid onto the bench. Without a word, Dax filled the second cup from the small glass pot and saluted his friend and bar manager.

Tomi had the good grace to wait until after finishing his cup of tea before peppering his boss with questions. "So, what's the word from our freshly departed pasty Scandinavian friend?"

"We may be dealing with some white supremacist Norse pagans."

"Fuck. I hate Nazis."

"Me too. But we can deal with that in a moment." He lifted the teapot and filled the glass pot.

It'd been a long time since he'd had to deal with Nazi bikers. The body he now resided in had been covered in white supremacist and Nazi-themed tattoos. He'd burned them off his body as he settled into it. The gods who'd banished him to earth might have forced him to live in a human body, but that didn't mean he had to saddle his human life with symbols of hatred before he even made it through a full night on earth.

"For now, let's finish the last few steepings of tea. Pagan fascists seem more like a conversation for whiskey."

Tomi snorted and lifted his glass to acknowledge the point, taking a noisy sip from the teacup. "Whiskey it is, boss."

FOURTEEN

JAMIE

Jamie stared at the line of cans. With her arms extended in front of her, the gun felt far more weighty than its pound and a half. Narrowing her eyes, she picked one of the cans and aimed. Her eyelids dropped as she squeezed the trigger.

She winced at the echo of the report bouncing around the stone of the abandoned quarry. She hoped the trees surrounding the quarry would dampen the sound that escaped, though they were far enough away from any neighborhoods that their practice should go unnoticed. Forcing one eye open, she found the can she'd aimed at. It still stood proud and insulting, unmoved and unshot.

Beside her, Cory snickered. "Nice shooting, Annie Oakley."

"Fuck off," she mumbled.

"You've got to keep your eyes open. Your barrel dipped right before you pulled the trigger."

She nodded and took aim at the same can. Try as she might, she barely kept from looking away, but at least this time, the bullet hit just in front of its target, sending rock shrapnel pinging off aluminum.

"That's a little better." Cory took a drink from his soda. "You've never shot a gun before?"

She snorted. "No. Bookies typically don't do betting on shooting competitions, so my dad never got into it." Sighing, she sat next to Cory, leaning her head against his shoulder.

He squeezed her arm. "I mean, you're getting closer."

She sat beside her best friend, staring at the empty cans and letting the quiet draw out. "I hate him."

"What? Who?" Cory asked.

"My dad. If it weren't for him, I wouldn't be here, freezing my ass off in this quarry, practicing to kill a man. His gambling is going to turn me into a murderer."

"You don't have to do this," Cory said quietly.

"What choice do I have? If I don't, they'll kill me and probably mom and dad or worse."

"You could run away."

"And live on the streets? I don't have any family that I know about. Besides, they can find me. They're not just a local motorcycle gang. They'll track me down and kill me." She shook her head. "You can still back out. I don't want to drag you along based on a promise you made before you had all the information."

"If I let you do this alone and you got hurt or failed, I'd never be able to forgive myself. I'm going to help you, but I'm also going to try to think of a way to get you out of this."

She patted his knee and stood up. "You're sweet, but I hate that I pulled you into this."

"I'm eighteen. I'm legally an adult and can make my own decisions. You're stuck with me."

Smiling weakly at him, she turned her back to him to face the cans. Cory's support warmed a tiny spot inside of her that lately felt devoid of anything but anger, hate, and desperation. Taking aim, she forced her breathing to calm and squeezed the trigger. The can pinged and flew off its rock, tumbling back to earth several feet away.

"Hey, I did it!"

Cory laughed. "Let's see you try it again."

She flipped him off and selected an empty to aim at. Trying to repeat what she'd done a moment ago, she pulled the trigger, and another can flew back. She turned around to gloat.

"Damn. Nice job." Narrowing his eyes, he leaned forward. "Was that the one you were aiming at?"

She tried to keep from flinching at his inquisitive stare. But when the corner of her lip twitched up, he broke out laughing. He'd found her out.

"At least I hit something."

"You've hit something every time. Rocks, dirt, more rocks. About the only thing safe from you is the thing you're aiming at." He slapped his knee then stood up. Throwing back the last swallow from his beverage, he walked over and set it up in place of the can she'd just accidentally hit. "Let's see if you can hit the one you're aiming at. Just wait until I'm not down range."

She chuckled as he jogged back and sat out of the way. They'd purchased a full box of fifty bullets for the .38 caliber pistol the biker had given her. After firing off half the box, they decided to leave the quarry, not wanting to press their luck any further. On the last full load of six shots, she'd hit her targets three times and been close on two of the other shots.

Cory grinned broadly as he stashed the ammo and pistol in his backpack. "You keep that up, and some of the cans will be mildly scared of you."

She scowled at him. "I'm not trying to kill a can. What I'm shooting at is a lot bigger." Though she wanted to sound tough, to her own ear, her voice sounded more nauseous. Shooting at a can was one thing, but taking aim at a human who hadn't done anything to her was an entirely different thing. She'd have to live the rest of her life, assuming she didn't get caught, as a murderer. But she'd live.

As they walked down the gravel road that led out of the quarry, she kept to herself, walking half a step behind Cory. When she was like this, he knew to let her be until she was ready to talk. It seemed like he was always working around her moodiness, but he never complained, even when that's all she seemed to be doing.

When they approached the locked gate that blocked the road, they slipped up the hill into the woods and walked through the trees until they reached a fence. Checking to make sure the coast was clear, they found a spot where someone had cut the chain link fence near one of its posts. Cory pulled it back enough for Jamie to slide through.

Squatting down, she slid through it until something tugged at her hoodie. "Gah!"

"Hold on, don't wiggle." Cory pulled on her hoodie, nearly knocking her off balance.

"Careful," she hissed. This would be the spot where they'd get caught if a cop happened to drive by down below.

"There."

With her hood untangled, she heaved a sigh of relief, slid out of the way, and held the patch of fence as best as she could from the wrong side as Cory slipped through. Unlike her, he made it through without a hitch, despite his size. She shook her head, annoyed at how graceful he was.

From there, they jogged out, moving away from the fence as quickly as they could. Once they felt they were far enough away, they angled toward where they'd parked Cory's car.

"At least it's stayed dry so far," Cory said.

"Why did you have to say that? You're going to jinx us."

As if responding to the curse, a drop of rain spattered on her nose. It was followed by a second on her cheek, then all its friends all over. Pulling her hoodie over her hair, she took off at a run, Cory following. By the time they arrived at the car, they were thoroughly damp and cold. Before climbing into the car, Cory grabbed the towels from the trunk and tossed one to Jamie as he sank into his seat.

"Since you jinxed us, you get to buy hot drinks to warm us up," Jamie said, patting her unruly hair dry. It was a futile gesture. Once her hair took in water, it was loath to release it in any kind of quick or convenient fashion.

"I guess that's fair, since my words totally control the weather." He cackled evilly. "Behold my power! I am the weather god, Cory! Bow in my presence, mere mortal!" He threw back his head for another exaggerated guffaw of evil.

Jamie chuckled at his antics until it built into a full, deep laugh. It was the first real laugh she'd had in a few weeks, though the positive effects didn't linger long. Her mind always brought her right back to the deep hole she was in.

"I needed that," she said as her breathing calmed.

"Glad to be your chuckle factory. Now I believe I owe you a tasty, warm beverage." Cory aimed the car back into town and toward the nearest coffee shop. "So… I found a burger joint."

"Ha! Your middle name should be 'burger joint.'" It felt good to fall into the routine of banter, even if it only took the edge of her roiling anxiety.

"Have my burger joints ever disappointed you?"

"There's always a first…"

He ignored her jibe. "Supposedly the special burger there is a pineapple bacon cheeseburger. It's got a whole ring of pineapple and a special sauce that compliments it." He rubbed his stomach. "We're going to need stakeout food. It's bad luck to do a stakeout without proper sustenance. You know, brain power and fuel and all." He gave her a quick wink before returning his attention to the road.

Jamie would never admit it to him, but she was looking forward to the burger. It had become a comfort food, which had become a symbol of stress relief after a run with her friend. She took care of the music while Cory drove. After they pulled through the coffee place's drive-through, she scalded her tongue trying to drink it too soon but gave up and just used the cup to warm her hands until it cooled enough to not boil her brain.

The rain slowed traffic as they navigated from the south side of Redemption City toward their burger destination and stakeout spot on the north side, but it did allow her enough time to drink the coffee before they acquired their burgers. She had to admit the burgers smelled amazing. She couldn't wait to dig in. Unfortunately, when they parked down the street from the address she'd been given by Ivar, her appetite disappeared in a gurgle of stomach acid. She took a bite, anyway.

"House of the Rising Sun Pub and Teahouse?" Cory snorted. "It's barely readable. He should have picked a shorter name. Do you think that's why…" He drew a finger across his throat and made a slicing sound.

"That's not funny, Cory." The mouthful of food tasted of ashes after his comment. She set the burger back into its wrapper and covered it before putting it back into her bag. "This isn't a laughing matter."

"I'm sorry, Jamie. That was inappropriate and insensitive." He reached over and squeezed her shoulder.

"And no. You can't have my burger. You don't get rewarded for ruining my appetite that way."

"That's a fair punishment." He looked longingly at her burger bag but pulled his eyes away and looked toward the bar. "So, what do we do? Just sit here?"

"Yeah. Let's wait to see if he comes out. We can follow him if he does."

"What if he's not there? This would be a lot easier if we could go into bars." He folded his arms across his chest and slouched in his seat.

They sat with the engine off and watched, occasionally wiping the condensation from the inside of the front windshield.

"Maybe we should try to go into the bar. That kind of place probably doesn't card people."

Jamie shook her head. "No. If they do, we'll be on their radar. They might have security cameras that could link us to everything."

"Yeah. You're probably right." He wiggled around, antsy from sitting in the car for so long. "I'm hungry."

"You just ate a burger and fries."

"Being nervous makes me hungry." He pouted, crossing his arms.

"Alright, Shaggy." She sighed. "Look. There's a convenience store. Go buy yourself a snack."

"Want me to pick up anything for you, Scoob?" He waggled his eyebrows at her.

"Ugh. If anything, I'm Velma. Now either quit wiggling, or go get a snack."

"Fine, Velma." He rolled his eyes and slid out of the car, waiting for a passing truck before darting across the street.

At least with him gone, the car quit bouncing around, and it was quiet. She stared toward the House of the Rising Sun, waiting. Even though they were here, ostensibly staking out her—mark? Potential murder victim?—she had no idea what she was doing. Would she just poke the gun out the window and fire when she saw him? Would she try to sneak up on him so she'd be close enough to actually hit him?

She didn't want to become a murderer. But what choice did she have? If she didn't, they'd come back for her, her father, and her mother. Now Cory was involved too, which meant his mother could become collateral damage. What was the life of one skeezy looking man compared to the five she held in her hands?

She held her hands up, looking at her palms and fingers. Fingertips… Fingerprints! She pulled a handful of napkins from the burger bag and unfolded one, laying it in her lap. Reaching into her pocket, she pulled out the six bullets she'd pulled from the revolver before they'd gone out to practice. She picked up the first one with a napkin, then used another to rub it down, hopefully wiping any fingerprints she might have left. She set it aside and then grabbed another to wipe down.

She was so focused on polishing her bullet that she didn't see Cory come back. When he yanked the door open and flopped into his seat, she nearly had a heart attack, scattering the bullets over the seat between her legs and onto the floor mat.

"Damn, feeling twitchy?" Cory asked, throwing some candy into his mouth.

"You scared me," she replied around ragged breaths.

"Sorry. Why are you playing with the bullets, anyway?" He reached over and plucked one off her lap.

"I was making sure I hadn't left any fingerprints on them. Now, I have to polish yours off, too."

He brought it closer to his eyes, squinting at it. "What are these marks around the bullet?"

She hadn't looked at them too closely, treating them as if they were venomous snakes. Picking one up, she inspected it thoroughly for the first time. "They look like Viking runes or something."

"They feel weird. Like they almost have a life of their own." He shook his head nervously. "I don't like them. Not that I like guns and bullets anyway, but these feel almost…"

"Insidious."

"Yeah." He handed her the bullet. "Wipe this one really well."

"Thanks for advice," she said sarcastically.

Once she was finished wiping them down, she checked around for anyone nearby or looking out a window. When she felt the coast was clear enough, she pulled out the gun and quickly reloaded it with the bullets Ivar had sent with the gun. After it was loaded, she stashed it back in the glove box. Cory had been staring at her the entire time, his gaze still fixed where her hands had been working.

"It's not too late to back out, Cory. You don't need to go down with me."

He shook his head and sighed. "No. I'm in. Plus, the bikers saw me come in with you. If this doesn't work out, they're coming for me, too."

She caught his gaze and raised an eyebrow. "Wish you'd stayed out of it when I asked you to?"

"Kind of, but it's too late now." He huffed. "Even if I had it to do over, I'd still back you up. We're in this together."

Reaching over, she grabbed his hand, squeezing it. "I hope you take this the right way, but I'm both sad and happy that you're here for me."

He squeezed back. "You and me. Together until the end."

Once they settled back in their seats to continue their vigil, Cory was more relaxed, though the near constant rattle of candy wrappers was getting on her nerves. She kept to herself, not wanting to mess with his coping mechanism so soon after reaffirming their commitment to each other.

"Do you think we're going to have to wait here all evening?" Cory asked.

"I don't know." Squinting toward the bar, she sat up and leaned forward. "Maybe not…"

"Do you see something?" Cory focused.

She pulled up the photo on her phone. She'd taken a picture of the original so she wouldn't have to carry it around. "Yeah." She held out her phone for Cory to look at. "Does that guy look like the picture?"

Cory looked at the phone then toward the figure walking away from them. "Maybe. It's hard to tell this far away in the dark."

"Let's circle the block so I can get a closer look at him."

"Right." He turned the car on and pulled out into the street.

As they neared the figure, Jamie prepared, staring at him as they passed him.

"Does it?" Cory asked.

"Kind of. Look. He's stopping at that bus stop. Circle the block then we'll follow the bus to see where he's going. Maybe we'll get a closer look."

"OK," replied Cory, though his voice lacked his usual conviction.

"I know. We're just going to follow him. That's all…"

FIFTEEN

DAX

"Hmm?" Dax moaned, sleep still grasping tightly to his awareness.

Thud. Thud. Thud.

Dax tried to shake his head to clear it, but something weighed his head down. Reaching up to rub his eyes, he found the obstruction. Morty had fallen asleep, stretched over his face, covering his eyes. Carefully, so as not to startle the kitten and his razor-sharp claws, he scooped him up and gently lifted him from his face. The kitten was still out, so he set him gently on the other pillow.

Thud. Thud. Thud. Someone was pounding on his front door. He swung his feet out of bed and grabbed the dirty t-shirt off the floor that hadn't quite reached the hamper and pulled it over his head. Stumbling out of the bedroom, he flipped on the lights to the living room on his way by.

Thud. Thud. Thud. Thud.

"I'm coming, damn it," he mumbled, but not loud enough for whoever was trying to beat his door down to hear it.

Peeking through the peephole, he found Tomi on the other side of the door. Dax pulled the chain lock then flipped the deadbolt before opening the door and stepping out of the way.

"About damn time, Dax."

Rubbing his eyes, he shut the door behind Tomi. "I was asleep."

"Deeply, I guess." Tomi strode to the recliner, sat in it, then stood up again and paced back and forth in front of the TV stand.

"I was dreaming." He shut the door and turned to face Tomi.

The edges of the dream still lingered, as did the serenity of it, despite the rude awakening. He'd been watching a sun rise from behind a gas giant, the particles of its ring scattering the incoming light to stunning effect. The total silence of the vacuum only enhanced the visual symphony. It felt like a memory, vivid and hazy around the edges at the same time.

"It must have been some dream."

Shaking his head, he narrowed his eyes at Tomi. "Why are you here in the middle of the night, pounding on my door?"

The noise had finally woken Morty, who was currently stalking one of Tomi's untied shoelaces as he continued his incessant pacing.

"It's Jason. He's…" Tom stopped, allowing the kitten the opportunity to pounce the shoelace. "He's dead. Someone shot him."

"What? Where?" That woke him up.

"Just outside of his apartment after his shift."

Dax ran a hand through his already messy hair. "How do you know?"

"The cops came looking for you. Detective Ryan wanted to talk to you. I tried to call, but you didn't pick up."

"You didn't lead the cops here, did you?" Dax asked, his voice stern and his eyes narrowed.

"Dax. I didn't think you took me for a fool." Tomi shook his head, pursing his lips. He bent down, peeled the kitten off his shoelace, and picked him up, flipping him over to rub his belly.

"Sorry. Let me get some clothes on." He returned to the bedroom and pulled on his jeans. The red lights of his alarm clock said three-thirty a.m. He groaned and returned to dressing. After throwing on some clean socks, shoving his wallet into a pocket, and grabbing his phone, he rejoined Tomi in the living room. "Let's go, if you can part from your new buddy there."

Morty was stretched out on his back in Tomi's arms, exposing every inch of his belly and kneading the air with his front paws. Looking embarrassed, Tomi set the kitten down gently. Shaking his head, Dax smirked. He stepped past Tomi and grabbed a coat from the closet, then opened the door, ushering Tomi out.

He followed his bar manager out of the apartment building and down to his car. "Did you grab Jason's address from the file?"

"Didn't need to. I've been over to his place a few times to play poker."

Dax let Tomi get to the business of driving so he could stare out the window. Why would anyone want to shoot Jason? He showed up to work, did a good job, and kept his nose out of trouble, as far as Dax knew. The regulars liked him, and he collected good tips. By all accounts, he was a likable guy. A few minutes later, the harsh reality of the red and blue flashing lights focused Dax's attention on the tragedy of losing an employee and an acquaintance.

After Tomi parked, they wordlessly exited the car and walked toward the tape line the police had set up. The ambulance still hadn't showed up to cart off the dead body, though there wouldn't have been much more of a rush if he'd actually needed the services. Nothing worked right in Red City. Or rather, everything worked to funnel money from the citizens to corrupt businesspeople and politicians.

With each step closer to the body, the aura of Jason's death drew him in like a tracking blood hound. It flirted with him, luring him to reach out and follow the tendrils and threads of the young man's life. It was one of the few powers he still had. He could read death, taste all its exquisite details and complexities, but he could do little else. Normally, he avoided even doing that because it reminded him of what he'd been forced to give up in order to avoid oblivion.

This time, he drew in the fullness of the sensation, letting it permeate all his senses. The lines of Jason's life were few but firm, leading back to a previous generation whose threads still moved forward. They'd lost a son. When he reached the end where Jason's connection to the tapestry of life had been clipped, he found the other end. His death had been premature...by decades. This wasn't right.

It wasn't Jason's time. Yet he lay in a heap on the wet sidewalk, a pool of blood surrounding his body. Gritting his teeth, he followed the line back to Jason and into his chest where the shot had severed his aorta, spilling his life almost instantly. A dark particle sat at the center of the prematurely cut line. He'd felt it before. Concentrating, he tried to wrap his awareness around it, to examine it more fully, but it was slippery, oily, like sentient sludge.

Its elusiveness was the clue he'd needed to connect the pieces in his thinking. He'd felt it before—inside his body. Jason had been shot with a similar bullet to the one that had caused him so much trouble. An elbow in the side brought him back into his own head.

"Never seen a dead body before?" Detective Ryan asked, looking smugly between the body and Dax. "Hey…" He pointed between Jason and Dax. "You two kind of look similar."

"Lots of people are tall and wear leather coats," Dax mumbled, trying to ignore Ryan.

He stared at Jason. There were superficial similarities. Jason had dark hair, was about the same height, and wore jeans and a black leather coat like Dax often did. In the dark, that passing resemblance might have proven deadly.

"I suppose I should get on with the formalities since you've been kind enough to grace us with your presence," Ryan said, pulling a notepad from his pocket.

Dax forced his gaze off his dead bartender, leveling it on the caustic detective instead.

"What can you tell me about Mr. Ortiz over there?" Ryan asked.

"Not much. He worked for me, but we weren't close. We often didn't work the same shifts. He showed up on time, did his job. The customers seemed to like him. Beyond that, I can't say much else."

Ryan looked up from his notepad. "Can't or won't?"

"As in, I don't have much more to say. He was my employee, not my pal."

"Did he have any enemies? Any customers he kicked out?"

"Nah," Tomi jumped in. "He got along with the regulars. There are always people asked to leave if they drink too much, but no one ever caused any problems."

"If you want, you can review the bar logs," Dax added. "Every employee has to fill out a note in it when they finish their shift to note such occurrences. Keeps us right with the liquor board if anything happens."

"I'll send someone along to collect those." Ryan flipped the page on his notepad and kept writing. Turning to Tomi, he asked, "What's your name?"

"Tomi. Tomi Chenevert. C-h-e-n-e-v-e-rt." Tomi always spelled his name out before people asked because inevitably if it was someone "official," they'd ask for clarification on the French Creole name.

"How well did you know the victim, Tomi?"

"Well enough. He was a good dude. We played cards together occasionally. He was a good co-worker."

"Any enemies you know of?"

"Nope. Everyone liked him. He was easy-going and inoffensive," Tomi replied.

"Nothing either of you can think of that might have gotten him killed?" Detective Ryan looked back and forth between Tomi and Dax.

Dax shook his head.

"Nope, not that I can think of," Tomi added, shuffling on his feet as he returned his gaze to his dead friend.

"OK, you're free to go. If I think of anything else, I know where to find you both." Detective Ryan turned around and headed toward a couple people standing next to a uniformed cop, probably other witnesses.

Tomi waited until Ryan was out of earshot before turning to Dax. "You ready to get out of here, boss?"

Dax nodded. "Yeah. I doubt they'll let me cross the tape line and inspect his body closer."

Tomi cast a last glance toward Jason then turned and headed back toward his car. Fixing his eyes on his former employee, Dax found the thread that had connected Jason to the tapestry of life and gripped it in his mind. *I'm sorry your time was cut short. I'll find out who did this to you and make sure they get what is coming to them.* Before he let go, he cleaned up the edges of the thread so nothing of the man would linger in this world and prevent him from moving on.

"Dax? You coming?" Tomi called.

He turned around sharply and strode toward Tomi. The two men made eye contact, exchanging an understanding. Someone was playing a deadly game with Dax and had made a grievous mistake murdering an innocent. It was a mistake Dax aimed to make them pay for.

Once they settled into the car, Tomi turned the car on and pulled away from the crime scene. After the flashing lights were no longer visible in the rearview mirror, Tomi aimed the car toward Dax's apartment.

"I figured we'd go back to the bar. That's where the liquor's at," Dax said, breaking the silence.

"I grabbed a bottle of whiskey from stock. I want to sweep the bar for bugs tomorrow. In your apartment, we can talk freely."

Tomi was right. They could speak freely in his place. As long as Tomi didn't let anyone know about his apartment, Dax was undetectable thanks to the layers of warding he'd laid in. It allowed him some semblance of privacy. They'd be able to talk treason without anyone hearing, even if they listened at the door.

Tomi grabbed the bottle from the backseat before locking his car, then followed Dax up to the fourth floor. After he locked the door behind them, he checked his wards to make sure they were still strong and secure. Tomi didn't know about the wards. At least Dax didn't suspect that he did. Tomi was sharp, though from all outward appearances, he appeared to be a non-magical human, but he might be able to find out his boss had such magic in effect. Tomi and his family were the only humans who knew anything about Dax's true nature, though even they didn't know the full story or even a small percentage of it. However, he more than suspected he had to add Manman Delphine to the number of those who were in the know.

Dax walked into the kitchen and pulled out a couple whiskey glasses and set them in front of Tomi, who promptly filled them.

Tomi held up his glass. "To Jason. Rest in peace."

Holding up his glass, Dax gently clinked it against Tomi's. "He will."

Tomi raised an eyebrow, then relaxed, nodding. "Good."

Despite selecting a good quality whiskey, Tomi belted it back and refilled his glass. Following suit, Dax hissed at the burn as the over-sized shot lingered on the way down his gullet. He set the glass in front of Tomi for a refill.

"This one's for sipping." He followed his own advice, then exhaled. "I guess we're going to have to find a new bartender to fill in for Jason."

"Yeah."

Tomi took another sip then made sure he had Dax's attention, staring into his eyes. "Do you think this has anything to do with the shot you took?"

"Maybe." Dax shrugged. "I'd like to get a closer look at Jason's body and see what tales it can tell."

"Ol' Rand Ryan seemed to think it might."

"Yeah. It seemed more than a casual comment."

"I'm surprised he didn't dig into it there."

Dax snorted. "Maybe there were too many other cops around. I'm sure we'll be hearing from the tenacious detective in a more private setting."

"He's like a damned bedbug—nearly impossible to get rid of." Tomi shook his head, looking disgusted. "But I don't see why he'd care if other cops were around. They're all corrupt and dirty."

Dax swirled his glass before taking a sip. "They are, but I think they keep their individual corruptions and vices to themselves out of courtesy. If the wrong person knows something, they might want a cut of whatever grift Ryan's running."

"What grift is there to run on us? We're barely making ends meet as is. If we're supposed to be his profit center, he's an even shittier grifter than he is a cop."

"Who knows what his plans are or for whom he's working? He's low rent, but that doesn't mean there's not a very big fish pulling his strings."

"Or more likely, several layers of progressively bigger fish."

Dax raised his glass toward Tomi to acknowledge the point. "Exactly."

"You're going to need to watch your back if you don't want another round of bullets in it."

"I don't fancy experiencing that again." He shivered. "The last bullet was a near thing. The next bullet might work better."

Tomi raised an eyebrow in curiosity. "What do you think would happen?"

"I don't know, and I don't care to find out." He threw back the rest of his glass and pushed it toward Tomi for a refill. "I'm going to put some music on."

SIXTEEN

DAX

Dax's phone woke him up, along with Morty, who was currently digging his needle-sharp kitten claws into Dax as he hissed at the noisy interruption to his sleep. He peeled the kitten off his chest and set him on the other side of the bed, then rolled over and grabbed his phone.

"What?"

"Good morning, sunshine," Tomi said, entirely too chipper for Dax's current mood.

"Again, what?"

"My, aren't we grumpy this morning?"

Dax ran his hand over his eyes, rubbing the sleep out of them. "Sorry."

"You still interested in checking out Jason's body?" Tomi asked.

They'd hoped to get a look at Jason's memorial service, assuming his parents didn't cremate him, but so far the body hadn't been released since it was part of an ongoing investigation.

"You know I am," Dax yawned. "Ow, fuck!" Now that Morty was awake, he thought Dax's twitching finger was the perfect play toy.

"You OK, Dax?"

"Yeah. Morty needs to mind his teeth."

Tomi snorted. "I never thought I'd see you get something as mundane as a kitten, not that I thought you'd get anything. The only things you seem to really love are punk rock and tea."

"I guess we can't all stay the same forever."

"You know better than me on that one."

Dax rolled his eyes. "Anyway, Jason…"

"Yeah. How do you feel about playing a cadaver?"

"Is this a joke? You know I don't have a sense of humor."

"That I am aware of. It's no joke. I found a way into the morgue, but it requires going in the, uh, let's just say the business end."

"OK, I'm listening."

Tomi cleared his throat. "Manman Delphine has a friend who's an EMT. He's, uh, 'friends' with the coroner. He can get you in, but you've got to arrive in a body bag. You OK being zipped into one?"

"I guess we'll find out. When we doing this?" He rolled Morty over, scratching his chest. The kitten attacked his hand briefly then flopped out, purring at the attention.

"Got any plans for today?" Tomi asked.

"Aren't I supposed to be covering the bar later?"

"Yeah, but if you get your ass out of bed, we can get moving."

"Alright, alright. Speaking of the bar, do you have any leads on a new bartender?"

"Yeah. If you don't mind a little nepotism."

Dax snorted. "As long as they're reliable and know what they're doing, I don't give a fuck. Bring them in to meet me. Where we meeting your friend?"

"Well, your place is out I'm guessing…"

"You're right."

"And the bar is out as a starting point. Manman Delphine's shop work for you?"

"Sure. Pick me up in thirty and bring coffee." He hung up before Tomi could argue.

He rolled out of bed, grabbed a shower, then shoveled a bowl of cereal down his throat. He scooped a smelly can of kitten food into a bowl before grabbing his leather jacket and heading out the door to meet Tomi at the curb. When Tomi pulled up, he slid into the passenger seat and held his hand out. Tomi placed a to-go coffee into it.

"You're lucky I like you, Dax. You can be disagreeable in the morning." He snorted and shook his head. "Not that you're terribly agreeable at the best of times."

"How many bosses would let you zip them into a body bag?"

Tomi chuckled. "You're a regular laugh riot. It's the best plan we have."

"It's a plan."

"OK. It's the *only* plan we have." Tomi pulled out of the parking space and took them to Manman Delphine's.

Tomi kept to himself, letting Dax work his way into his coffee. He was grateful Tomi respected his need for a bit of quiet in the morning, at least before his first cup of coffee. The two of them had been stretched thin, picking up the extra shifts over the last week with Jason gone. The other bartenders kicked in when they could, but they only had a limited amount of time they could spare. He'd have to give them and Tomi bonuses if he could scrounge up the money. He should have asked for a bank account when he was banished, though he'd known little of the intricacies of human society then and even less about finances.

He looked at Tomi out of the corner of his eye. If it weren't for Mama Adele and Tomi, he'd probably never have made it off the streets he'd been dumped unceremoniously onto several years ago. He was glad Tomi allowed him his grumpiness. Being exiled and forced to live as a human wasn't an easy situation, and he was less equipped to deal with it than most from his station. He'd have to tell Tomi that he appreciated him, but he wanted to do it with something more tangible than just words. Sighing, he quickly covered it up by taking a drink of his coffee.

When they pulled up to Delphine's, Dax finished his coffee and set it in the cup holder of the console. "We going inside?"

"It would be rude to use her shop as a meeting spot and not stop in and say hi," Tomi said.

"And your mama would blister your ear for being rude."

"You're not wrong," Tomi replied, chuckling. He reached into the back seat and grabbed a plastic container.

"More gumbo?"

"Nah. Samosas. Mama's been experimenting with Indian food lately. She's threatening to make a jambalaya samosa."

"It'll probably be good." He felt slightly disappointed that Adele had sent food for Delphine and not him. He loved her cooking.

"You know it." As if reading Dax's mind, Tomi added, "Don't worry, I've got a container for you too."

Dax's senses were assaulted by the aromas of the herbs and spices and tropical hardwoods of Delphine's wares. It was a rich and lively smell compared to the smell of his working-class bar and his neutral apartment, though Morty's litter box added a touch more variety to the scent life of his abode.

"Tomi! Is that your mama's cooking I smell?" Delphine called, stepping out from behind the counter. She gave Tomi a kiss on the cheek then took the container from him and set it on the counter. "Dax. It's a pleasure seeing you again."

Dax felt awkward but leaned in to reciprocate the hug as she kissed his cheek as well. "It's good to see you as well, Manman Delphine."

"Please, call me Delphine, Dax."

He nodded. "Of course."

"Make yourselves comfortable, boys." She checked her watch. "Boudreaux will be along shortly."

Last time, Dax hadn't had much time to check out her wares. Since he had time, he thought he'd peruse the selection, not that he was in the market for any voodoo supplies or other magical accoutrement. He quirked his head to the side, a thought teasing him. "How's business, Delphine?"

"Steady. Why do you ask?"

"Polite curiosity. Do you do a lot of trade in the..." He wasn't sure how to phrase it, but it wasn't like he was in mixed company. Delphine was a powerful manbo, and Tomi's mother believed in voodoo and was part of Delphine's flock, though he'd never pressed Tomi to see where his beliefs lay.

"Spit it out. You won't offend me."

He nodded, acknowledging her point. "How much of your trade is amateurs versus actual practitioners?"

"Cher, the amateurs and the magical tourists keep the doors open for the serious practitioners who prefer to keep to themselves in a city like this," she replied.

"Fair enough." He didn't delve deeper since she'd made it clear that was an area where she respected the privacy of her clients, which was important if she wanted to keep her doors open and didn't want to run afoul of any magical communities.

He knew Red City had a variety of magical communities. It was one of the reasons he'd been exiled here, though he'd not sought them out or explored the other supernaturals of the city. He didn't even know if the mundane city officials knew such beings existed. Since he'd arrived, he'd pretty much kept to himself and kept his head down. If he was honest with himself, and sometimes he was these days, keeping his head down hid the pouting about his situation.

He wandered past the wood carvings and masks, admiring the detail and quality of the work. When he found himself by the tarot cards again, he squinted at them, his hand hovering over one of the decks open so customers could see the artwork. It was a different one than he'd looked at the last time he'd been here.

Giving in, he dropped his hand onto the deck and picked up part of it, flipping it over. He rolled his eyes and snorted. It was the death card again.

"Normally I wouldn't bother you…"

He jumped, Delphine's presence behind him startling him.

"If you wouldn't mind not touching the decks… I had to toss out the last one you touched. Weirdly enough, it would only flip the same card on the first draw." She looked at him sternly, a note of knowing mischief in her eyes.

"I guess getting my cards read would be a worthless endeavor."

Delphine chuckled. "Maybe, maybe not. You just might need to consult a powerful reader, not one of those charlatans who throw cards at a party. But be aware that if you do seek a reading, they'll need to do a larger spread to receive a true reading." She paused and looked him and up and down. "Your aura might be too strong, but you never know until you try."

"Is that something you could do?" He raised an eyebrow, assessing the manbo.

"No, that's not where my talents lie. But if you're curious sometime, I could check and see if I know anyone that might be able to read you and who would be willing to risk the encounter."

"I'm not that dangerous," he replied.

"Aren't you though?"

The door jingled.

"Delphine!" A tall, muscular Black man wearing a knit beanie and an EMT jacket stepped into the store. His voice filled the space. Spotting the manbo, he changed directions and put out his arms wide as he walked toward them.

"Boudreaux! How is it possible that you get more handsome every time I see you?" She stepped into his arms, returning the hug. They exchanged a kiss that was more than casual but less than intimate, at least to Dax's eye. She turned to Dax, gesturing toward him. "Boudreaux, this is Dax. Him and his friend Tomi are the gentlemen you'll be helping today."

Dax stuck out his hand when Boudreaux did and shook it. Tomi sidled up and greeted Delphine's friend.

"So, which one of you gets the sleeping bag?" Boudreaux asked.

Dax raised his hand. "I'm guessing that's me."

Boudreaux looked Tomi up and down. "I think you can borrow my partner's backup jacket. You look about the same size. You two ready to go?"

"What do I owe you for this?" Dax asked, before answering. He still owed a favor to Manman Delphine. He wasn't interested in increasing his favor debts to new people.

Delphine spoke up first. "I'm buying Boudreaux dinner tonight. You can add this to the favor we already agreed upon."

He narrowed his eyes as he gauged the manbo's words. He was already unhappy about being in her debt, but he weighed owing her slightly more versus owing a favor to a new unknown quantity.

He'd have to rely on Delphine and Adele's trust in her friend. "Agreed."

"Good." She winked at him. "Don't worry. I promised I wouldn't make the repayment too arduous." She reached out and caressed Boudreaux's smooth cheek. "Take care of my friends."

The EMT gave her a lop-sided grin and a sultry gaze. "Anything for you, Delphine. Gents, follow me."

He led Dax and Tomi out to the side street, stopping at a parked ambulance. Opening the door, he ushered Tomi and Dax in, then shut the door behind them. After he climbed into the driver's seat, he tossed back a jacket that matched his. "Throw that on, Tomi. Then you can help your friend into the bag. When we get there, you let me do the talking—especially you, Dax. And if you could try not to breathe to heavily or loudly when we get there."

"Um, so we're just going to drive up and roll Dax in?" Tomi asked, a skeptical eyebrow raised.

"Pretty much."

"Won't they kind of notice a body missing once he takes off?"

Boudreaux laughed. "You've clearly never dealt with bureaucracies, have you?" He chuckled and shook his head. "I'll do the talking and get the coroner out of the way so your friend can poke around. I'll leave you to keep an eye on things. Then when you're ready to go, you come find me and tell me dispatch got the drop wrong. He's supposed to go to county, not city. Then, boom." He wiped his hands off, then showed his empty palms. "We load the body back into the bus, and no one's the wiser."

"Are there any cameras we have to worry about?" Dax asked.

He leaned across the front of the ambulance then tossed back an adjustable ball cap for Tomi. "Put that on and keep your gaze low." Then he reached into one of the cabinets and pulled out a small black device. "Probably should keep that with you inside the bag. Turn it on when we pull in to unload you. It's a WIFI jammer." He laughed. "The bastards running procurement and physical plant skimped and only bought wi-fi cameras instead of going with a shielded, hard-wired system."

Dax nodded appreciatively. "That's good for us."

"And not so good for them," Tomi added.

"You cats got the plan, then?" Boudreaux asked.

"Sure. Should I go into the bag now?" Dax pointed to the unzipped bag laid out on a gurney.

"It's probably for the best, though we won't zip it all the way until we park. Tomi can pop back through this door and zip you up. I'll open the door, and we'll roll you in."

Dax had never been in a sleeping bag or a body bag for that matter. Tomi leaned over and held it open as Dax sat on it and then stretched out, tucking his feet and arms under it so Tomi could zip it most of the way up.

Boudreaux pointed to the straps dangling from the gurney. "Strap him down so he doesn't roll off the gurney while we're moving." He turned and buckled in, then started the ambulance.

Once Dax was settled, Tomi grabbed the zipper and closed up the body bag, stopping at the shoulder. After he buckled Dax down, he slipped through the small door to the front and strapped himself into the passenger seat.

"Hang on tight!" Boudreaux called as the ambulance surged out of its parking spot.

Dax gasped as his body was chucked around. He hoped the straps held, and he wouldn't need the ambulance for real.

SEVENTEEN
DAX

Dax sighed in relief when the ambulance bumped into the loading dock and the engine turned off. The deal was Boudreaux would get them into the morgue; he didn't promise it would be a smooth ride. Feeling around, he found the jammer and turned it on.

Tomi, a grin on his face, slid into the back. "Ready?" he whispered.

Dax nodded, not trusting himself to open his mouth. With a wink and a zip, darkness shrouded him. He wasn't afraid of the darkness —it was his domain, his birthright. But being confined in the heavy plastic bag after being tossed around without any control, his hot, moist exhalations laying heavily on his face with no place to escape, had sparked a bit of claustrophobia he didn't know he had. His finger twitched, then his shoulder. If he didn't get control of his body, the coroner would think they were bringing in a rising zombie rather than a dead corpse.

He took the expedient option and tucked his human façade into the aether. Without lungs to pull in air and a heart to move the oxygenated blood around, he didn't need to breathe. Without a nervous system and muscles to receive the signal, he wouldn't twitch. So, he laid perfectly still, a dressed skeleton in a body bag.

"What do you got for me today?" a feminine voice said. "Oh, hey, Boudreaux. It's good to see you." Her voice had shifted from all business to slightly flirty.

"Hey, Winnie. Just another customer for you," he replied.

"Whatever brings you my way… Where's Miguel? Taking the day off?" she asked, noticing Tomi.

"Yup. Got a trainee today. Why don't you and I head to your office and take care of the paperwork? Petey here can take the body down to the fridge," Boudreaux replied.

"Um, trainee, remember. Where's the fridge?" Tomi asked.

"Just follow the signs that say, 'Cadaver Storage.' Find an empty drawer to slide it in. You can't miss it."

"Ah, cool. I see," Tomi replied.

The conversation between Boudreaux and Winnie dwindled, along with their departing footsteps. When doors clattered, Tomi started them rolling. Dax jolted when they pushed through some doors. He might have moved at the shock of the impact if he weren't becoming increasingly distracted.

Something felt profoundly wrong, and it intensified the longer they were here and proceeding toward the morgue. At first, he thought he heard shuffling but dismissed it because it could be Tomi walking. The eerie moaning was harder to disregard. If he were wearing his human skin, he'd have goosebumps. Since the bag effectively blocked his vision, he pushed out with his awareness.

What he found punched him in the gut. Threads. So many frayed, uncut, unknotted threads.

"Ah, the elevator," Tomi mumbled to himself as they rolled to a stop.

When the door binged, Tomi pushed them inside. As soon as the elevator jolted to life, the oppressive feeling of too many threads grew with each foot descended. Every now and then, he thought he heard words mixed in with the moaning. Some he thought might be English, but others were harder to distinguish.

"Man, it's fucking creepy in here," Tomi said.

That wasn't the word he'd have used. Death was his domain. But after so many years being detached from his purpose, exiled in a human city where he was surrounded by death both violent and natural, he could understand Tomi's verdict. Though, he didn't know what he'd do if the tethered spirits stuck in this place figured out who he was or, more accurately, had been.

When the elevator bumped to a stop, Tomi pushed him into an icy cold room. The noise had been in the background, though persistent on the way here, but now it was more than white noise. It dominated his senses. It took him a minute to notice Tomi was speaking to him.

"Dax…Dax… You ready, man?"

"Yes."

Light assaulted his eyes when Tomi unzipped the body bag.

"Holy fuck!" Tomi staggered backward, clutching his stomach and covering his mouth with his other hand. "Dammit, Dax. Warn me next time. I nearly messed my drawers." Tomi faced away, breathing heavily.

He'd forgotten to return to his human skin after they were safely away from the coroner. Before he gave Tomi a heart attack, he slipped it on and then he understood.

While he had sensed the threads and the noise they created, his human senses, combined with his links to dead, assaulted him. He shivered aggressively, his hair standing on end. He could see the threads, see the rough treatment they'd been subjected to. He blinked. When he opened his eyes, he saw the gauzy shapes attached to the threads.

Closing his eyes, he extracted his body from the bag and dropped to the ground, nearly falling as the gurney rolled out from under him.

"Shit. Sorry about that. Forgot to lock the wheels."

Tomi's voice faded into the background. Dax had opened his eyes. He'd been noticed. Slowly spinning while he tried to find an escape route, he tried to block out the sound pummeling his ears. Moans stacked with screams, wrapped inside pain. And it was all directed at him.

"What's wrong, Dax… Oh fuck me… You see ghosts, don't you?

Shit. Shit. Shit." Tomi's eyes were wide as they darted around, trying to see if there were any ghosts coming for him.

Dax's breaths came in short gasping wheezes as his body overloaded. Around him, the tethered spirits focused all their intentions on him as they surrounded him, making him the eye of the storm, but there was no calm as the wind of their dismay was directed at him.

His vision started to fade around the edges as he spun and gasped, his friend forgotten. Instinctively, he shucked his humanity and pulled the cloak he'd first tested the other night around him.

Silence.

Peace.

He could tell that the vortex still swirled around him, but he'd erected a small barrier, a small cone of silence around himself. But like the wind had, the spirits picked pieces from the edges in dots and streaks. His panic burned into anger. He shoved out on the cloak hard, thickening the walls with his sense of injustice at the uncut threads.

"Oh, fuck, what now…" Tomi said, his own breathing hurried and shallow.

Dax had expanded the cloak around the entire room, encompassing Tomi and the morgue drawers.

"I know better than this," Tomi mumbled. "I've seen this movie. I know I shouldn't have followed the white man into the haunted morgue basement. And it's always the brother that gets killed first…" He mumbled an unintelligible string of what sounded like profanities.

Though the cloak wouldn't last forever or for very long, Dax had bought himself some time. "Tomi. Nothing can harm you down here, not with me here."

He wasn't actually sure of that, but the staff managed to work here.

"Damn, man. You sure?"

He nodded. "It was just overwhelming. I've never been in a place like this with my…" He gestured to his human body. "The sensory experience was…unexpected. Let's find Jason and get out of here.

"Right. Right. Right." Tomi leapt into action, checking the clipboards on the outside of each drawer. "You going to help?"

"Sorry, at the moment I'm working on something else." He wasn't sure how long he could maintain the cloak, especially at this expanded level. He could feel the pressure of the spirits pushing on it, testing its integrity. It felt like his ears needed to pop, and he couldn't quite fully expand his chest.

"Uh…gotcha. You focus on that." He returned to his task, clipboards rattling against the side of the shiny morgue drawers. "Found him." Tomi pointed toward a drawer, holding up a clipboard.

He didn't appear to want to open it, so Dax grabbed it and pulled it open. A black bag like the one Dax had arrived in lay on the stainless-steel shelf.

"I can't watch this, man." Tomi turned around, facing away.

Dax could understand Tomi's hesitance to see the cold, dead body of his friend and whatever the coroner had done to it. Despite the urgency of their errand, he paused once he saw the pale, empty face of Jason. He was unclothed. Cut lines and staples covered his chest.

He hadn't been able to get a close look at the wound at the crime scene. The cops had kept their police line too far away. With a shake of his head, he reminded himself to get on with it. He knew it was too much of a hope that the body would have been left unmolested or the evidence bag kept nearby, but if his suspicions were correct, he wouldn't need them.

His eyes homed in on the irregular tear where the bullet had entered Jason's body. With his hand held flat, he hovered it over the wound and reached up to place his other hand over the spot where he'd been shot. He thought he felt a similarity.

Licking his lips, he retracted the flesh on his hand and poked a bony finger into the wound, making sure the edges of the wound touched his finger bone. He should have brought his bullet with him. But the traces he felt along his finger were too familiar to be a coincidence. Whoever had put a bullet into him had come back and put one in Jason, probably thinking it was Dax.

"Fuck."

"You got what you need? Because I want to get out of here," Tomi asked, his voice sounded steady but strained.

"Hmm, give me a minute." He felt something else, something that shouldn't be there.

A tiny thread remained. It shouldn't have. He'd cut it. He'd felt it snap. Reaching out, he pinched the thread between his thumb and forefinger. Something of the bullet coexisted with Jason's life thread, coiling around it. He followed the thread and its rider. Taught and entangled, it disappeared through the edge of the barrier.

Closing his eyes, he sighed, deflating slightly. Somewhere on the other side of the barrier he'd erected to protect himself, Jason's spirit moaned and howled, demanding that Dax set him free. He'd failed his former employee. He thought he'd freed him, but something of the bullet had defeated him, tying Jason's spirit to his cadaver.

Withdrawing the finger from Jason's chest, he kept a firm grip on the thread as he shucked his human façade. Pulling his scythe from the place in the aether where he stored it, he made sure he focused entirely on the thread, marshaling all his strength, such as it was these days, and slashed it. The thread snapped, zinging away from the cadaver.

Looking back to the body, he poked his finger back into the hole but found it empty save for the trace of the bullet. Apparently, he'd broken the bullet's enchantment and freed his former employee. He pulled his finger from the wound and made sure the finger was clean before pulling on his human skin. Tomi didn't turn around until Dax slid the drawer closed.

"Can we please get out of here now?" Tomi asked, a faint sheen of sweat glistening on his forehead under the bill of his hat.

"What?" Dax had become distracted as the sounds grew steadier. He looked toward where Jason's thread had snapped. It had torn a hole in his cloak, and the spirits were using it to tear a wider space. "Yeah. Yeah. Let's get out of here."

He crawled back into the body bag as Tomi held the gurney still, then pulled in the cloak until it just surrounded him. Tomi would be fine. The spirits here weren't interested in his human friend, not when someone who could release them was there.

He wanted to, but he also didn't want to test the limits of his power or the limits of the leash that had been imposed upon him. Someday, someday he'd come clean out this pit of despair, but right now, they needed to get out while their cover still held. He didn't know how long Boudreaux could keep the coroner busy.

Once they entered the elevator, he returned to his skeletal form so he wouldn't show his breathing. As they ascended, the pressure around his cloak diminished, though it didn't entirely disappear.

"Hey, Petey, you're supposed to deposit, not withdraw," Boudreaux said, a touch of humor in his tone.

"Didn't you get the message? Dispatch fucked up. We're supposed to take this one to county."

"Dammit. I wish the pencil pushers would pull their heads out of their asses. Load him up." He paused. "Sorry for the hassle, Winnie."

"No worries, we never got around to the paperwork, so no harm, no foul. See you Saturday?" she asked.

"You know it."

"Good. I'll make waffles and bacon for Sunday brunch."

Tomi pushed them back into motion and a minute later, he was secured in the back of the ambulance. As soon as Tomi pulled the zipper, he slipped his skin on. Once the cool air rushed over his face, he sighed in relief. His body felt thin and overly stretched. He'd never tried switching forms that many times in such a short time window. He didn't like it.

As they pulled into traffic and put some distance from the morgue, relief washed through Dax as the maelstrom of trapped spirits disappeared behind them. Today had been eye opening in ways far beyond just confirming his theory about who'd shot Jason. He just hoped his excessive use of his powers would remain unnoticed.

But he also wondered why so many souls had been left tied to one place. Surely the psychopomps would want their due and come collect them. How had they been neglecting their duties this much? He sighed. He'd have to check out the other morgues to see if they were suffering from a similar surfeit of tethered spirits. As if he didn't have too much on his plate already...

EIGHTEEN

"Hey, Mom, we're going to head out to a movie," Cory called into the kitchen.

"That's nice. What are you going to see?" she replied.

"I think that new action flick, right, Jamie?"

She rolled her eyes at her friend.

"So, car chases and gun fights?" his mom replied.

"Maybe some explosions, too." He laughed.

"Have fun. Let me know if you're going to be late."

"Alright, Mom." Cory pulled the door open and ushered Jamie out.

She climbed into the passenger seat of Cory's Kia and buckled up. As soon as they were on the road, she turned to him, an eyebrow quirked up. "Car chases and gun fights, eh?"

Cory laughed, sounding overly satisfied with himself. "I thought it was funny. Plus, she doesn't care about action movies, so she won't ask many questions about it."

She snorted. "You better hope there's actually an action movie in the theaters right now."

He turned his head, blinking slowly at her. "Jamie. There's always an action movie in the theaters."

"I guess so." She fiddled with the music, finally settling on one of her soothing playlists.

Though it didn't seem to help much these days. The gun in her pocket seemed to weigh far more than the nearly two pounds it professed to weigh. It seemed to be reaching the proportions of a neutron star, crushing her dreams and her waking hours until its gravity was the only thing her brain could focus on. Its weight reminded her that her life depended on murdering someone.

"Where do you want to park this time?" Cory asked.

"I don't know. Um, let's just do a drive by first," she replied.

"Gotcha."

Now that they were near the bar, she forced her brain to focus on their task. It was dark and rainy, nothing unusual there, but she'd still be able to peer down the dark alley where he always seemed to park his motorcycle. Sure enough, it was there.

"It's there. Pull around the block then park in front of that market." That would put the car facing the direction their target usually went when he left the bar.

"Good. Because I might get hungry later and need a snack, and I don't want to walk in the rain."

She rolled her eyes. "You're always hungry for a snack."

He chuckled, pulling off the road, and parked. "Mom says I'm still a growing boy."

"You're eighteen. You've got to be as tall as you're going to get."

"I don't want to take any chances."

She laughed, and it felt good. She'd done precious little laughing since she'd walked in on bikers roughing up her dad. Cory viewed his job as keeping up her spirits. He'd been doing it for most of their lives, but she knew he felt particularly helpless with the current situation, so he supported her and tried to make her laugh.

He turned off the engine and slouched into his seat. Soon, the windows fogged up, the cold rain chilling the inside of the car as they expelled their moist breath into the air. Though it made watching a bit more difficult, it obscured their presence from people walking down the street, not that there were many in this weather.

As they sat, Cory checked the time on his phone, then stared out the other window, sighing forlornly. Jamie tried to ignore him as she stared out the window, alternating her gaze between the entrance to the bar and the alley next to it. A steady stream of people headed in and out of the bar, but none of them looked like the tall, skinny white man with the large nose. After a while, Cory's fidgeting shook the parked car as his foot thumped on the floorboard. If he didn't knock it off, someone might wonder why a car with its engine off was vibrating. They didn't need a nosy cop wondering what they were doing out this late in this part of town.

She huffed in annoyance. "Cory, go get yourself a snack. And for god's sake, download a phone game or something."

He grinned and gave her a jaunty salute. "Yes, ma'am!"

Once the door shut, she exhaled a deep sigh. She was glad for his company, even if he was a pain in the ass, but she still couldn't help feeling annoyed. It wasn't his fault, really. He was a fidgety guy and needed to burn a lot of energy, hence their regular runs. Since they'd been burning time planning their—she was loath to call it murder, but that's what it was—murder, they hadn't been out for one. She missed it, too. She almost always felt better about life after a good run through the woods in her wolf form. Two weeks was too long between runs.

"Shit," she mumbled to herself.

The headlight of his motorcycle poured out of the alley. If Cory didn't get back soon, they were going to miss their opportunity to try to find his home. Peering toward the door to the market, she made a snap decision and jumped out of the passenger side and ran around to the driver's side. She fired up the car and put it in gear, rolling forward so the car was directly in front of the market's door.

"Come on, come one…" she said to herself.

The headlight shifted in the alley, appearing to move forward. She'd hate to leave her friend behind. There he was. He noticed his car and bent over, peering into the vehicle. Reaching across the car, she grabbed the handle of the passenger door and pushed it open.

"Get in!" she yelled.

Cory sprang into action and practically dove into the car, though he made sure to protect his fountain drink and bag of salty, fatty snack foods. He pulled the door shut behind him just in time. The motorcycle pulled out of the alley and onto the street. Giving him a second to straighten his bike out and pull away, she eased into the street behind him. She was just someone who'd stopped at the market for snacks and was now heading home. No big deal.

Cory carefully set his bag on the floor and pulled his seatbelt around, but when the belt got tangled around his arm holding the soda, he nearly lost it. Fortunately, he saved it without a disastrous spill and managed to get his belt buckled without further mishap.

The snack bag crinkled as Cory reached in and popped a handful into his mouth. "This is very exciting."

"Don't talk with your mouth full. It's gross." She focused on the road ahead and the motorcycle, knowing that Cory had probably just stuck his tongue out at her with a mouthful of half-chewed food.

"Ugh." He swallowed. "You always ruin my fun."

"Well, you're getting a first-hand view of a car case." She looked down at the speedometer — twenty-five miles per hour.

"It's titillating. A rocket-fueled, mayhem making, adrenaline ride." He said this all tonelessly. "Woo. Hoo."

She chuckled. "It's not my fault he's a conscientious driver… rider…whatever."

"Oh, look, he's using his turn signal. Oh, no. The excitement. I hope we can keep up with this wild, reckless driver."

Her chuckle turned into a laugh. "Stop it! I'm trying to pay attention, and you're making me laugh." She turned on her turn signal and made a safe turn, resuming her slow speed chase.

Cory exaggerated a loud, fake yawn. "Wake me up if this thing gets exciting." He filled his mouth with another handful of crunchy snacks.

They followed the man through a couple more turns onto quieter roads, but when they approached the larger, busier road intersecting the one they were on, he gunned it through the stop sign and took a hard left across traffic.

"Wake up. It's chase time." She wasn't sure why she said it, but it made Cory snort with laughter as he tried to keep himself from spraying food debris from his mouth.

She pushed down the pedal, and the Kia leapt forward at a moderate clip. Once she approached the stop sign, she looked both ways as she rolled through it then mashed the pedal down as she aimed for a gap between cars approaching from her left. Her stomach dropped, and her throat tightened as lights bore down on her and horns screamed.

The old Kia bounced into the middle lane then into the lane they wanted. They'd only lost a bit of distance on the motorcycle, though he was attempting to weave his way through the cars in front of them to put some distance between them.

"Holy shit, Jamie. You're going to kill my baby…" He patted the dashboard. "Don't worry, baby, I won't let the mean lady hurt you."

Ignoring her passenger, she turned off her safe driving brain and squeezed through a narrow passing space, accelerating to weave back into the other lane. With each honk annoyed at her antics, her adrenaline rose. She'd never done something like this before. Neither had Cory as far as she knew, though he seemed to be taking it in stride as he sucked on the giant soda. However, the knuckles on his hand gripping the dash were white.

A moment of triumph brought a faint smile to her lips as she gained a position. There was only one car separating them from the motorcycle. A pair of trucks blocked the motorcycle from slipping by them. Instead of moving into the other lane to get closer, she decided to keep the car in front of her, hoping the motorcyclist wouldn't see them and think that maybe he'd lost them.

Now that they were both cruising at traffic speeds, she backed off a little bit so she wasn't quite riding the tail of the car in front of her. The brake lights in front of her flared, and the rear of the car rushed toward them. She slammed on her brakes and yanked on the wheel, aiming for the middle lane. She narrowly missed ramming into the car.

More brakes screeched and tires squealed. The motorcycle darted into oncoming traffic, sending cars swerving around it. Screaming, Jamie held up an arm, blocking the view of the car hurtling toward her, its lights streaming through the window. Fortunately, the car stopped before smashing into them. Weaving through the mayhem he'd created, the biker looked directly at her, staring as he rode by. When he passed, the roar of his engine announced his departure.

She heaved panicked breaths as she tried to calm her body. Blinking rapidly, she watched people step out of their cars, assessing their vehicles and the other drivers. The lights blared in her eyes. She jolted when someone knocked on her window. When she didn't lower her arm or roll the window down, they knocked again. She could barely hear their mumbled voice, the blood pumping too loudly through her ears.

With a shake of her head, she rolled the window down. "What?"

"Are you alright, miss?" a woman asked, bending over to look into the car.

Jamie, unsure of the answer, looked at herself. Other than the seatbelt locked tightly against her chest and shoulder, she thought she was OK. "I think so. Just a bit scared."

"Damn motorcycles. Always causing traffic problems. I hope the cops get him. Well, if you're OK, I'm going back to my car," the woman said.

"Thank you, ma'am. We're fine." She rolled the window up. "Are you OK, Cory?"

"I spilled my drink…" he mumbled, sounding on the verge of tears.

"What?" She turned and looked at him, a smile cracking her face.

He'd spilled his giant cup of soda indeed. It dripped down the inside of the window, pooled on the dashboard, streaked the side window, and had drenched Cory. Streams of sticky soda ran out of his hair and down his forehead. His shirt was soaked. After the adrenaline dump of nearly becoming part of a massive car pileup, she couldn't help but laugh at her soggy friend. She really didn't mean to, but he looked like a half-drowned kitten, his hair falling into his face.

"Yeah, yeah. Laugh it up at your poor old friend, Cory. Just here to make you laugh." He sounded miffed at her jocularity, but she couldn't help it. He shook his head violently, flinging soda all over the car and onto her.

"Hey!" she called, raising her arm to block it.

"Serves you right." Rolling down the window, he dumped the rest of the soda onto the street, then tossed the empty, crushed cup onto the floor of the car. He reached down and grabbed his bag of snacks, stuffing his hand into the bag. He lifted a handful, but liquid dripped from his hand and down his wrist. With an annoyed growl, he crushed the mushy snacks and flung his hand back into the bag.

She stifled her laugh, forcing her lips shut, and looked away so she didn't start laughing again. As the cars tried to move apart so they could unblock each other and traffic, she waited until a spot opened up, and she was able to pull away from their disastrous first attempt at a high-speed chase.

They stayed silent as she worked her way back to their neighborhood. Cory wasn't in the mood as he fumed about being soaked in cold, sticky soda. If she thought it were possible, steam would be rolling off his head.

"You're helping me clean this mess up," Cory said, finally breaking the silence.

She thought about explaining how it was his fault for buying the super-duper bucket o' soda while they were on a stakeout, but she was sure her observation wouldn't be appreciated. He was helping her when he didn't have to. She owed him some cleaning time; it was the least she could do.

"I know. We'll get your baby all cleaned up and sparkling again." She parked in front of Cory's house, then turned and looked at her friend, a twinkle in her eyes. "At least you have an exciting car chase story to tell your mom."

Cory flipped her off and headed toward his house, no doubt to grab a shower. She sighed; the silliness had been needed, even if Cory was grumpy about it, but reality settled back in. She still hadn't completed her mission. She still hadn't killed a man.

NINETEEN

JAMIE

Jamie opened her mouth to saying something to Cory but snapped her jaw closed with a clack of her teeth when Travis wandered over to their table, his hands hidden in the pockets of his black leather jacket.

"Hey, dorks," Travis said, flopping into the empty chair between them without invitation.

"Can we help you?" Cory asked.

"You kids seem to be having a good time." He smirked briefly before shifting to what he thought was an intimidating face.

Normally, Jamie might have found it intimidating, but now that she'd seen the masters for whom Travis ran errands, she was less impressed.

"What do you want, Travis?" Jamie pursed her lips.

"You were given a task. My associates want to know why you haven't accomplished it, yet."

Travis's arrogance rankled her. Without that leather jacket with the Thor's Hammer over the left side of the chest, Travis would just be any other loser twerp, barely making it through high school.

She sat up straighter, furrowing her brow. "We weren't given a timeline. We'll get it done when the time is right. This isn't like getting a gallon of milk for your mom."

"My, aren't you getting brave? Not the meek little nobody you used to be." He snickered. "Be careful you don't mouth off to the wrong person, Jamie."

"Tell them we're working on it. This isn't an easy task."

Cory nodded. "Right. We'll get it done. We'll actually follow through."

He'd tried to sound confident, but Jamie, who knew him better than anyone else, heard the trepidation and barest hint of a quaver he tried to cover up.

"Tell Ivar we've been preparing. We want to do this job correctly and not blow it. He can have the job done quickly and wrong or he can have it done properly. He can't have both quickly and correctly all at once."

At the mention of Ivar, Travis flinched slightly and paled nearly imperceptibly. If Jamie hadn't been paying attention, she'd have missed it.

Rallying himself, he puffed up. "I'll tell them. You just better hope they accept your answer."

She inhaled and prepared to say something obnoxious but bit her lip and exhaled. "Thanks, Travis. We're trying to do our best. I appreciate you taking the time to carry our message to Ivar."

He nodded and stood up. "We'll be in touch." Then, he walked away.

Cory twisted around to make sure Travis was gone and not lurking around one of the bookshelves. When he was sure the bikers' flunky had disappeared, he chuckled weakly. "You handled him."

"Yeah," she replied, then added half-heartedly, "I really handled him."

TWENTY

JAMIE

They'd tried casing the bar a couple more times, but he wasn't there one night, and they lost him the other time when they tried to stay further back in traffic. Jamie was beginning to lose hope of ever finding his house. And with each failed attempt, the encroaching panic over the promised retribution grew. Would they come for her first, or would they start with her mom or dad?

The bar and the street in front of it felt like too public of a place, but they'd had no luck finding his address or following him home, and with Ivar breathing down their necks via his high school protégé, they didn't have much time left. She imagined if they didn't complete the job soon, it wouldn't be Travis, but the much scarier Ivar coming to check on them. Or to just drag her away to repay her father's debt in some other manner.

"So, what are you going to do?" Cory asked, fidgeting as they sat in the car before leaving Cory's neighborhood.

"I don't know. I don't know." She growled in frustration. "I just may have to do it there. At the bar. But if I do it, I'm going to need you ready and alert. We're going to need to get out of there fast." She frowned as her stomach gurgled. Since Travis had turned up the heat on them, her stomach had become sour, constantly churning with anxiety and fear.

Cory took a deep breath and nodded nervously a couple times. "I know. I've never let you down, and I'm not going to start now."

She sighed. He was her best friend, and her one true companion and ally. And she was making him an accessory to her crime. An accomplice. Every time she tried to get him to leave her on her own, he refused and doubled down. She wanted to tell him he didn't understand what he was getting himself into. She barely did. But he was eighteen, and so was she. Legally, they were adults.

Besides, people got murdered every day in Red City. The cops hardly ever arrested anyone unless the victim was someone rich or important. She doubted a grimy biker who owned a shitty dive bar was in either of the classes the police actually cared about protecting. As long as they didn't get caught doing the deed, she thought they could get away with it. They'd even gone to the junkyard and found some old license plates from a junker to throw on the car for the days they cased the bar. They had an unregistered gun, a beat-up car that looked like a thousand other beat-up cars, and no real connection to the bar owner.

If they weren't stupid, they could do this.

And that only added to Jamie's general disgust with everything. She didn't want to be a murderer. She just wanted to go to school and get out of her parents' house, but there was only one way to do that now. And that was through the man in the photograph.

Cory slapped his hands on the steering wheel. "Alright. Let's go." He turned the ignition and directed the car on the now familiar path toward the House of the Rising Sun Pub and Tearoom.

Her eyes tracked and focused on any point of light outside the window—an open sign, a porch light, a strip club's neon sign. When they arrived on the street with the dive bar and market, they parked next to a dark patch of sidewalk that seemed to have no streetlight. For some reason, there seemed to be fewer streetlights, and the lack of other nighttime businesses that helped render the street darker. It reminded her of her own neighborhood. Poor people, poor infrastructure. She guessed for this kind of dark work, that was a feature and not a bug.

As had become their standard procedure, they drove by the alley to check that his motorcycle was there. It was.

"Want me to park on the other side of the street so you can watch directly into the alley?" Cory asked, his voice subdued.

"Yeah. Let's do that."

Cory pulled around the block and parked across the street, so her window was pointed toward the alley. "You just gonna roll down the window and wait?"

She'd never been very specific about her plans. Despite spending more time at the quarry, she was still at best an inconsistent marksperson. And right now, the motorcycle in the alley seemed like it was a long way from where she sat. If he managed to get rolling quicker than she could get her shot off, she'd have to try for a moving target, and she had no confidence in her ability for that. And they only had so many of the special bullets Ivar had given them.

"Shit. I can't do this."

Cory reached for the keys, but she laid her hand on his.

"No. I've got a different idea. Go get yourself a snack, then I want you to pull around the block and let me off over there."

"OK…" Cory hesitated.

"Go, Cory. You're going to need to be ready to drive at the drop of a hat." Now that she had a plan, she was ready to go into action, and she didn't need Cory wasting time.

"Right." He jumped out of the car and strode purposefully toward the convenience store. He reemerged three minutes later with a small bag. Setting it aside, he started the car and drove around the block, stopping where she'd directed him to earlier. "What's the plan?"

"I'm going to wait in the alley. I don't think I can shoot well enough to hit him at this range." She swallowed the acid in her throat.

Cory stared at her for a few moments before he nodded. "So, thought. These blocks aren't too big around here. Should I drive around so I'm not just parked and waiting? Then I'll be rolling so you can come out running, and we'll be off instead of waiting on the side of the road."

She thought about it. Though she didn't like not being able to see her getaway car waiting in front of her, his idea did have merit. If a bunch of cars happened to pass by, they'd be stuck for valuable seconds. If he stopped, he could stop traffic with the car, then they could get moving. Plus, she was a fast runner, even in her human form. It could work.

Reaching into her pocket, she pulled out her gloves and pulled them on then drew the hood over her head. With a quick pat at her other pocket, she ensured the pistol was indeed there.

"Let's go with your plan. Just be sure to have the doors unlocked. Maybe roll down the windows too." Her mouth was dry, too dry. She looked at the water she'd brought, but the thought of putting anything into her mouth made her want to throw up. She'd just have to live with cotton mouth for a while.

"Good luck," Cory said, his eyes sad.

She nodded then stepped out of the car. Stuffing her hands into her pockets, she walked toward the alley, keeping her head down. With a quick look around to make sure there was no one on the street, she ducked into the alley, trying to walk casually as if she belonged there. With no light in the alley and no streetlamp on the sidewalk, the alley was deeply dark. She was thankful for her enhanced night vision. Otherwise, she'd have tripped over the garbage.

However, she was less than thrilled about her enhanced sense of smell. The alley smelled of piss, stale beer, and garbage. She shrugged. It felt appropriate. Cold-blooded murder shouldn't smell like roses and a spring day. At the least the rain had slackened to a steady drizzle. The streets weren't a river of rain runoff. She didn't fancy being soaked to the bone then slipping and falling as she tried to run away. Now, she just needed her target to step out and climb on his bike.

So she waited.

She was a much more patient person than Cory. His idea to drive around had the added benefit of keeping her fidgety friend from becoming distracted by boredom and snacks, though he no doubt had a bag open on the passenger seat so he could feed his nervous habit. He liked driving. It had been his limited freedom as a teen. It was a task he could focus on.

Not sure when she'd need it, she kept her hand on the handle of the gun, though she was careful not to rest her nervous fingers on the trigger. She didn't want to shoot herself with nervous shaking.

But the longer she waited, the worse her stomach churned. The smells didn't help either. She lurched toward the dumpster, bracing her hand against the brick wall, and unloaded her nearly empty stomach until only acid burned in the back of her throat. She spit onto the ground, trying to clear the taste from her mouth, but without anything to drink, she was stuck with the vile taste.

Once she was sure she could hold her stomach, she walked to the other side of the alley and tucked into a deep shadow to wait. The vomit didn't add to the bouquet of the alley, but at least her stomach felt more solid.

She tapped her glove covered finger on the cylinder of the gun with its six special bullets. Something of the bullets' essence reached her even through the glove. Though they felt dangerous and somehow dark or evil, their presence kept her alert. The focus also seemed to settle her stomach, at least for now.

A thump on the door caught her attention. Securing her grip around the handle, she withdrew the gun but kept it low against her side, her finger resting on the trigger guard. She stayed tucked into her shadow, but her whole body vibrated, ready to jump into action. Instead of a dry mouth, it now flooded with saliva. Adjusting her head to the side, she spit while keeping her eyes firmly fixed on the heavy door.

A crack of light emerged as the door opened. The sound of music and voices spilled out with the light. Then the door opened wide. She lifted the gun, pulling back the hammer, and waited.

TWENTY-ONE

DAX

Dax backed his motorcycle into the alley, tucking it under the awning he used to keep it dry during the rainy season. Then he slipped in the side door, stashing his stuff in the office. Tomi was working the bar tonight, and his cousin was supposed to be in attendance for an informal interview. They needed a bartender, and Tomi said she had the skills and his trust.

He worked the morning and day shifts when the crowd was older and more blue collar. The evening crowd was a whole different animal with a diverse mix of twenty-something punks and alt-rock kids. The evening crowd drank hard, liked the jukebox loud, and had a great time. Though Dax wasn't part of the crowd, he still like to observe it from the outside. Somehow, the energy was infectious.

Tomi had kept out the element that wouldn't appreciate the diverse crowd they fostered. A zero-tolerance policy for anyone with white supremacist symbols enforced with a brandished bat went a long way to keeping that element away.

Dax pulled up an empty barstool in the corner where the bar met the wall. Before he'd even gotten fully situated, Tomi had a cold can of Rainier open and sitting in front of him. He nodded his thanks and took a drink, swiveling around to watch the crowd talk, flirt, and have a good time. It was a mostly full house tonight, something their bank account would appreciate. And the better the bar did, the less likely he'd have to find more specialized ways—assisting people in need of a transition to the afterlife for a fee—of using his powers to make money like he had in the past.

Since there was a gap between Dax and the next occupied barstool, a short Black woman slipped into the space. She had her afro clipped up in a frohawk. Her black band T-shirt—he didn't recognize the band displayed—had the collar, sleeves, and hem cut to reveal more skin. Tight black pants and thick-soled Doc Martens finished her ensemble.

"Tomi, whiskey, please!" she called, leaning onto the bar.

Tomi, a smirk on his face, slid a bucket glass onto the bar and poured a healthy shot from a bottle on the back bar. The young woman grabbed it and threw it back, sliding the empty back toward Tomi.

Turning, she faced Dax, a broad grin on her face. "I'm Little Suzie, and I'm punk as fuck!" She threw up both hands and gave him a set of devil's horns. "Woo!" She sauntered off, heading to the jukebox.

Dax stared after her, his jaw hanging. The sound of Tomi laughing drew his attention back to the bar.

"What?" Dax asked, the beginning of a smile quirking up one side of his lips.

"Nothing." He turned and walked to the other end of the bar. "Hey, Suz. Come over here when you're done there." He gestured toward Dax with his head.

Focused on the jukebox, she lifted her left hand and gave Tomi a crisp middle finger. Tomi laughed some more. After feeding the juke, she wandered back over, hopping up onto the barstool next to Dax.

"What you want, Tomi?"

"Suz." He gestured to Dax. "This is Dax. He owns the place. Dax. This is Suzie. She's my cousin. She's punk as fuck." Tomi grinned broadly, having too good of a time with the situation.

Suzie's eyes widened as they flicked between Tomi and Dax. "Shit... Sorry, Mr...."

"Just Dax is fine." He couldn't help but grin at her. "Tomi says you've bartended before."

"Hell yeah. For a few years," she replied.

Tomi slid a pint of Pabst in front of her.

"Ever worked shifts on your own?" he asked, taking a swig from his Rainier.

"You know it. Worked at a few small bars like this. I can handle myself. I may be punk as fuck, but I can fuck up a punk if needed." She emphasized it by punching her fist into her open palm.

He chuckled. "Not sure you'll need to worry about that. We keep the crowd pretty friendly here. Any questions about the job?"

"Tomi says you're good to work for and the pay is good. I'm new to town and need a job. As long as you're not an asshole, and you keep out racists, I'd love the job."

He stuck out his hand. "You're hired."

"Shit? Really?" she looked shocked, her jaw hanging open a little.

He nodded.

She took Dax's hand and shook it. "Fuck yeah! Tomi—"

Tomi slid her another shot of whiskey. "I know, cuz. 'Tomi, whiskey.' Oh, I don't remember if told you, but Mama wants you to come over for Sunday dinner."

She rubbed her belly. "You know I'll be there." Taking her shot and beer, she winked at Dax and wondered off to find some new friends.

"So?" Tomi asked.

"I like her. She'll fit in well here."

Tomi looked relieved, but before he could continue the conversation, he was drawn to the other side of the bar to fill more orders. After that, there was little time to talk. The bar was hopping, and Tomi was hustling, so Dax nursed his beer, then gave up his stool and headed to the office.

"I'll talk to you tomorrow," he called as he passed Tomi.

"Sure thing, boss," Tomi said, not bothering to look up as he poured pints.

With his coat on and his helmet in hand, he opened the back

door, pausing for a moment to take in one last dose of the energy before leaving. Stepping out into the night, he let the door go.

He stopped abruptly, a dark premonition smacking him in the face. Turning, he stared into the shadows as a glint of light shined off dark metal.

Narrowing his eyes, he thought he recognized her as she stepped forward out of the deepest part of the shadows.. The girl in the car…

She opened her mouth. "I'm sorry…"

The first bullet slammed into the wall above his head. Before he could react, the second smashed into his helmet, sending it skittering away from him. The third…

Searing agony exploded in his chest just to the left of his heart. He staggered backward and fell on his ass, then to his back, his head snapping back onto the hard ground. As stars burst in his eyes, he tried to process what was going on. She'd shot him. She'd ambushed him and shot him. He'd been fucking shot again. In his own alley.

Pain quickly transferred into burning hot rage. He forced himself off the ground. As he twisted around, still seated, he watched the girl sprint out of the alley and dive into a car. However, the car didn't move. He clawed his way to his feet, staggering against his motorcycle.

Infuriated and ready to deal some retribution, he threw his leg over his bike and kicked the bike to life. He revved the engine, the loud roar stoking his fury as he gunned the engine.

TWENTY-TWO

JAMIE

Jamie stared down at the man she'd just shot. He lay sprawled on the pavement of the alley—dead.

With a shake of her head to clear it, she took a few tentative steps toward the entrance of the alley, sidestepping around the body. When he moaned and moved, she gasped. She'd shot him right in the chest. He should be dead. Then he tried to stand.

His eyes locked on her. But where he'd had normal eyes before, they now burned with a hellish fire. Her teeth chattered as she gasped in shallow breaths. His face looked thinner than it had before. It might have been a trick of the eye in the low light, but it looked almost like she could see his skull.

She had to run. She stumbled forward then ran.

A car screeched to a halt in the middle of the street. It was Cory. He reached into the back seat and pushed open the door behind him. With a clear target in front of here, she sprinted out as fast as she could, the gun still in her hand. At the last second, she dove into the back seat.

"Go!" she yelled.

Cory hit the gas. But the car sputtered and stopped.

"Cory!" she hissed, sitting up and pulling the door shut behind her. "Now. Go, damn it!"

Cory turned the key, but the car only made a grinding sound, then stopped even doing that, making a weird electrical whine.

"Cory…"

"I know. I know. I'm trying." He cranked the car again. "Come on, baby…"

The old Kia fired to life. Cory laughed hysterically as soon as the engine started. Jamie just sighed in relief, sagging into the seat. Grabbing the gear shifter, he yanked it into drive and mashed the pedal. The car dribbled forward, crossing the oncoming lane, then the striped center line. Jamie twisted in her seat to watch the mouth of the alley and screamed at a set of headlights bearing down on them. The car jammed on its brakes and swerved, screeching to a halt and barely missing the bumper of Cory's car. The car stopped in the other lane, blocking it diagonally.

A motorcycle roared to life. The sound, loud and terrifying, bounced and ricocheted out of the alley, sounding like some monster bellowing its rage.

Cory's car picked up steam gradually, pulling away from the scene of the crime she'd just committed.

"Can't you go any faster?" she asked frantically.

"I'm trying. This isn't a race car…or even a good one." His voice had gone up an octave under the stress.

She held her breath, staring at the entrance to the alley. On cue, a motorcycle sped from the alley, dodging around the car as it tried to pull back into the proper lane.

"Oh shit! He's chasing us." Her voice joined Cory's, hiking up into a higher register.

"What do I do, what do I do, what do I do?" His arms shook as he white-knuckled the steering wheel.

"Just drive. Calm down and drive."

"Where?"

"Away. Anywhere."

He yanked the wheel, the tires screeching as he turned to the right. She slammed into the door. Scrambling up, she kneeled on the seat, facing backwards so she could watch. The motorcycle swung a wide arc into the other lane and pulled back into the lane behind them.

The man had lost the helmet he carried at some point. His medium length hair flew out behind him. She rubbed her eyes; the flames in his eyes burned hotter than before. What was he?

"Oh, fuck… What's wrong with his eyes?" Cory gasped out.

"Keep your eyes on the road. I'll watch him."

The motorcycle surged forward as the rider popped a wheelie.

"Turn!" she screamed, bracing herself. She had no idea if they were near a street, but if they didn't do something soon… She stared at the menacing front wheel and undercarriage of the big custom chopper motorcycle.

Her only warning of the turn was a scared moan and a grunt as Cory pulled the wheel. This time, they lurched to the left. Heaving a sign of relief, she unbraced as the motorcycle's front wheel bounced back to the pavement, the biker blasting through the intersection.

"Did we lose him?"

"Maybe… Fuck. No." She sagged in on herself.

The biker had somehow made the turn, pulling over the sidewalk at the corner by speeding back into the lane behind them.

"I have a plan," Cory called from the front seat. "Keep an eye on him."

She didn't need the instruction; she couldn't take her eyes off the flame-eyed biker. As they passed under a streetlamp, she squinted and tried to focus behind the biker. It looked as if he had a frayed-edged cloak fluttering behind him. But what truly worried her was the dark flickering blade that played at the edge of her vision, floating above his head. Not floating, it was attached to a pole that the biker held in his right hand, the base of which was propped next to his boot covered foot.

With each second she stared into the flaming eyes, her terror grew, filling her gut and spilling through her veins to permeate every part of her body. Her mouth felt as dry as a desert. She tried to move her tongue around, but it felt like sandpaper.

"Turning," Cory shouted.

She didn't get braced in time and tumbled into the door, one of her knees slipping to the floor. "Thanks for the heads up." She crawled back onto the seat. The demon biker was still there. Shaking her head, she gaped, her mouth hanging open. The man's face looked thin…transparent. She could see a skull transposed under his flesh. The fires in his eyes burned hotter and brighter, almost white blue. Now, a hood shrouded his head, staying up despite the wind pulling the more solid cloak out behind him. But the gleaming blade of the scythe drew her eyes like they were magnets.

He surged forward, popping up on his back wheel again. Before she could yell a warning, she just screamed incoherently as the front wheel of the motorcycle slammed onto the trunk. Her eyes went wide as he swung the scythe down.

Metal screeched on metal as the scythe plunged through the roof of Cory's car. He joined her in screaming. Yanking the wheel back and forth, Cory swerved. Jamie shoved herself down, rolling onto the floor to get away from the brutally sharp blade.

She managed to find some words. "Do something!"

"I'm trying," Cory squeaked.

As the tires squealed into another turn, she slammed into the door, her head striking it. Her vision burst into stars. The car bounced, and the metal of the roof screeched as the scythe slipped out. Trying to clear her vision, she pulled herself up and peeked above the seat. The bike was still behind them, though at least Cory had shaken him off the trunk. Wind whistled through the gaping wound in the roof.

With a moment's reprieve, she pulled her phone out of her pocket and poked the camera above the back of the seat while keeping her head down. She started recording a video to document that she wasn't hallucinating, and a demonic horror was actually chasing them. She had no idea if it would help explain to Ivar why she'd failed, but it couldn't hurt.

"Turning," Cory said.

She braced, grabbing one of the head rests and spreading her knees, but kept her cellphone camera rolling. The tires screeched again. She was honestly surprised they hadn't blown a tire or lost a wheel entirely. The Kia's best days were years behind it.

"Turning again," Cory said. He sounded more confident to her ear, or at least less panicked. "OK. OK, OK, OK."

The car accelerated. In the distance, she heard a faint, steady dinging that grew steadily louder as they moved toward it. Keeping her phone aimed backwards, she turned her head.

"Oh, fuck! What are you thinking?" she yelled.

The dinging originated from a railroad crossing. Cory must have mashed the pedal because the little car found some extra guts and accelerated tepidly.

"I hope we're going to make it." Cory cringed down into his seat as if that would do anything if they didn't make it in time.

As they cleared the last of the buildings along the street, the train came into view. Though it wasn't at full speed, it wasn't creeping along either. She gave up on her video. Flopping onto the seat, she reached for a seatbelt and hurriedly yanked it across her body. She fumbled getting the tab into the buckle but managed it, barely.

The train laid on its horn, at first a couple warning pulls, then the conductor just let it blare, trying to warn them off.

"How close is he?" Cory asked, the panic back in full force.

She turned her head catching the horror out of the corner of her eyes. "I don't know. Maybe thirty feet?"

He patted the dashboard. "Come on, baby. Give me all you got."

She didn't think the Kia had much more to give. The engine sounded maxed out with an odd knocking and a new squeal she hadn't heard before. She couldn't look anymore. She hunkered down and closed her eyes tight.

The sounds were bad enough, but she was gripping onto the door and the seat in front of her so she couldn't spare hands to cover her ears. The train, accompanied by its horn, drew closer. The roar of the loud motorcycle also drew nearer. And the poor car screamed as Cory tried to coax more speed from its empty well.

"Ahhhhhhhh!" Cory screamed as they hit the slight incline up to the tracks.

As the train bellowed its imminence at them and the tires

rumbled over the tracks, she opened her eyes and wished for all the world she hadn't. The front of the train bore down on her. It had to be no more than ten feet away and then they slammed down on the pavement on the other side.

Her heart beat in triple time as her breath came in ragged, shallow gulps. Cory's scream, though it still sounded, was losing steam like a kettle removed from the burner. She tried to turn around to see if they'd lost their pursuer, but the seatbelt snapped tight. Slamming her fingers into the release, she twisted around and saw only the train passing behind them.

She thought she saw glimpses of his infernal eyes in the narrow gaps as each rail car passed. She followed the train backwards. Knowing her luck, it would have been the shortest train of all time. However, the train appeared to go on forever, or at least long enough to allow them to make good their escape.

"Cory. Slow down." She reached up and gripped his shoulder. "Slow down. We won't get away if the engine explodes."

"Did…did we make it?"

"Yeah. I think so. It's a long train. But if we don't slow down, the car's going to fall apart or a cop is going to pull us over. Then we'll be fucked." When she felt the car decelerating, she turned around to check on the biker one last time. She no longer saw the mini-infernos where his eyes had been. Either he'd turned his eyes off, or he'd turned around to go home or find another way around the train.

In the terror of the chase, she'd almost forgotten that this had all started when she tried to kill a man. Almost…

TWENTY-THREE

DAX

Dax let out an incoherent bellow of rage as he brought his motorcycle to a screeching, shuddering, swerving halt as the train cut him off from his prey. Time was, he'd have simply passed through the offending solid object to continue his hunt, but as tied to his mortal flesh as he was, that wasn't an option. He sat and fumed as the bike rumbled under him.

When the wind picked up again, tugging at this black hooded cloak, he realized he'd let too much out in the anger of his pursuit. If he weren't careful, he might make a bigger scene than just a reckless chase through a few neighborhoods. As he gathered himself in, the pain of the bullet reminded him it existed, sending searing tendrils of agony through his body.

Tossing one last look through the brief windows between train cars, he watched the beat-up Kia disappear into the distance. By the time he found a clear crossing, they could be anywhere. Besides, even if he did find a place to cross, he didn't know how long he could keep going with a gaping wound in his body.

It hurt to breathe. Each breath felt like an icepick being driven into his lungs and twisted. A half-cough brought the taste of copper to his mouth. He had to get home, and fast.

Turning around, he headed back into the shadows of the build-ings. Once he saw a street he recognized, he navigated his way home on the shortest route possible. Each bounce of his bike, every move-ment of his body hurt like sin. He was getting closer, but it required every ounce of willpower not to succumb to the pain and tumble off his motorcycle.

For the second time in as many weeks, he stumbled off his bike and staggered to the elevator. He cast a prayer of thanks to whatever deity claimed elevators as their provenance that the blasted contrap-tion was working. Sagging against the wall, he braced and locked his knees to keep himself upright as he smashed the key to his floor. If he slipped to the floor, he wasn't sure he'd be able to get up again.

When the door dinged open, he staggered out, careful to keep from falling. He had to trail along the right side of the hall in case he needed to rely on the wall for verticality. When he reached his door, he propped himself up against the jamb with his forehead, since he needed to use his good arm to unlock the door. Shutting the door behind him, he left the chain lock dangling, but turned the deadbolt.

The bathroom. He had to make it into the bathroom. He leaned up against the vanity and shimmied out of his leather coat, careful to keep his left side as still as possible. He flung it into the shower. His t-shirt, he cut off with a pair of shears he'd acquired for just such an occasion. When he tried to kick his boots off, using his toe to his heel, he nearly fell, but caught himself with his left arm.

He groaned as the corners of his vision blacked out, the jolt to his shoulder and left side of his body sending screaming pain radiating out from his wound. Once he breathed his vision back from the edge, he shimmied out of his pants, flipping them into the shower with his foot.

Turning to look in the mirror, drying blood was smeared over his chest and ran down onto his stomach. He found the bloody rosette of the wound, a bit of blood still oozing out. It had landed in his upper chest on the left side, just missing his heart. What puzzled him was why the pain felt like it was also coming from lower, near the bottom of his rib cage. Between the initial wound and the pull of the bullet's location, a line of damaged flesh connected them. Somehow, the bullet had drifted down in his body—probably during the shift and mad chase.

When he'd lost control and drifted between forms, his flesh hadn't been solid enough to keep the bullet where it had started. It had moved through his lungs, melting his flesh as if the hot bullet had been dropped through a cold stick of butter. It didn't matter right now though. He had to get it out of his flesh before he could even begin dealing with the damage it had caused.

Gripping the edge of his vanity, he concentrated. A scream broke from his lips as his body tensed, muscles and viscera clamping around the bullet. He nearly blacked out. He stopped and concentrated on his breathing until his vision mostly cleared. There was still too much darkness around the edges, though. If he tried much harder, he'd black out completely. If he did without removing the bullet, it would continue to work its dark magic on his mortal flesh.

Worse, if it was like the last one, he wouldn't heal quickly, and he could bleed to death. Though there wasn't much blood coming from the wound, he bet there was a lot more happening internally. To emphasize it, he coughed raggedly, spraying blood over the counter and onto the mirror.

Scratching at the door momentarily broke into his awareness. Morty wanted in. Unfortunately, the kitten would be in the way as he tried to disentangle his flesh from his bones. As he turned back to stare into the mirror, the reflection of light off the silver of the shower head in the tub drew his attention. The tub.

Bracing himself against the vanity with his good arm, he moved his foot over, then slid his other foot backwards so the tub was behind him. He placed his hand on the tub and sank onto the edge. He wanted to take a deep breath, but it would hurt more than what he was about to do.

He pushed backwards and fell into the tub onto his butt. His shoulders struck the back. Despite trying to contain it, a scream forced its way from his lips and blood dribbled onto his lips and chin. Sagging into the tub the rest of the way, he swung his legs in until he lay on his back. The pain of the fall and the scream trimmed the edges of his vision in black until he only saw the shower head gleaming above him. The tiny sparkle of light reflecting off silver served as a focal point as he panted shallowly, trying to stay conscious.

He wasn't sure how long he lay there, flirting with oblivion, but when the grungy lines of the grout between the tiles came into focus, he realized he hadn't succumbed. When he felt as ready as he could under the dire circumstances, he closed his eyes and started gently. He looked at the shifting barrier around his aura that kept him locked into the weakened form of his exile, seeking cracks that appeared and disappeared so fast as to almost never have been.

As he slipped into the rhythm of the barrier, he could nearly anticipate the weaknesses in it. Jamming in bits of his awareness, he was able to hold a few open, essentially using his limited power as a straw. Sometimes he missed the openings and other times he managed to get another piece of himself wedged through the gaps.

He wanted to rest. Needed it. But he couldn't, or the barrier would eject him, and he'd have to start anew. Once he figured he had enough, he sent out feelers to the broader surroundings to find any energy he could. When he came across a delicate and familiar flame, he excluded his kitten from the field he hunted. Careful not to gorge, he sipped as little as possible from as many sources as he could.

Life filtered through the tiny pores of the barrier and into him. The energy tasted sweet. For a moment, he almost lost himself and unleashed his need. He'd have to risk it with what he'd already taken or endanger those around him and himself. If he took too much, his jailers might notice and seek to strengthen the barrier.

Pulling his awareness back within the barrier, his essence snapped back to him like a dozen small rubber bands released simultaneously. He winced but used the snapback to focus his awareness.

Since he'd felt it before, he located the bullet and its magical tendrils and isolated them. Then, he reached out with all his siphoned power and forced his awareness between the bullet and its dark magic. Expanding his proverbial shoulders, he pushed out, stretching the elusive and slimy cords tying the bullet to its mission. He'd hoped to save some of the energy, but when he'd pushed as hard as he could and his flesh was still attached to his bones, he unleashed every last bit of purloined power.

The magic frayed like a heavy steel cable pulled beyond its tolerance. Threads snapped and burst out flying and flaying. He could no longer hold in his scream. It echoed off the tiles and mirror and walls and the other hard surfaces, creating a distorted hell of pain as his vision faded away. He could no longer tell from where the pain came. It dominated his entire body.

When the magic of the bullet finally broke, his flesh fell away, but not before every last nerve ending in his body burned in agony. The plink of metal on enamel-coated cast iron drew a thin, raspy gurgle of a laugh from between his fleshless jaw. He dropped his bony fingers of his left hand to his side and scrabbled around until his fingers bumped up against the bullet. Closing his hand, he ignored the burn of the bullet on his bones and chucked it out of the tub.

Without the bullet in him and his damaged flesh hidden away, he felt relief for the first time since before he was shot. But he had no more energy to give. His bony arm fell across his chest as he passed out.

TWENTY-FOUR

DAX

"Argh." The simple exhalation burned.

Cracking his eyelids, Dax discovered a tiny weight on his chest. Morty had sunk his claws into his skin and was now in the process of turning in a circle so he could lie down in the crook of the arm that had fallen across his chest earlier.

Sometime while he was unconscious, his flesh had returned from the aether, and Morty had shoved his way into the bathroom. He must not have pushed the door enough for the latch bolt to catch. Despite the agony of each breath, he couldn't hold on to the waking world.

He woke periodically when Morty dug his claws in before settling again. Each little paw contained razor sharp needles that jolted him back to the realm of the living. But it never lasted long before he went under again.

Once again, Morty clawed him to awareness, but this time, the kitten scrambled out of the tub, screaming his tiny kitten scream as he bounded out of the bathroom door. The screaming continued but faded as he moved through the apartment. Dax nearly disappeared into the blackness, but the kitten's screams grew louder again. They were joined by the familiar voice of Tomi.

"Where is he, little dude?" Tomi asked.

Morty burst through the door and jumped up, scrabbling at the edge of the tub until he pulled himself onto the ledge. He screamed in Dax's face but nearly fell off when he spun around to scream at Tomi.

"Holy fuck," Tomi exclaimed. "There's blood all over the place."

Dax opened his mouth to speak but only a gurgling rasp escaped his lips.

"Don't talk. Shit. I think your lungs are filling with blood. I'm gonna have to call an ambulance." Tomi pulled out his cellphone.

"No…" Dax rasped out.

"Fuck, man. You need big time medical help. A poultice isn't going to fix that."

"No…authorities…" Fortunately, those syllables required the barest minimum of effort.

"Fine." He dialed his phone. "Mama, we need the manbo for some serious healing. It's urgent. Dax's place." He knelt on the tile floor. "Shit. The kitten is covered in blood. Has he been laying on you?"

Tomi disappeared into the other room and came back with a ratty blanket, draping it across Dax. "I don't want to move you, but that tub has to be cold. This is the best option I could find." He carefully tucked it under Dax's chin, before turning to the kitten. "Not for you."

He scooped up the kitten and set him down in the bathroom sink. Fumbling around under the sink, he found the cat shampoo and turned on the water. Morty's earlier insistent screams were replaced by shrill yowls of protest and annoyance as Tomi lathered him up and washed the blood out of his fur.

Dax drifted in out of consciousness while Tomi cleaned and dried off the kitten. When he was done, he set the kitten outside the bathroom door and shut him out.

"There. That'll keep him out of trouble," Tomi said.

Dax's chest hurt, and he couldn't draw a good breath. Mostly, he just tried to focus on staying awake. When Tomi's phone rang, Dax jolted a little, groaning then gurgling in pain.

"Hold on, Dax." Tomi sounded genuinely scared as he answered his phone. "Hello?" He put it on speaker phone after a couple second.

"Dax, this is Delphine. I've got Boudreaux on his way. He'll be there shortly. He's going to take you to a doctor friend of mine."

Dax tried to shake his head, but the corners of his vision nearly blinked out, so he stopped.

"He's trying to say no," Tomi supplied. "He can't speak. I think he's got a lot of blood in his lungs."

Delphine cut in. "Dax. You're going to have to trust me. I'm afraid modern human medicine is your only recourse right now. If I were to try to heal you, it would require me ask one of the lwas to intercede on your behalf. And I've gathered that you wouldn't like to have your activities and infirmities announced in certain quarters, am I correct?"

He opened his eyes wide, giving his head the lightest of shakes to avoid passing out.

"That is correct," Tomi said.

"Then you're going to have to do this the other way. Boudreaux was an army medic in Afghanistan before becoming an EMT. He'll get you stabilized. The doctor is a friend of the community who will keep things off the books. You and I can sort everything out when you're healed. Now quit fighting me and just worry about staying alive." Her voice had finally slipped from patient to annoyed, but it had worked.

Dax made eye contact with Tomi and gave him a slight nod.

Tomi relaxed a little. "He's on board."

"Good. Take care of him, Tomi."

With the loss of blood and his short-circuiting body, he couldn't be sure, but it had sounded like the manbo had added extra weight to her command to Tomi.

"I always do, Manman Delphine. I need to go downstairs, or Boudreaux won't be able to find the place." He hung up the phone. "Dax, you just need to hold on for a few more minutes, and Boudreaux will be here."

He nodded faintly at his friend. Tomi reached down and

squeezed his hand, then took off. With a plan in place, he tried to focus on just staying conscious until help arrived, but he faded in and out.

Blinding pain woke him when Boudreaux applied a bandage to his chest. Between them, Boudreaux and Tomi moved Dax out of the bathroom and onto a gurney. Together, they wheeled him down to the street toward the flashing lights of the ambulance he'd ridden in a few days ago when he'd only played the part of a cadaver. The irony was not lost on him. He'd have laughed if it wouldn't have caused him blinding pain as he drowned in his own blood.

Before they loaded him into the back, he waved Tomi over and lifted the oxygen mask off his face. Concentrating on using as little lung effort as possible, he whispered, "Morty."

Tomi patted his hand. "Don't worry, Dax. I'll make sure your kitten is taken care of."

He set the mask back in place and let them load him into the back of the ambulance. He just hoped the ride was smoother than the last time.

TWENTY-FIVE

DAX

A week after being released from the quiet clinic he'd been recovering in, Dax sat at the bar nursing a lukewarm can of Rainier, grimacing after with every sip. Thinking about the sudden swirl of events he seemed to be the epicenter of, he'd lost track of time and let the cold can warm in his hands.

He'd lost a week of time on his back, healing from the wound to his chest. The doctor Delphine had sent him to did a great job, and his own healing did the rest, but something of the bullet lingered, keeping him from healing quite right, just as it had the last time, though this wound was far worse. When he thought about it, the girl's face popped into his head. She'd apologized before shooting him, but the pain had burned hotter than the infernos of several hells.

Looking down at the can, he didn't know why he kept drinking from it. He knew what it cost him at wholesale. He could afford to dump one partial can and order a fresh one, but he kept at it anyway. It was probably thirty cents' worth of cheap beer, but it was his and he'd be damned if he was going to waste it.

"Looks like you're really enjoying that, boss. Want a new can?

Or something to go with it to cover the taste?" Tomi tipped his head toward the whiskey shelves.

"No. I'll—"

A series of vibrations from his pocket interrupted him. Pulling his phone out, he saw an unknown number calling him. He shrugged and hit the ignore button, setting the phone on the bar top. Instead of leaving a voice mail, whoever it was called again.

He rolled his eyes and picked it up, pointing the screen toward Tomi. "You recognize that number?"

Tomi leaned forward and squinted at the screen. "Nah. But then again, I'm a millennial. I don't have a bunch of phone numbers memorized."

Dax hovered his finger over the screen, the tip moving back and forth between ignore and answer. Sighing, he hit the answer button. If they were this persistent, he'd might as well answer before it become too annoying.

"This is Dax. What do you want?"

A snort and short chuckle greeted him, followed by rolling the of Manman Delphine. "Hello to you, too, Dax. How are you feeling after your little misadventure?"

"Well enough. Still not one hundred percent, but I'm ambulatory," he replied.

"I'm glad to hear it. Now back to what you so graciously started the conversation with… It's not so much what I want but what you want."

Relaxing somewhat, he picked up his can of beer and took another swig, grimacing at the warm, flat liquid. "And what do I want, Delphine?"

"You want to repay the favors I've done for you with a favor of your own. Then it'll be off your conscious. And isn't a clear conscious what we all want at the end of the day?"

Dax couldn't help smiling at the humorous and sardonic tone Delphine took with him. But then he wondered what kind of favor the manbo was going to want from him and whether it would be mundane or supernatural. He certainly owed her enough after the three favors she'd helped him with, including saving his life. "I can't disagree with that." Looking around at the customers nearest him, he stood up and tossed a coaster on top of his can, indicating he'd be back. "How can I achieve that admirable goal?"

He headed toward the back of the bar, unlocking the tearoom and slid in, relocking the door before heading to the back of the room.

"Is there a reason you're being circumspect with your responses?" Delphine asked.

"Sorry, I was just surrounded by curious customers. It's safe to talk now," he replied. "What is the manner in which I can clear my debt to you?"

She chuckled. "I wouldn't consider it a debt, but a favor...or three among friendly acquaintances."

He couldn't decide what might be the more potent and potentially dangerous option of the two—debt versus favor—and which would allow him a cleaner repayment. In human terms, a debt could conversely be paid and the tie between parties ended. Favors, though. They could lead to an endless entanglement of spiraling favors. It would all just depend on who the favors were owed to and what they chose to make of them whether the spiral elevated both parties or dragged them down into the depths.

He was glad to know she might consider him a friendly acquaintance, though. Despite her protestations and humble demeanor during their first meeting, he could sense a deep power flowing beneath the surface...for a human. He had few friends in Red City after years of lying low and living an unnoticeable life since being banished to the city. And since then, he'd never tried to flex his proverbial muscles to see what power he'd been left with after being betrayed and exiled. He didn't want to find out how short the leash he was being kept on was.

"How can I repay the favors, friendly acquaintance?" he asked.

"I appreciate your plainspoken nature, Dax. I'll accord you the same respect." She paused, taking a deep breath. "I know what you are... Or rather, what you were, though I don't know quite where the two intersect."

He stared at the back wall, his breathing steady but shallow.

He'd suspected that might be the case after their meeting. She knew her business and afforded him a respectful curtsy when they'd finished. If she had even a portion of the power he thought she might, he'd have been disappointed in her diligence if she'd not tested around the edges of his aura, such as it was these days.

"Fair enough. Assuming you're correct. How does that play into your favor? My powers are few and weak these days, nor do I care to exercise them in case I draw the wrong kind of attention."

She sighed. "Though I do appreciate the verbal fencing, this might be better discussed in person. Adele tells me you have a penchant for making and drinking excellent tea. If you're available tomorrow, I'll stop by your tearoom. You can make me a cup of tea, and we can discuss it in person."

"Very well. Tomi comes in at noon tomorrow so he can cover the bar while we talk."

"Adyeu, Dax."

"Adyeu."

TWENTY-SIX

JAMIE

Normally, a run through the woods in her wolf form with Cory would relieve the tension of whatever was bothering her at the time, but not today.

Cory had finally talked her into leaving her house to get some exercise after her attempted murder. She hoped the run would help her get a decent night's sleep—they had been few and far between in the aftermath of her failed assassination attempt. Those flaming eyes haunted her. She'd woken up in a cold sweat more than once.

But as his eyes never seemed to leave her be, her conscience dogged her more. She'd tried to kill a man. In cold blood. She'd stalked up behind him and blasted him with the gun as he turned around and saw her. If she thought about it, she could still feel the pressure of the trigger on her finger and the recoil of the pistol. The odor of the gunpowder came back to her particularly strong, wrinkling her nose. Then the wheeze of the air leaving his lungs as he fell backwards...

She shook her head and sped up, dashing through the woods at a breakneck pace. Behind her, Cory yipped at her to slow down. But he didn't need to exorcise the guilt and shame from his soul like she did. He didn't need to run himself to exhaustion in the hopes of gaining a moment's peace.

The one good piece of fortune was that no one had come looking for her. The man or monster or whatever he was hadn't showed up at her door. Neither had the cops. Though would a creature who could summon hell fire into his eyes go to the cops? Or would he take his own vengeance? There was no way someone like that would let this go.

He'd turned into a robe-shrouded skeleton and chased them on his hellish motorcycle. She shivered, nearly losing her step, as the memory of the screech of his scythe piercing Cory's roof ripped to the surface. Of that entire encounter, the train had been the least terrifying.

She tried to dig deeper and find more speed, but she was nearing the end of what her body could give in its current condition. A growl rising in her throat, she slowed down to a trot, looking around for a place to collapse. The panting growing louder behind her alerted her to Cory's approach. When he drew next to her, he bumped into her in the friendly manner he always did. But instead of bumping back, she felt a low growl rumble in her throat. Cory backed off.

Sighing, she turned and trotted back toward where they parked. She wasn't sure why that had been her reaction, but it had happened before she could stop it. She'd owe him an apology as soon as she had her human vocal cords available. They loped back, though Cory kept a respectful distance between them as they ran.

As soon as she slipped her clothes on, she turned to Cory. "I'm sorry for growling at you. I'm not sure what came over me."

"No need to apologize. It's been a hard time for you after…"

Cory had refused to acknowledge what they'd done in direct words, always cutting off or using some obtuse framing. Though he hadn't pulled the trigger, he'd been there for the dangerous and violent aftermath. Somehow he'd explained away the damage to his car as random vandalism. His mom had bought it because she trusted him.

And that, too, made her feel even worse. After all the trust Linda had placed in her as her son's best friend, she'd betrayed her too, leading her son into danger and making him an accessory to attempted murder.

"I know, but I'm sorry, anyway. You're the only support I have. I shouldn't be a jerk to you." She pressed her fingers into her temples, trying to massage away the constant tension headache that had been plaguing her. "You're too good of a friend. I don't deserve you."

"That's bullshit. You're an awesome friend. Don't let your parent situation dictate what you think you deserve." He pursed his lips and shook his head. "This whole thing sucks. Why hasn't anything happened?"

"I don't know. I can't stop wondering…" She hadn't even heard or seen anything about the shot or chase in the news. She'd checked the news and their websites and social media to see if anything had been mentioned, so she'd know if the cops were looking for her. "If this guy is so scary that the bikers themselves aren't going to go after him directly…"

"Yeah. Why are they using you? Do they think you'll be less of a suspect?"

"I don't know. That's just it. Surely they have better ways to kill someone. Do you think they're scared of him? I mean"—she shivered—"I know I am. Honestly, I'm more scared of him than I am of the bikers."

"I don't know about that. I'm scared of them both about equally." He ducked his head as if he should be ashamed of being afraid.

"What if"—she took in a deep breath then huffed it out—"I go to him and tell him who sent me. Let him deal with the bikers."

Cory spun around to her. "What the fuck? Are you insane? He'll kill you on the spot. And if he doesn't, the bikers will track us down and make us pay. Slowly. And painfully." He shook his head. "No way. This is the stupidest idea you've ever had." He tried to smirk at her in humor, but it came out as more of a grimace than anything. "And that's saying a lot."

She decided to play along and keep her thoughts to herself. He'd probably never agree because he felt he was still tied to his promise to help, but this might be a way to help him without endangering him even more. "Yeah. Like choosing you as a friend." She gave him a friendly punch in the arm. "But you turned out alright." She sighed. "I guess you're probably right."

"So, what *are* we going to do?" he asked.

"I don't know. Let me think about it, and then I'll discuss it with you once I have an idea or two." She ran a hand over her forehead. "I'll come up with some way to save our bacon."

"Mmm, bacon…" He pantomimed drooling. "Speaking of which, I'm in need of a burger, and I know just the place to get a bacon burger."

Of course he did. Cory was a simple creature. And the more she thought about it, the more she realized she might have to break her promise to him if she wanted to get them both out of this alive. The bikers would never let go of them, especially if they could hold a murder over her head. But this way… Maybe, just maybe, she could make it to the end of this alive without actually having to murder someone. And if it meant saving Cory, she'd even be willing to take all the wrath from the man she'd shot. He didn't deserve to die because she came from a family of fuckups.

TWENTY-SEVEN

DAX

Delphine sniffed deeply at the hard disc of pu-erh tea. "Dark, earthy, and complex. Like me." She chuckled. "I'll take a cup of this, please."

Nodding, Dax set the kettle to bring it to a boil. He'd already set up most of the tea service but had to wait for Delphine to choose her tea before selecting the pot. She'd selected one of his most prized teas, though he'd never have offered it to her if he didn't wish her to have it. He'd hoped she would select it. Few did, and this was a tea he felt needed to be shared—it was an indulgence he rarely chose when he brewed tea for just himself.

Delphine, giving him her attention, relaxed while he explained the process and ceremony as he performed it. Once he poured the tea into their cups, he sat down.

Cupping the small tea bowl in both her hands, she lifted it and nodded toward him before taking a deep sniff. A small smile quirked up the corner of her plump lips. She blew over the steaming cup until she felt it was ready for a noisy sip.

Sighing contentedly, she looked up from her cup. "Delightful. I hope you know I risked leaving my home without lipstick so it wouldn't interfere with your tea. I'm glad I did. This cup was worth it."

He chuckled lightly, nodding to acknowledge the courtesy. "There are plenty more steepings and plenty more character to explore in this tea as it evolves and changes with each cupping."

Delphine smirked, her eyes twinkling. "Again, much like me."

Unsure how to respond, he retreated into a sip or two of his own, savoring the deeply complex and rich flavors and aromas of the post-fermented, aged tea.

"Thank you for choosing this one," he said, finally breaking the silence. "It's one of my favorites, but I rarely get the opportunity to drink it."

"Why? It's your tea. Life is too hard and short, especially in a city like this. Well…for most of us." She raised an eyebrow and held his gaze for a few moments. "We should enjoy ourselves while we can. Undrunk tea makes no one happy."

"But some things are better shared—their beauty often serving to remind you of what's missing."

"Beauty is still beauty whether it's witnessed with another or by oneself." She shrugged. "Life is precious. Something too many take for granted." She punctuated her statement by downing the last of her tea and exhaling happily as she set the cup back on the tray for the next round.

He obliged her and set the tea to boil. Filling the silence, she chatted about how she'd landed in Redemption City as one of the people who'd had to leave New Orleans because of Hurricane Katrina.

After several more cups, she straightened up and fixed a serious gaze on him. "I understand you're in the business of transitions for those people who are willing to pay…"

He nodded. "On occasion, I've augmented the meager income of this place by using what powers and skills are still left in my reper-toire. Though, I don't do it often so I can continue to avoid notice."

He still had some limited powers over death. Early on, he'd discovered a method that would allow him to sell the service to those looking for an out, while staying under the radar. Though he rarely performed the service except when the bar's books were dangerously out of balance.

"I understand. I do much the same, though my meager abilities are rarely worth noticing."

He snorted. "Since we're being frank, you're not required to maintain your façade of meekness in my presence."

Delphine sat back and gave him a knowing smile, placing her hand over her chest. "Allow a lady her secrets."

Chuckling, he raised an eyebrow. "As you wish." He reached over and set the kettle to boil again. "Back to your point—I have been known to help facilitate a paradigm shift in the occasional client's relationship vis-à-vis this world and the next."

"Fah! You sound like some puke in a suit. It's unbecoming of one of your dignity."

Shaking his head, he tried to keep the look of annoyance off his face since it wasn't directed at the manbo. "I have been left with little of that in recent years."

Pursing her lips, she stared at him for longer than felt comfortable. "That is not something that can be taken away from you… unless you allow it to be so."

Delphine held his gaze until the intensity of it and her words became too much for him, and he looked away. She'd called him out on his self-pity, something no one else had, though none but Tomi and his family knew who he was, and even they only knew a fraction of the truth. Well, them and whoever was trying to kill him. But right now, he couldn't afford to dedicate too much time delving into his own feelings, not with Delphine staring at him, waiting for him to do something.

Sighing, he raised his eyes until they met hers. "Who am I helping find an easier peace and why?"

Delphine relaxed, setting her elbows on the table and allowing them to take her weight. "A friend because there is no one else who can, nor can they afford other alternatives."

"Can you acquire something of theirs? Something that has significant meaning to them, preferably something that's had extended physical contact."

Instead of answering, she reached into her purse and pulled out a bracelet made from shaped and polished stones that varied in tones from beiges to deeper browns. He couldn't tell what kind of stones they were, geology was not his area of knowledge or interest. Cupping his hands together, he extended them so Delphine could drop the bracelet into them. Even before she handed over the bangle, he could feel the sense of its owner seeping into the air around it.

The stones felt smooth and cool to the touch with a nice weight that spoke of solidity. Folding one hand over so the bracelet was clasped between his palms, he closed his hands over it and extended his thoughts. The owner and the bracelet had been together for a long time. He could follow their life together back to a small hillside village in Haiti through New Orleans to where they ultimately ended up in Redemption City. The stones had soaked up decades of struggle, hope, and love so strongly he felt he could follow the threads from beginning to end.

"Will that do?" Delphine asked.

He nodded then stood up, opening his eyes before heading toward his wall of tea and teapots. Winding the bracelet between the fingers of his left hand, he reached out and grabbed a tin of tea, opening it. Chinese green tea—after a quick sniff, he closed the tin and put it back in its spot. Next, an Indian Assam black tea. It too was rejected quickly. After he pulled down a Bai hao Zin Zhen, he paused and took another sniff. Then to confirm, he held the tin in his left hand with the bracelet so the sense of both could mingle.

Nodding to himself, he set the silver needle white tea down and turned to the manbo. "When and where?"

Raising an eyebrow, she stared back at him for a moment, the corner of one side of her mouth quirking up. "Tomorrow evening. I'll text you the address."

TWENTY-EIGHT

DAX

Tomi pulled up in front of a tiny house in a quiet neighborhood. While there weren't many larger houses, and even those that were would best be classified as humble, the neighborhood lacked the more obvious signs of neglect most of the other neighborhoods of the city featured. Few boarded windows or abandoned homes sullied the appearance of the area, even if some of the houses were a bit overdue for paint jobs, including the one they sat in front of. The last rays of the dying sun shined on the cheery faded yellow house. They'd caught a rare dry winter day.

"You ready, boss?" Tomi asked.

"Yes." Dax pulled the door handle and stepped out.

Tomi popped the trunk then joined Dax at the trunk, grabbing a jug of purified spring water and a kettle. Dax carefully lifted the tea kit he'd assembled for such occasions and shut the trunk.

"Welcome," Delphine said, stepping from the house onto the small front porch.

Dax nodded at her, adding a faint smile. A short Black man, maybe five feet six inches tall, stood just behind her and to the side.

He had tightly cropped hair that was mostly white, though a few streaks of black could be seen.

"I'll set up the kettle in the kitchen and get it heating up," Tomi said, sliding between the manbo and the elderly man.

Tomi knew the heat settings for the tea that had been selected. They'd done this several times over the years since they'd been working together. Dax trusted him implicitly.

"Dax, this is Samuel. You'll be assisting his wife Esther." Delphine squeezed Samuel's shoulder.

"Welcome to my home, sir," Samuel said through a thick Kreyòl accent and a small bob of his head. He gestured for Dax to enter the house.

"Thank you, Samuel," Dax replied, stepping into the small living room.

Dated wallpaper and well-worn furniture dominated the decor, though the walls were covered in framed photographs, probably of Samuel and Esther and their family and friends. He set down his large bag out of the way as Tomi stepped out of the kitchen and found an out-of-the-way place along the wall to stand.

Samuel shut the door behind Delphine and himself. "I'm going to make sure Esther is ready."

For the first time since he'd passed the threshold of the house, Dax opened his senses and slowly took in a deep breath through his nose. He'd felt the undercurrents of suffering and impending mortality as soon as he stepped onto the property, but now he could sort through and get to know the more nuanced notes. Tracing backwards, he followed a thread that contained too much pain for too long. The illness had not been a quick one. Cancer. He stopped at the point where the tumors had started instead of following the strong thread back to its origins.

Looking the other way, he found entirely too much thread remaining before what would be the inevitable end. He understood why Manman Delphine had chosen to use the favor to help out this family. It was a gift of kindness. Turning to meet the eye of the manbo, he held her gaze, relaying his understanding and the depth of his appreciation for her actions. As a spiritual leader, she took the health and lives of her charges seriously from the creation of their threads to the very frayed end.

Dax straightened his spine, erasing the normal slouch he maintained and let loose his aura. Catching a glance of his reflection on one of the many framed photos, his skin and muscle became slightly translucent, allowing his skull to be barely seen underneath it. The hollow, spectral flames ignited in his eye sockets.

Averting her eyes, Delphine pinched the sides of her skirt between her fingers and curtsied deeply. Behind him, a gasp drew his attention. He turned and found Samuel bowing deeply at the waist.

"She is ready, sir." Samuel's voice trembled.

Tomi stepped away from the wall and grabbed Dax's bag, disappearing into the room behind Samuel. A couple minutes later, he reappeared and nodded toward Dax before stepping out of the way. Dax followed Samuel into the room.

A hospital bed sat in the middle of the room. Along one side, oxygen and an IV extended their lines into the bed's inhabitant. On the other side of the bed, two small stands were set up—one contained Dax's tea equipment, and the other held an unlit cigar sitting in an ashtray and a glass full of a clear liquid, probably white rum from the bottle standing behind it.

Esther lay in the bed in a semi-reclined position, thanks to the adjustable bed. A brightly colored and patterned dress poked out from under the blankets and matched the head wrap she wore. Despite the brightness of her eyes, she looked gaunt, her skin sallow and thin-looking like old parchment.

Esther fixed her eyes on Dax as he stepped into the room, looking him up and down in his jeans, black T-shirt, and leather jacket. Looking at Samuel and Delphine, she said something in Kreyòl.

Samuel's eyes shot open wide. "Esther!"

Delphine chuckled, shaking her head, then looked at Dax, raising an eyebrow.

"What did she say?" he asked, sighing. "Time was, I would have heard her words and known them in my head, but no more."

"She asked why we brought the scrawny white man into her room," Delphine answered, a grin spreading across her face.

Behind him, Tomi snorted.

Dax ignored his friend and took a step toward the bed. "Esther, I'm here to help you, if you'll consent to it. May I take your hand?"

She narrowed her eyes and stared at him for a moment before giving a small nod. He closed the rest of the distance and gently took her frail hand in his, closing his eyes and reaching out with his senses. Though she kept the extent of her pain off her face, he could feel the depth and profoundness of it. As he delved deeper, linking his consciousness with Esther's, she shuddered weakly and let out a small moan of pain. She hadn't taken the full dose of her pain medication in order to be as clear minded as her current circumstances would allow her for his visit.

The bracelet Delphine had brought had given a good picture of her predicament, but the personal touch filled in the rest of the story —a slow, long-suffering cancer that had stubbornly refused to give into modern medicine or a strong-willed desire to live. There was nowhere in her body not tainted by the tumorous cells. And while the thread leading forward wasn't terribly long, it would be filled with excruciating pain and the further diminishment of her remaining faculties.

As he pulled back his awareness, he heard the steady, mumbled cadence of words coming from Esther and felt her tension holding his hand. The one phrase he did recognize was a name—Bawon Samdi. Time was, he could have called on Baron Samedi, also known as Bawon Samdi to some Haitian believers in vodou, but their ties had been severed. Esther sought the comfort of the death god she knew and believed in, called upon the mercy of the lwa of the dead to ease her spirit into the next world.

Setting her hand down gently, Dax withdrew from the room. Delphine followed.

"She calls for Bawon Samdi, but I do not bring her comfort." Dax shook his head.

"Is there something you can do, can you..." Tomi trailed off, making a slow rolling hand gesture.

"I no longer have the power or connections to call him here." He narrowed his eyes and pursed his lips. "I might be able to come up with another option, but I wouldn't be Bawon Samdi."

"Death has many faces. It is comfort she is looking for," Delphine said. "If you can give that, then you will have given her both what she wants and what she needs. The ultimate power is yours, even if you wear another face to wield it."

She was right. He took his leather jacket off and handed it to Tomi. "If you don't want to see more than you're ready for, I suggest you return to the room."

Delphine chuckled. "I've seen a naked man before, even a few scrawny white ones."

It was his turn to get one over on the manbo. Instead of stripping down to his skin, he pulled in the façade until he was nothing but a skeleton wearing a T-shirt and jeans. Delphine gasped, covering her mouth with her hand, and took an involuntary step backwards. He laughed, the hallow, airy, gasping sound raising goose bumps on Delphine's and Tomi's arms.

"I've seen him do that too many times, and it still gives me the wig." Tomi took the pieces of clothing as Dax handed them to him.

Once he was naked as a skeleton, he pulled the ragged, black hooded robe from the aether and wrapped it around himself, though he left the scythe. Concentrating on the image of Baron Samedi, he forced the robe into the semblance of the lwa, picking an image from the last time he'd seen the Baron. When he was finished, he stood in black pants, a velvet purple tailcoat, a silver waistcoat over a white shirt with a black bowtie covered in a purple paisley pattern. On top of his skull sat a matching purple top hat.

Once the clothes settled over his bones, he sagged toward the wall. Tomi quickly dropped the clothes and caught Dax before he fell.

"What is wrong with him?" Delphine said quietly.

Tomi shrugged. "I don't know."

"It takes a lot of energy and will to force myself into an image that isn't mine. The only form I was left with, besides the human skin I took, was the scythe wielding reaper in his robe. I should be fine in a moment," he said in the hollow, airy voice his skeleton form used. Tomi's grip started to relax. "But don't let me go, yet. I don't think I'd bring much comfort to Esther if I collapsed into a pile of bones."

Once he felt steady enough, he gathered his balance and stood on his own, letting Tomi step back. Straightening his coat and setting the top hat to a slight angle to give himself a jaunty appearance, he strode boldly into Esther's room with a hitch in his step.

He laughed as he approached the bed. "What a fine woman we have here. What say you send your man away and I'll show you a good time, cher?"

Esther chuckled weakly, a bit of color seeping into her face. A couple of coughs slipped into her laugh until they took over, sending the elderly woman into a hacking fit. Once the spell ended, she wheezed but smiled. "I'm too old for such games, you old lech."

Filling the air with his dry, wheezing laugh, he picked up the offered cigar and clamped it between his teeth. Samuel stepped up and held a lit lighter in his hands, offering the flame to Dax.

He waved off Samuel. "I appreciate the offer, but we'll save the lovely lady's lungs from another fit." To punctuate it, he pulled the cigar from his teeth and grabbed the glass of rum, taking a large swig.

Bobbing his head, Samuel stepped back. "I'm sorry we didn't have time to steep it in peppers, as you like."

"It's a fine rum. Besides, Esther is spicy enough on her own." He leered at her, laughing, then took another drink of rum, draining the glass. Samuel picked up the bottle and refilled the glass. "Bring me a chair, Samuel. Tomi, the water."

He sank into the chair, drinking more of the rum. "Will you share some fuckin' tea with me, Esther? I know this may not be typical, but it will ease you along the path to the place of dark water."

"I would be honored, Bawon." She covered her mouth, trying to suppress a cough.

A minute later, Tomi brought in the steaming kettle. Dax set down the empty rum glass and clamped the cigar between his teeth before taking the kettle from his friend.

"First, I'm going to heat up all this shit." He poured hot water into the cups and the empty pots.

As he worked his way through the ritual, he described what he was doing, sprinkling in plenty of obscenities and lecherous comments. This tea ceremony had been his creation after he'd been exiled. It allowed him a way to work around the restrictions placed on him.

Esther seemed far more relaxed and content with this image than she had with the white man's skin he wore, his comments bringing an occasional weak smile to her face. When the tea was finally ready, he poured it into the two clay cups. The white tea had a lower water temperature requirement, so it was soon ready to be consumed.

"Do you need help, Esther?" he asked, handing the cup over.

She shook her head and took the cup with trembling hands.

"Do not finish the full cup, but leave the last swallow in the glass."

She nodded again, taking a small sip. "Thank you, Bawon."

"Now drink that fucker down!" He raised his glass toward her then took a noisy sip.

She tittered, but it was cut off by another bout of coughing. Delphine swooped in and took the teacup from Esther's hands before she could spill it. Once she calmed, trying not to gasp too hard and spark another fit, the manbo returned the cup.

"Try not to laugh, cher," Delphine said, squeezing Esther's shoulder.

Dax felt bad about drawing the painful sounding cough from her, but she'd asked for Bawon Samdi, which meant lewd comments and profanities. He'd have to keep his reservations to himself and allow the poor woman the comforts she expected. To cover, he raised his cup for another sip, ensuring he didn't accidentally drain it.

Esther took her time, enjoying the fine cup of tea and letting go of an occasional contented sigh. A small, peaceful smile spread across her face. The cups weren't big, only about three ounces, so she checked regularly to make sure she left a bit in the bottom. When she reached the end, she handed it to him. With one hand, he took it from her thin hands, the bones of his fingers clacking against the hard clay.

Removing the lid from the teapot, he poured the splash from Esther's cup over the leaves then added the last bit from his, letting their combined essences mingle among the aromatic and wet leaves. Tomi, holding the hot water kettle, leaned in and carefully filled the teapot with water. Dax returned the lid and quietly counted in his head the few seconds for the second infusion.

He found the second cup to be his favorite infusion. The tea had been awoken after the rinse and the first brew and provided a unique strength of character. He'd always used the second infusion since he'd created this ceremony. Pouring the cups, he let them sit while they cooled enough to be consumed.

Ensuring he had Esther's attention, he leaned forward slightly. "Are you ready to proceed? You can withdraw at any time with no consequences, until the very end. I will give you a last chance warning."

"I understand." She reached toward the cup to signal her consent.

He carefully handed her the cup she'd already drank from. Picking up his own, he took the first tentative sip. Closing his eyes, he swished the liquid around in his mouth. He could feel Esther's essence mingled with his own in the liquid. He shuddered lightly as a wave of her pain spread throughout his body. Instead of tamping it down, he drew in another sip of tea, prepared for the bitter throbbing sensation of months of Esther's pain. She was on the edge today without her pain meds. Only her anticipation of his visit and now his presence kept her from dipping over the edge. With his third sip, he pulled forth not just the memory of her pain but a small portion of today's, granting her a bit of relief before they continued.

If he'd been in his human flesh, he'd be trembling and sweating. But in this guise, the pain was more contained, though still potent in the hollow core of his rib-encased chest. Without the padding of cheeks and lips, his teeth ground and clacked. He wasn't sure why, he had no sweat glands or skin for them to cool, but he felt the dampness of a sweat trapped inside his clothes.

When he swallowed the mouthful of tea, he gave a raspy sigh as the pain subsided into a back corner of his awareness. Leaning closer and focusing on Esther's face, her eyes were wide, but she looked less droopy than she had before.

"Did you do that?" she whispered. "Take some of my pain away?"

"Wi, cher." He let his jaw drop slightly, hoping it looked close enough to a grin. "Now finish your tea, but take your time to enjoy the fine brew."

She nodded and put the cup to her lips, taking a deeper drink, though she appeared to heed his advice and took her time savoring the delicate white tea. As much as he wanted to focus on his own cup, the constant burning of her assumed pain kept him from entirely sinking into his drink. Leaning back, he relaxed into the chair, affecting a casual, room-commanding slouch. After a couple more sips, the tiny cup was empty. He set it down. A moment later, Esther set hers next to his, her hand steadier but still trembling some.

Folding her hands in her lap, she stared down at them. "Now what, Bawon?"

"We proceed to the last stage, if you give your final consent."

Samuel, standing quietly in the background, let out a quickly stifled sob. Delphine, while Dax had been finishing his cup, had set up a chair on the other side of the bed.

Still looking down at her hands, Esther spoke, her voice sounding tired and tiny. "Will it hurt?"

Normally, it would. There were prices to pay for the exercising of such powers, and he didn't wish to be the one paying for it when he was providing the service.

Reaching out with a bony hand, Dax rubbed the knuckle of his forefinger along her cheek. "Non, cher. Not for you."

Delphine narrowed her eyes. "'Not for her'? Are you bargaining? Is there a cost to be paid?"

"I'll gladly pay it," Samuel said. "I'll take her pain."

"No, Samuel," Esther said firmly. "You will not bargain for this."

Dax shook his head. "No. No bargain."

"No tricks?" the manbo asked.

He was not a trickster god, unlike Baron Samedi, but he couldn't tell if Delphine was unsure of his actual intensions or was playing her part as a manbo interceding between one of her flock and the vodou trickster god of death.

"No tricks. Esther has already paid for the bargain with a lifetime of devotion." He sat straight in his chair, looking for Tomi. "Ah, there you are. Please clear the tea and the table. They'll only be in the way."

"Right." Tomi quickly took away the breakable tea pot and cups, then returned to his station near the door.

"Are you ready, Esther?" Dax asked, leaning closer and reaching out to take one of her hands in both of his.

She looked at Samuel. A steady stream of tears fell from his eyes, streaking his dark brown cheeks.

"Is this what you want, my love?" he asked, his voice trembling.

"I'm so tired. Let me choose my time, when I still have my wits about me." She stared at her husband, pouring all the love she held for him into her eyes. "Come here, you old fool."

Samuel stepped forward, bending over and placing a hand on each of her cheeks. He ducked in for a gentle kiss, but when he tried to pull back, Esther deepened the kiss, though she was only able to for a few moments before sagging back into the bed, breathing heavily. Watching them, a hollow pit opened in the hollow of his empty ribcage.

He'd seen their struggles together, fleeing poverty and disasters in Haiti to New Orleans then to Red City after Katrina nearly washed NOLA back into the sea. Through it all, they'd had each other. Through lost family members, dead friends, hunger, uncertainty, and innumerable privations, they'd been each other's rocks. And now…

She turned to Dax. "I am ready, Bawon Samdi."

He captured her gaze. She gulped at the intensity of his eyeless stare, a hint of flames igniting in the empty sockets. "You have invited me into your home to perform a service. Do you consent for me to proceed?"

Esther nodded and sat up straighter, a bit of steel reinforcing her spine. "I do."

"You may lay down and be comfortable." He kept his grip on her hand as she let the mattress and pillows take her weight.

Manman Delphine took Esther's other hand, grabbing Samuel's hand and adding it to the pile. The old man tried to contain his sobs, wiping his cheeks with his free hand. Dax took in the scene, containing a mournful sigh as the pit in his chest deepened. After soaking in the love on display, he focused his essence on Esther, her being burning strongly inside him after drinking the tea mingling their essences. The mix inside the elderly woman called out and linked to him, uniting them.

As he concentrated, blocking out everything else, her heart beat in his chest. Her lungs expanded his ribs. Bracing himself, he brought the pain out from the corner he'd stashed it in and let it link up with the cancer devastating the poor woman's body. But when it tried to flow back towards her, he pinched the connection shut, trapping it behind a barrier that could only flow from Esther.

With the pain effectively trapped, he focused in on her life thread, tracing it the short fraying distance to its terminus. He pinched the present moment in one metaphorical finger and thumb and drew the end point toward the present. Though the thread was weak and frail, it held strong, the exertion to pull it squeezing his body. Grinding his teeth, he pulled harder until it finally budged.

Pain, searing and jagged, coursed down the tether uniting them, storming the beachhead he'd set up earlier. Sweat that didn't exist coated his body and dribbled down his forehead and back. With a last effort, he pulled in her pain and yanked her thread, bringing the terminus into contact with the present he had pinched between his fingers. He could no longer contain his own pain.

A rough, raspy scream escaped from his mouth, filling the room. Delphine let loose her own ritual wail of grief, Samuel joining her, though his wail was deeper and richer for the loss of his life and his love. But soon, the pain he'd taken on behalf of Esther overwhelmed his ability to focus on his surroundings. He needed to finish his task before he lost even his ability to do that.

With the terminus pinched to the present, he knotted them together then drew his scythe in his mind, though a flicker of its outline cast a shadow against the wall opposite him. Poised with the blade on the knot, he drew in Esther's life force, letting it fill and buoy him until the last bit of it left her thread and resided inside him.

Slashing down, Dax severed Esther's thread.

Air sighed from her lungs as the weight of her chest compressed her torso for the last time. He tucked away his scythe and drew in a deep breath, exhaling the pain that had nearly overwhelmed him.

Lurching up, he staggered toward the door, barely making it to rest a hand against the door jamb to prevent himself from collapsing. Tomi slid up next to him, catching his other arm in his hand, and guided him through the door into the living room.

"Are you OK?" Tomi whispered, the wailing from the room behind them quieting.

"Yeah. I will be in a minute." He collapsed onto the couch Tomi had led him to.

It had been a long time since he'd taken on someone else's pain like that. He didn't want to do it again anytime soon. Blocking out any noise from around him, he focused on returning his mind to a more stable place. But when he couldn't seem to find his balance, he realized he'd forgotten to release Esther's soul. It created a background buzz like a refrigerator with a noisy motor.

He took in a deep breath then let it go slowly and with it, Esther's soul to continue its journey to the next phase of its being. His shoulders slumped, and he let out a small chuckle. The fullness of containing such a rich, vibrant life now left him empty without it filling his center, but it had left behind a bit of giddy energy in its wake. It had been an honor to help Esther transition and a mercy to let her do it on her own terms.

"Are you sure you're OK, boss?" Tomi's brow furrowed as his eyes moved back and forth nervously. "You don't seem... Well, I'm not sure."

Extending an arm, he let Tomi pull him to standing. "I feel positively capital."

Behind them, Delphine cleared her throat. "Is it done?"

Dax turned to face the Manbo, still wearing his Baron Samedi façade. "It is, Manman Delphine. She has departed this realm peacefully. It's safe to begin the next part of her funeral rites."

She bowed her head gracefully. "Thank you."

"It was an honor to help her. Are we even?"

"And then some," she replied. "Can you see yourself out? I must return to Samuel."

He nodded, turning toward the door.

"Um, Dax. Aren't you forgetting something?" Tomi held out the stack of clothes Dax had worn in.

"Oh." He looked over his shoulder to ensure they were alone. Delphine had returned to attend to Esther's body. Letting go of the façade, he sighed in relief to be back in his own body, though the cool room raised goosebumps on his pale skin as he hurriedly dressed.

Without another word, Tomi led him out to the car, opening the door and shutting it behind him. As Tomi buckled his seatbelt, several cars pulled up and parked near the house they'd just left, probably showing up to help with the next phase in Esther's death rites.

After Tomi stuffed the key into the ignition, he paused, looking at Dax. "You seem to be in better shape than expected after the scream you let out. I thought I'd be carrying your ass home." He paused, licking his lips nervously. "Are you sure all of her soul has moved on? There's nothing…lingering?"

"I'm sure. Everything has left my being and moved on. After the drain of the pain and the process, the soul has left me energized."

"But—"

Dax held up a hand, interrupting Tomi. "Does the wind turbine keep a piece of the wind when the breeze blows through?"

Tomi shook his head uncertainly.

"Her soul has moved on to its next step." He looked out the window as Tomi started the car and pulled out onto the street. "But something of Esther will always linger."

TWENTY-NINE

DAX

"Dax!" several of the regulars called as he strode through the front door.

He'd taken to parking out front since getting shot in the alley was becoming a regular occurrence. He hadn't seen the girl who'd shot him since the incident, but no doubt she'd be back to finish the job. Assuming his mad dash after her hadn't scared her away.

Normally, he didn't come in on the evening shifts, but he wanted to be on hand while Tomi trained his cousin Suzie. Dax wound his way through the scattered tables and leaned up against the end of the bar, neither sitting as a customer nor moving behind the bar to tend to them.

"Hey, boss. You remember, Suzie," Tomi said, gesturing to his cousin.

Suzie stood just over five feet tall before adding the height of the thick black Doc Marten's platforms she wore with ripped fishnet tights under a black leather skirt. The black Bad Brains T-shirt she wore was cut at the waist and neck to reveal a bit of her midriff and cleavage. Her afro was clipped up into a fauxhawk like it had been the last time he'd seen her. The white gauges in her ears stood out against her dark brown skin.

"You call him boss, cuz?"

Tomi shrugged.

Dax extended his hand. "You can call me Dax. Everyone else does."

"Thanks for the job, Dax. I appreciate it," Suzie said, taking his hand.

"No problem. Tomi says you're a great bartender and trustworthy, so I'm glad to have you."

"Need a beer, boss?" Tomi asked, bending slightly as if ready to scoop a can of Rainier from the undercounter cooler.

"No. I'm just going to do some paperwork in the office. Call if you need me." He quirked a corner of his lip up at Tomi's cousin. "Welcome aboard, Suzie."

Turning, he walked into the back hallway, stopping at the office. Since he was going to be working, he left the door unlocked. After he got comfortable, he turned on the security camera that covered the bar and the seating area and pulled up his accounting software to make sure the numbers were coming out right. But anytime there was motion on the security monitor, he'd flick his eyes up to see what had caught his attention. Each time, it was a regular coming or going.

About an hour after sitting down, he pushed his chair back, rubbed his eyes, and leaned back in his office chair, extending his arms above his head to stretch his upper back. He watched the security monitor. It was a good night. Most of the seats were full, the music was bumping, only slightly muffled as it penetrated the walls, and Tomi was busy behind the bar showing Suzie the ropes.

Dax had kind of blanked out staring at monitor when someone entered through the door, which wasn't unusual. But once the door shut behind them, they stood and didn't advance into the bar. Moving closer to the screen, he squinted. The young woman looked familiar. Soon several of the regulars turned to see why she was standing there. He didn't like it.

He climbed out of his chair and stepped out of the office. When he entered the bar, he stopped, mouth agape.

"You!" he pointed to the young woman.

She had put two bullets on two different occasions into him that had done more damage than nearly anything he'd encountered. Burning rage kindled in his gut and spread. The woman cringed but didn't back out.

The patrons swept their gazes back and forth between Dax and the young woman standing near the entrance. A few sat with their eyes wide and their mouths dangling open as they leaned away from Dax.

Tomi looked between the woman and Dax, his eyes going wide. "Suz, you got the bar." He quickly stepped in front of Dax, blocking him from the view of the bar patrons. "Dax. Dial it in. Your eyes. Go to the tearoom. I'll figure out what's going on."

Grabbing Dax by the shoulders, Tomi turned him around and shoved him back into the hallway.

Suzie stepped onto the step stool they kept for pulling things off the highest shelves. "Get your drink orders in, bitches! I'm Little Suzie, and I'm here to get you drunk!"

"And laid?" someone from the crowd called back, accompanied by a couple chuckles.

"I'm a bartender, not a miracle worker," Suzie replied. That got a lot more laughs.

Trusting his bar manager and friend, Dax walked stiffly to the back and yanked the sliding door to the tearoom open. He flicked on all the lights, then paced back and forth, trying to keep from losing himself. Why was she here? She hadn't pulled a gun when she saw him. She just stood there, looking terrified. Yet, she didn't flee either.

"Wait here," Tomi said from outside the tearoom before stepping in. He slid the door closed then beckoned for Dax to follow him to the back corner.

"You better have a good reason for bringing her back here, Tomi," Dax ground out through clenched teeth.

"She says she wants to talk to you. She has important information about who's trying to kill you." Tomi kept his body language relaxed and his voice calm, probably hoping to get Dax to bring the temperature of his anger down to less aggressive levels.

"I know who tried to kill me. She did!" He emphasized it with a violent point toward the door.

"She's a kid, not some mafioso orchestrating your assassination. Listen to her. Please." Tomi filled his expression with his earnest plea.

Dax let out a small growl that finished as a sign. "She has to keep her hands clearly visible at all times."

Tomi nodded and opened the door, waving the girl in. She shuffled in, her gaze on the floor and her hands clenched in front of her.

"I'm sorry," she mumbled.

"What?" Dax's voice rose. "You're sorry? You nearly killed me."

"Dax. Keep your voice down." Tomi gestured for Dax to lower his voice. He turned to Jamie. "You better say your piece before things get out of hand."

"I'm sorry. I didn't want to kill you. I was forced to."

He moved his baleful stare to Tomi then to the girl. "What about Jason? Were you 'forced' to kill him, too? One of those bullets was pulled from Jason." He stabbed his finger toward the girl. "She murdered our friend."

"Whoa, whoa, whoa." She held up her hands, palms facing him, and backed away. "I haven't killed anyone. I swear. When I shot you was the first time I fired the gun other than target practice."

He wheeled around, stalking closer to her. "You followed a man who looked similar to me from this bar. You stalked him back to his apartment building. Then you put one of those bullets into his body, tying his soul to his corpse."

She shook her head frantically, her eyes wide as saucers. "I swear… I didn't kill anyone. You're the only person I've ever shot." Her back hit the wall as she ran out of space.

Tomi wedged his body between his boss and the girl. "Boss. Dax." Tomi held his gaze, trying to calm him. "I don't think she shot Jason. At least give her a chance to speak."

"What if she has nothing of value to say?" He raised an eyebrow and sneered.

"Well, you can't do anything about that. She walked in the front door. You can't make her disappear without it coming back to us."

Dax growled low in his throat. "Fucking fine."

"Why don't you sit down? I'll make you some tea." Tomi gestured cordially toward the central table with its two long benches.

Nodding, he stepped around Tomi and sank onto the padded cushion. He rested his elbows on the table and clasped his hands in front of them, gripping his hands so tightly his knuckles were white.

Tomi stepped out of the way. "You can sit down, but no fast moves. As you can see, Dax is a bit jumpy."

She nodded, moving toward the table and the bench opposite from Dax.

Tomi stepped toward the tea bar. "Would you like some tea?"

"Please." She sat down but leaned as far back as she could without falling out of the seat. She flicked her eyes up briefly to Dax's. They went wide and then she promptly found a spot on the table to stare at.

He glared at her forehead, while Tomi hummed a tune in the background as he set the water to boiling and prepared the tea. A few minutes later, he set down a blue ceramic teapot and three cups. After he filled the cups, he took a seat next to the girl.

"Who are you and why are you here?" Tomi asked. His voice held an edge to it, but it wasn't pitched entirely toward intimidation.

She reached into the pocket of her hoodie and pulled something out.

"Whoa! Slowly, now," Tomi said, staring down at her hand. "I don't want that going off accidentally and hitting me." He scooted away from her slightly.

Making sure she kept the barrel pointed away from everyone, she gripped a revolver around its barrel and wheel. She set it down carefully and pulled her hand away slowly.

Tomi picked it up and opened the wheel. The first cartridge he pulled out was spent. He set it in the middle of the table on its base, then pulled out the next—also spent. The next one was unfired as were the next two. The last of the six had been fired.

Dax stared at the hateful things—three fired, three unfired—

lined up like soldiers. One of them had put a bullet in his left lung. Another had put a round in his right shoulder.

Tomi picked up the gun and flipped it over. "Serial number's filed off." He set it back down, pushing it toward Dax.

"Why are you here?" Dax said.

The girl, she looked like she still had the softness of youth, crumpled into herself. "…Help."

He didn't hear what she'd said other than the one word. "Why should I help you? You shot me. Twice. You waited in ambush across the street and then fired three bullets at me about a month ago."

He pointed to his right shoulder. "One hit me right here. Another skimmed my helmet."

She stared at him, her eyes wide and her jaw hanging open. It quivered as if she wanted to say something but couldn't.

"Then you showed up again. Set up another ambush and fired three more shots at me. One of them hit me in the lung and I nearly drowned in blood."

"I…" She licked her lips, took a breath, and sat up a little straighter, though she didn't quite make eye contact with him. She shifted her gaze to the bullets. "Those are the only bullets they gave me. And…and I only tried to…"

"Kill me?"

She nodded. "They gave me six bullets. I swear. I only shot three bullets at you."

Tomi, his eyes intent, sat straighter, his gaze firmly fixed on the girl. "What day was this?"

Dax looked between them both, confused. If what she said was true… "It was—"

Tomi raised his hand to forestall Dax. "What day?"

"Sixteen days ago."

"And where were you at on the morning of the twenty-fifth?" Tomi asked.

"What day was that?"

"Tuesday," Dax replied.

"I was at school. You can check with anyone. They take attendance." She gulped and slumped a bit, her back curving.

Tomi and Dax exchanged a glance. Tomi spoke first. "I believe her."

"And Jason?" Dax asked.

Tomi nodded. "If she didn't shoot you the first time, it's possible whoever did went after Jason, mistaking him for you."

"I know what you are," Jamie said quietly.

Dax sat up straighter, narrowing his eyes. "Then you know mercy is not what I deal in."

Tomi sipped his cup noisily.

Dax snorted lightly and picked up his cup, inhaling the steam. "Gunpowder?"

Tomi winked and smirked.

Rolling his eyes, Dax shook his head and took a drink of the green tea. "Drink your tea, child. I can't very well kill you now with the whole bar witness to you being here." She nodded at him and picked up the cup. "But that doesn't mean I won't come looking for you."

She choked lightly on her tea and blanched. Setting down the cup primly, she finally made eye contact. "I can tell you who gave me the gun and the bullets."

Tomi set his cup down and picked up one of the unfired bullets, inspecting it. When he finished, he handed it to Dax. Unlike the two bullets he'd pulled from his body, this one still felt fully potent and alive. None of the runes had been damaged by the firing process. He'd have to see if Gunnar would take a look at the unmarred bullet, though he may not want to have any more to do with him, especially if things were getting more intense.

"I'm assuming this information isn't free." Dax stared intently at her.

She took a deep breath then dove in, speaking rapidly, "I want you to not come after me and my friend or our families."

"That's not a small ask, not after what you did to me." He shucked his jacket off his shoulder and pulled the V-neck collar down and over, displaying the angry red scars of the gunshot wound and the line where Boudreaux put in the chest tube to drain the blood. "Those runes aren't just scratchings on the bullet. They're dark magic, and you put one right here." He pointed to the bullet wound.

The girl shrank into herself again. "I'm sorry," she mumbled just above a whisper.

"Sorry?" Dax's anger rose. "Do you think a sorry will fix this?"

Tomi cleared his throat. "Let's see what she has to say. She's brought us the gun and the bullets. That's a good starting point."

Dax gave a curt nod.

"I'll be right back," Tomi said, sliding out from the bench and disappearing out to the main bar. He returned and set three shots down, one for each of them.

The girl looked at it then looked at Tomi. "I can't drink this. I'm only eighteen."

Dax snorted. "You're worried about breaking the law and drinking? You committed attempted murder. Did you drive?"

"No, I took the bus."

"You carried a gun on a bus?" He shook his head. "Have you ever drank before?"

She nodded.

Tomi lifted his shot and held it up toward the girl. Rolling her eyes, she picked hers and held it up with an annoyed smirk. Dax picked his up and just threw it back, letting the burn of the cheap whiskey blend with his anger and annoyance. Tomi and the girl followed suit.

"Gah," the girl cringed and coughed. Reaching for her tea, she took a deep drink.

Tomi chuckled, setting his glass down.

"Can't you get in trouble for serving a minor?" the girl asked.

Dax chuckled and turned to Tomi. "She's got spunk, if nothing else." He narrowed his eyes and looked at the girl for a few seconds. Sighing, he relaxed a little. "I'm willing to tentatively offer conditional amnesty, depending on what I hear."

"Since that's out of the way. I'm Tomi, and the boss there is Dax."

"What are you?" she directed the question to Tomi.

"That's for me to know and you to mind your own business."

She sniffed the air. "You're not a wolf shifter…"

Tomi laughed. "You need to be more careful. You just gave away part of your identity."

She scowled and blushed.

Tomi turned to Dax. "She is green. You might as well give us your name."

"Jamie."

Dax rested his elbows on the table and leaned toward Jamie. "Now tell us why you shot me and how you came by the desire to commit a felony."

Before starting, she took another drink from her tea, tipping the last into her mouth. Tomi refilled her cup from the pot, then topped off his and Dax's. Once she had no other choice, she broke into her tale of pagan Nazi biker gangs and her dad's gambling debts. When she was done, Dax was astonished.

It appeared Tomi was as well. "You're a better daughter than your father deserves."

Dax had only witnessed families from the outside. Tomi, his mom, and his sister were the closest thing he had to a family.

"What do you say, Dax? Should we let her slide this time?"

Dax scowled at his friend. "You weren't the one bleeding out in a bathtub."

"Don't forget the part where your kitten kept you alive with claw jolts to the chest and was so covered in blood I had to give it a bath."

Dax clenched his jaw. "Fuck you, Tomi."

Tomi grinned broadly.

On second thought, Dax wasn't sure about Tomi being his family. He had an asshole streak at times.

Jamie's jaw hung open as she stared back and forth between Dax and Tomi. "You...you have a kitten? And it saved your life?"

Tomi wiped the grin off his face, shifting to a heavy, serious expression. "Yeah. He does. And it did."

"I'm sorry about your kitten." Her brow furrowed as her eyes flicked down at the table and up to Dax. "The...the grim reaper has a kitten?"

Tomi snorted and chuckled, then broke down into a hearty laugh. When he calmed down enough to speak, he said, "Yeah. Weird, huh?." In between snorts, he said, "He named it Morty!" He slapped the table and wheezed, gasping for air around guffaws.

Dax's cheeks heated until they were burning. For the first time since she walked in, the corners of her mouth tipped up until she snickered a couple times, trying to keep it from overwhelming her until she held her hand in front of her mouth to cover the laughter, though the sound mingled with Tomi's.

Shaking his head, Dax sighed and held up his fist before raising his middle finger toward Tomi. He thought about letting slip the flame-eyed demon that had chased the girl through the city, but then decided against it. Frightening her would feel good for a moment, but at this point, it would be bullying. She was legally an adult, barely, but she was still a child—a child playing in waters too deep for her abilities. He wanted to hate her for the pain she'd caused him, but... Tomi's gallows humor, laughing at the ridiculousness did more to deescalate him than just about anything. Tomi knew how to help Dax feel grounded, helped him approach some semblance of human.

When they stopped laughing, Dax sighed and let the tension slip out of his shoulders. "Jamie. Your offering of information is accepted. I will forgo your death, the death of your friend, and the deaths of your families." The girl perked up, a bit of lightness slipping into her spine and lifting her shoulders. "But. There is now a link between us. You're not free of this yet. You've failed at your task. I'm very much not...eliminated."

Tomi, ever cognizant of the feel of the room, instantly became serious. "He's right. All the bikers have to do to confirm Dax is still alive is send someone in for a beer."

"And that means you and your people are still in danger," Dax said.

That sapped a bit of the starch from her spine. "What can I do?"

Tomi snickered. "I guess y'all are both in the same boat. Some pagan asshole bikers want you dead."

"Um," Jamie licked her lips. "Norse pagan, Nazi wolf shifter bikers."

Tomi whistled and tilted his head. "That sounds like some serious shit, Dax. You're kinda fucked."

Dax slowly shifted his gaze to Tomi, raising an eyebrow. "And you're a known associate. And I'm guessing these aren't what one would call multicultural bikers with a DEI program. You're just as fucked as I am."

Tomi grimaced. "You had to drag me into this."

Dax barked a harsh laugh. "Your ass is already in this, my friend."

Tomi shrugged. "I have been since you saved my mama and my baby sis." He sighed. "So, where does that leave us?"

Dax looked between his friend and the girl. "In a bad place."

THIRTY

JAMIE

"You did what?" Cory asked, twisting on his basement couch to stare at her.

Jamie pursed her lips. "You heard me. I went to him and asked for mercy in exchange for the bullets and who sent me."

"Why didn't you bring me? We promised each other to do this together. There was a pinky swear involved." He folded his arms across his chest and scowled, though on his face it lacked the weight it would on a naturally less friendly person.

"I didn't want to risk your life if he decided to just take revenge right there. I've already risked your life and your mom's life enough because of my deadbeat dad. Your mom would never forgive me if I got you killed."

"If he killed me, you'd be dead, too. Not much she can do to you then."

"That's not the point. Your mother has treated me almost like her own daughter. I couldn't take you away from her. I know we swore an oath, but sometimes a person has to break an oath to do the right thing. I owe your mother so much. You're going to have to forgive me for this one." She pleaded with her eyes, hoping he'd understand.

Sighing, he shook his head and rolled his eyes. "Well. Are you going to tell me what happened?"

"You forgive me?"

"If I must..." He unfolded his arms. "Now tell me what happened."

"He's not going to kill us. At least I don't believe so."

Cory's brow furrowed. "What's it going to cost us to deal with this"—he searched for the term he wanted—"demon? White nationalist wolf-shifter bikers are bad enough. This doesn't sound like an improvement."

Jamie shrugged. "I thought I was going there to offer my life in exchange for yours. He didn't take it, though he was plenty mad. His friend stopped him from doing anything. I don't know if he'd have killed me right there. Not in his business."

"What was he like?"

"His friend?"

Cory rolled his eyes. "No. The demon."

"His name is Dax."

"What? That's not a very scary name."

"I don't care what name he goes by. Until you've sat three feet from him with those eyes staring at you..." She shivered. "They're like looking into an infinite abyss, but when his anger sparks—flames."

"Does he flounce around in his holey robe and open beer bottles with his scythe?" He pantomimed it for her entertainment.

Chuckling, she shook her head. "No. He just looked like a normal dude. Tall, skinny, a bit gawky." She narrowed her eyes. "I'm not sure who's really in charge, him or his friend."

"What do you mean?"

"I don't know. He didn't seem very good at being a human. His friend did most of the talking and kept him in check."

"I mean, he could have just been too pissed to talk. I know I sometimes have trouble communicating when I'm angry."

"When were you ever that angry?" She raised an eyebrow.

He gave a half shrug. "It's happened."

She narrowed her eyes, pressing her lips into a fine line. "You've been so angry you burst into an avatar of death and chased someone through the streets of the city on a giant motorcycle with a deadly scythe, your eyes burning with the eternal flames of damnation? You've been that angry? Almost might have killed someone on the spot? Happy-go-luck Cory? The biggest dork I know. *You've* been that angry?"

He deflated, a smirk spreading across his face. "OK. Maybe not that angry. Hey. Wait. I'm not a dork. You're a dork." He ran a hand through his hair. "I'm glad you're not dead, but what have you got us involved in now?"

She flopped onto the couch, sagging into the back cushion. "I don't know. But I almost killed a…a whatever. I shot a man in cold blood, and he didn't die. He nearly killed us." She stared off for a moment, her brow furrowing. "I've never been so scared in my life… When he chased us. They're just dirtbag bigot bikers. He's a… I don't know."

Cory joined her on the couch. "Yeah, that was a rearview mirror I don't ever want to see again."

"Right?" She looked up at her friend. "I can't become a killer. Not for Nazi bikers. I don't know if Dax is innocent—hell, I don't even know if he can be killed—but he hasn't done anything to us, despite what I've done to him."

"Do you think he'll actually look out for us?"

She shrugged. "I don't know. I'd just be happy if he decided to look up the bikers."

"Oh, man, can you imagine that? It would be —"

Jamie's phone ringing interrupted him. "It's my mom." She answered. "What, Mom?"

"Oh, it's not your dear old mom," a man said.

She recognized the dark, oily voice of the man who'd given her the gun and the photograph. Ivar. "What do you want?"

"A little birdie tells me you went to visit your target, and that you walked out alive after talking to him for a while. You know what happens to birdies who sing right?"

She didn't reply, unsure what she could say.

When she didn't fill the space, he spoke again, "I've got your mommy and your deadbeat daddy here. I'm sure they'd love a little family reunion. Now, if you'd like to see them alive, I suggest you join us in your apartment in…oh…fifteen minutes." He hung up.

She stared at her phone, her jaw working. Looking at Cory, she could barely breathe. "They know I went to see Dax. They've got my parents."

"I heard. You've got to call the cops."

She snorted, a look of disgust spreading on her face. "Do you think the cops don't know about those bikers? That they don't condone it? They won't help."

"Then what? Dax?"

Looking around, trying to grasp at ideas, she finally settled her gaze back on Cory. "I've got to go, or they'll kill them."

"OK. I'll drop you off then go to the bar and ask for help. He's got to be willing to help since you stuck your neck out for him."

Her mouth worked like a fish out of water until she just shrugged. Cory grabbed her jacket and got her moving. Together, they climbed into the poor Kia. The rear window had been replaced, but the trunk and the roof still bore the wounds Dax had inflicted on it with his scythe. Cory had duct taped the gashes closed so the late winter rain wouldn't leak in.

She tapped her finger nervously on the door arm rest as she stared out the window. When they arrived at her building, the car had barely stopped rolling before she leapt out and was moving.

"I'll hurry!" Cory called behind her.

She hoped he did. Yanking the door to the building open, she flew up the stairs, her legs and arms pumping until she slid to a halt at her floor. With a quick shove, she jogged through the door into the hall, breathing heavily. Bikers stood outside her door, just like they had when this had all started.

Trying to collect her dignity, she slowed down and walked in with her head held high. "I'm here."

Ivar stepped out of the kitchen. "And so you are."

He nodded to a couple men who stepped up and grabbed her by the upper arms. They frog walked her into the kitchen and forced her into an empty chair. Her parents were tied to the chairs, and gags had been stuffed in their mouths. After they forced her into the chair, they backed up, flanking her.

Ivar leaned up against the door jamb. "You're a braver kid than your gutless dad, that's for sure. He'd have never betrayed us."

Their attention was drawn when more men came in, dragging a struggling Cory between them.

"Caught her little boyfriend here trying to make a run for it," one of them said.

He had several bruises blooming on his face, and blood dribble from his nose.

"Where was your little friend going?" Ivar asked, looking nonchalant.

She kept her lips clamped.

"Really? Still going to fight?" He gave a quick nod.

While the two bikers held Cory, a third stepped up and punched him in the gut. Cory wheezed, drool dribbling from his lip. The biker followed up with a hard backhand to Cory's jaw that cracked like a whip. Groaning, Cory sagged, his knees giving out, but the men kept him upright. Ivar held up a hand casually, stopping the beating.

"Feel like answering now?" Ivar asked, looking like he didn't care one way or the other.

The biker raised a fist, cocking it back and waiting. She didn't know how much Cory could take, but she couldn't ask him to take any more punishment. Not on her behalf.

"The bar," she mumbled.

"Where?"

She looked up, struggling to restrain the venom she felt for Ivar and the situation from showing in her eyes. "The bar. I don't think you have the guts to go up against him. That's why you sent me instead of doing it yourse—"

Someone struck her at a nod from Ivar. The backhand rattled her teeth and wrung her head like a bell. The two flanking her reached forward and kept her upright, preventing her from sagging forward.

A cruel grin spread across Ivar's face. "Get these three out of here. They have an appointment with the boss. But we're going to have a little friendly chat with her friend before we join you."

With two bikers for each of them, she was dragged out of her family apartment with her mom and dad. The last thing she heard before they were shoved in the elevator was the impact of a fist and Cory crying out in pain. She cringed at the sound of her friend's pain. Tears burned in her eyes as the doors slid shut. She'd done this to Cory, and even if he lived, she'd never be able to forgive herself for it.

THIRTY-ONE
DAX

The Ramone's song blaring out of the jukebox sounded starkly louder without the general din of glassware and conversation. Everyone stared at the bloody youth wobbling just inside the door as if his presence had paused the action, the only movement everyone's heads and eyes following along as his body swayed in a tight circle, his feet stationary. Then, as his body tipped, the action resumed. Yells of "Catch him" or "Move!" or general screams drowned out the jukebox.

Chairs scooted back violently, one tipping over, as the young man slammed down onto the tabletop, scattering glasses that shattered onto the hard floor. In a flash, Tomi leapt from his bar stool next to Dax and shoved his way through the crowd. Everyone now stood after jumping out of the way or standing so they could see what was going on.

"Come on, make way!" he called, shouldering aside the regulars. "Suzie, grab the broom and mop so we can get this mess cleaned up. Dax, come here and help."

"Should we call 911?" someone asked.

Dax unwound his legs from the stool, the crowd parting to make way for him. Squatting down next to Tomi, they turned him over carefully. He looked familiar. A twinge below his left shoulder solidified the feeling. He was the boy in the car with Jamie.

The boy's eyelids fluttered, then opened, his eyes going wide as he looked from Tomi to Dax. He licked his lips, looking like he was attempting to speak. "H…help."

"Do we call 911 or what?" someone else asked, sounding annoyed.

"No." Dax said firmly. "Tomi, let's move him back to the tearoom. If we need to get him medical help, we'll give Boudreaux a call. Suzie, clean up the glass. Tomi will help you after we move him into the back. Then a free round—"

The cheers of patrons drowned out Dax's next words. Once the noise died down enough, he raised an arm and called out loudly. "Pabst or Rainier only!"

There were few mumblings. Most of the crowd was probably already drinking cheap beer anyway, nor was this the kind of crowd that would turn their nose up at a free beer.

"If we help you up, think you can walk with us, kid?" Tomi asked quietly.

The boy nodded.

"Alright, on three…" Tomi counted it off, then they hoisted him up, each of them sliding under a shoulder.

The crowd made way as he and Tomi walked-dragged the kid toward the back of the bar. In anticipation, Suzie had already unlocked and slid open the door to the tearoom.

"I'll go first," Tomi grunted, angling to the side so he'd pass through the door first. With his foot, he hooked a chair from one of the two-top tables near the wall and pulled it out. Together, they lowered the boy onto it, letting him slump against the wall and the table. "I'll be out front helping Suze if you need me." Tomi pulled the sliding door closed behind him.

"Thanks, Tomi." Dax said, staring down at the boy.

With a sigh, he turned and walked behind the small bar and grabbed a bar towel, wetting it down. When he returned, he narrowed his eyes and squatted in front of the kid. Some of the cuts spread about his face looked like they'd already stopped bleeding, a few of the smaller and shallower ones even looked almost closed.

Though he still slumped to the side, his breathing looked steadier. He knew there were other supernaturals in Red City. Many of them, if he remembered rightly from the before times. He didn't feel like invading the boy's mind to find out who or what he was, not that he was sure he could even do that anymore. Though, he was probably a wolf shifter, if his association with the girl was any indication. But if this had to do with her, allowing the boy to come clean would be a good first test.

Holding out the damp bar rag, he cleared his throat to get the kid's attention. "Do you feel strong enough to clean yourself up a bit? Or I can do it if you need me to."

The kid swallowed and took the rag, his hand trembling but more sure than it had been a few minutes ago. The boy started with his hand, grimacing and groaning as he dabbed gently. Once those looked reasonably clean, he took a deep breath and cringed as he started on his face, letting out gasps of pain as he patted around the wounds.

Dax stood, a sparkle in the kid's hair catching his eyes. Reaching over, he plucked a piece of glass from his hair, then set it on the table. "Be careful. There might be more shards scattered about."

The boy nodded his head, another piece of glass falling into his lap to emphasize the point. When he finished with the bar towel, he held it out then thought better of it, setting it on the table next to the shard of glass. Then he picked the one from off his leg and set it next to the other one.

"You're Jamie's friend." It was a statement, not a question. Dax snagged the other chair and pulled it out into the aisle between the large center table and the table the boy sat at. Lowering himself into it, he leaned forward, resting his elbows on his knees.

The kid nodded.

"What's your name?"

"Cory."

"How old are you?"

Cory licked his lips, keeping his eyes lowered. "Eighteen."

Same as the girl. "What happened to you?"

"I got beat up."

Dax snorted. "No shit. Why and who are the questions I want answered."

The young man nodded his head, though it looked a bit wobbly. "Jamie said she told you everything?"

Dax gave a single, crisp nod.

"It was the biker gang. They took Jamie and her family. Then…" He choked, holding back a sob. He took a moment to collect himself, breathing deeply. For the first time since he'd walked into the bar, he raised his head, making eye contact with Dax. "Then they kicked the shit out of me and then tossed me out in front of your bar with a message." He reached toward the inside of the left side of his jacket.

Raising a hand, Dax leaned back, his jaw clenching and his eyes narrowing in warning. "Slowly now. I don't want there to be any misunderstandings. I don't feel like being shot again."

Cory nodded nervously, swallowing hard. He grabbed the left lapel of his jacket with his left hand and slowly opened it, revealing a pocket with an envelope peeking out. "May I?"

Dax extended his hand toward Cory, his palm up. Cory slowly pulled the envelope from his pocket with his right hand and set it on Dax's palm. After he let go of the envelope, he slowly backed up, placing one hand on the table and the other on his thigh.

Leaning back in his chair, Dax flipped the envelope over. It was sealed with a glob of black wax, a Norse black sun emblazoned in it. He stared at it, a burning anger building in his gut. He didn't know how long he focused on it, but a whimper from the boy drew him out of his fugue. With a shake of his head, he forced the heat of his rage down. The heavy sound of Cory's scared breathing drew his attention up. The kid, arms splayed out, looked like he was attempting to push his way through the wall. He must have let too much of his anger near the surface. When he looked back down, the wax had started to melt, sending dribbles of black wax rolling down toward the envelope's edge.

"Sorry about that," Dax mumbled. Though the kid had helped his friend try to kill him, he still felt bad for scaring him.

Focusing on the envelope, he tried to pop the seal, but the wax was too soft after he let the flame of his rage reach his eyes. It did peel up, leaving a bit of wax on his finger. He set the envelope on the table next to Cory and opened the folded sheet of paper.

If you value the life of the girl, you'll turn yourself in to us. If you agree to our terms, send a reply. The paperweight we dropped with this message knows the location.

"I assume you're the paperweight referred to herein?"

Cory was still a bit wild in the eyes but had peeled himself off the wall, though his eyes flicked toward the door regularly. He gave a quick shake of his head. Dax held the letter out toward the boy, facing the writing toward him.

"Yeah. I'm the paperweight," Cory mumbled, looking at the floor. He took a deep breath and straightened his back. "It's that biker bar out on Bedford Avenue."

Dax knew which one Cory was talking about. It was in a rough neighborhood, rougher than most in a city full of run-down neighborhoods. The bar fronted a large, fenced compound with a wrecking yard on one side. He'd heard rumblings about the biker gang that owned the bar and the wrecking yard but had never had any cause to head out that way. He didn't need to drink with racist bikers. And it seemed like there were too many violent gangs in this city to keep track of.

He stood up and paced toward the back of the tearoom, rubbing his chin, the rough, black stubble providing texture to focus on. The bikers wanted him dead for some reason. He'd done nothing to antagonize them. Well, not in a lot of years. But he was pretty sure they'd have no way to link the body he inhabited with the gang, even if they were the same bikers. This body no longer had the tattoos that had covered the racist biker he'd killed. He thought he'd got away with it scot-free. Until they'd tried to put magical bullets in him, he was sure they had no idea who he was.

There were plenty of blue-collar dive bars in Red City. There was nothing special about his, other than his misguided attempt to also have a tearoom. He'd done everything in his power to lie low, not wanting to draw the attention of those who'd banished him or the earthly authorities who ran the festering hive of corruption he'd been banished to.

With a crisp turn, he stalked back toward the boy. He tried not to flinch but slowly leaned away from Dax the closer he got.

"Now. Tell me what I need to know. Who are these bikers?" He picked up the envelope, aiming the partially melted seal toward Cory. "Besides white nationalists."

Cory's eyes widened as he tried to avoid looking toward Dax.

Dax snorted. "Do you think they're going to let you live after all you've seen and been involved in? Just because you keep your lips closed when I ask about them? I don't know how you got wrapped up in all this, but it's clearly not because you're the sharpest scythe in the field."

Cory looked down at the floor and mumbled something quickly.

"What?"

"They're wolf shifters."

"Wolf shifters? How do you know that?"

He sighed and paused for a few moments before sitting up straighter. "Because I'm a wolf shifter, too."

"Come again for Tomi?" Tomi said, sliding the door shut behind himself.

Dax turned toward his friend, raising an eyebrow. "Everything calmed down out there?"

"Yeah. Free rounds always seem to work. Hope we can make up the sales though."

"It's cheaper than giving the authorities another reason to stick their noses where they don't belong."

Tomi shrugged. "I guess, but bankruptcy isn't exactly cheap either. Now, what did he say about being a werewolf?"

"Ungh." Cory shook his head.

"You got a problem, kid?" Tomi asked, narrowing his eyes as he approached them.

"I'm not a werewolf. I'm a wolf shifter. They're different, you know." Cory sounded disgusted at the mix up.

"You're a man. You're a wolf. Werewolf. It's in the title."

Cory crossed his arms and looked like he wanted to pout. "They're different. I'm not a werewolf."

Shaking his head and rolling his eyes, Dax slid back onto the chair he'd sat in earlier. "What's the difference? For my inquisitive friend over here." He gestured casually toward Tomi.

"I can just change into a wolf. My body doesn't break and reform into a wolf. I don't have to shift at the full moon. I'm not an out-of-control monster. I'm a wolf shifter."

"Huh. I guess you learn something new every day." Tomi grabbed a chair and straddled it, crossing his arms on the back of the chair.

"What else do you know about them?" Dax asked the boy.

He shrugged. "That's about it. It's not like I'm in their gang. I just know they're Nazi wolf-shifter bikers."

Dax narrowed his eyes and stared at Cory as he squirmed uncomfortably in his chair. When he'd decided the kid really didn't have much else to add, he shifted his gaze to Tomi.

"So, what does that have to do with us?" Tomi asked.

Dax snorted. "Well, according to our young squire here, not only are the bikers who want me dead fascist scum, but they're also wolf shifters."

Tomi whistled, his eyes wide. "That makes things a bit more interesting."

THIRTY-TWO

Jamie was growing tired of the sniveling. She just wanted to brood in peace, but her dad blubbered, alternating between begging for mercy and making outrageous promises if they let him go. Her mom just sat stone still and dead eyed.

She hoped Cory had escaped and taken his mom to safety. She couldn't stand the thought of her father's life of being a fuck up ruining another family. It was bad enough he'd dragged down her and her mom. Though, her dad might have been the only one who didn't understand how fucked they were, even if he begged. The optimism of a degenerate gambler.

When the last biker left the room, shutting the door behind him, they were left alone in the room where'd she'd first been handed a gun and a photograph.

"Dad, shut up. I'm tired of listening to you."

Her mom stirred from her seeming stupor. "Don't speak to your father that way, Jamie."

Her nostrils flared. "Oh, give it up, mom. This is my father's doing. This is where his gambling has brought us. This is what years of you enabling him has earned our family. In debt to *Nazi* bikers. Your husband sold me to them when they came to collect. And now, they're going to put bullets in our head and dump our bodies to be lessons for other degenerate gamblers like dear old dad."

Her mother's mouth hung open, her lower jaw quivering. Instead of speech, a few gasps of air sounded through her vocal cords. Finally, she found some control and turned toward her husband. "Is this true?"

He didn't even bother looking at her, instead dissolving into pathetic sobs. Her mom deflated, tears falling from her eyes as she did her best to shift her bound body away from her husband.

After a while, she asked, "Did they…harm you?"

Jamie shook her head, her gut clenching at the memory of that evening. "No, they threatened it. But they had another plan for me."

She didn't know why she didn't want to tell her mom. Maybe in some deep-down part of her soul, she still wanted her mom to see her as her little girl. Maybe she just didn't want to face the fact that she'd tried to kill a man and failed, then betrayed those who'd sent her to do it and that's why they were strapped to these chairs, bait for a monster they wanted dead.

She'd seen the white of his skull. The hateful flames of perdition in his eyes. That gleaming scythe haunted her dreams, its blade dragging her into nightmares.

"What do they want from us? I…I can pay the debt." A spark of hope gleamed in her mother's eyes.

Jamie sighed nosily. "It's long past that time. They wanted me to perform a task, and I failed. Now we're bait."

"Bait for what?"

"Something scarier than these creeps who hold us." She hung her head, staring blankly at the floor. Going to him was an act of desperation, but right now, he was the only hope she had of seeing her next birthday.

The sound of the door opening and the heavy tread of Ivar, the noise of clinking glasses, jocular shouts, and laughter trailing along with him drew her attention away from her downward mental spiral. Her dad blubbered louder, developing a hiccup to add to his pathetic lack of composure.

"Have some fucking dignity, man," Ivar said, crouching in front of her dad to make eye contact with him. "Be more like your daughter. At least she's got some balls on her.

In response, her dad reran his litany of empty promises and begging.

Ivar sighed dramatically. "Your mewlings are worth less than the scraps of paper your IOUs are printed on. Shut up." He shoved out with both hands, tipping her father's chair over abruptly.

He landed with an exhaled gust of a breath and the hollow snap of his head smacking against the wood floor. That shut him up, or at least reduced his sobbing and begging to a semi-conscious whimper until that too quieted to a steady breathing interrupted by hiccups.

Next to her, her mother breathed shakily. "P…pl…please, sir. I can pay the debt. I have the money."

Ivar stood up, staring at the heap of failure on the floor. "Honey, we're long past the point where that's the currency we're dealing with. I suggest you introduce your bottom lip to your top lip and let them stay acquainted for a while."

Her mom's mouth shut quickly, her teeth clacking as she snapped her jaw closed.

Taking the two steps to Jamie, he stopped in front of her, filling her downturned eyes with his scuffed, black motorcycle boots. She inhaled sharply when he patted her on the cheek a couple times.

"You better hope your new pal decides to show up. Or you'll have betrayed us for nothing."

Jamie lifted her head slightly, raising her eyes so they stared into Ivar's flannel covered naval. "Maybe you should wonder why I did it. Why he's scarier than all of you put together."

Next to her, her mother groaned, lowering her head.

"Ha! Too bad your wretch of a father isn't awake enough to hear you. He could use a lesson in showing some spine." Before she could blink, Ivar backhanded her across the jaw.

Stars exploded across her vision as her head snapped to the side. A moment after the shock of it, her jaw throbbed and her ear whined.

"Now, it's time for you to learn a lesson about when to speak and when not to." Ivar turned around sharply and stalked out of the room, slamming the door behind him.

"Jamie," her mom whispered harshly. "You're going to get yourself killed with that smart mouth of yours."

"What do you care? You spend all your time cleaning up the messes made by the idiot you married. If you'd kicked him out years ago, we wouldn't be here right now." She'd said it quietly enough that only her mother could hear it.

Her mother let out a strangled noise, then started crying quietly.

THIRTY-THREE

DAX

Tomi pulled over once the distant neon glare of the biker bar resolved into a view of the bike filled parking lot. "This close enough?"

Dax squinted, rolling down his passenger side window slightly. "I think so."

"I hope some cops or bikers don't drive by and see me parked like this. They'll know we're up to something," Tomi said warily. "Though it already looks like the lot is full. Fuck. I hope there aren't more on the way."

Secretly, Dax agreed with him, but he had an idea that might help, assuming it even worked. "I'm going to try something. If it works, drive on and park in the neighborhood."

"How will I know it's working?"

"You'll know." Dax closed his eyes and took a deep breath and held it.

While Tomi tapped the steering wheel nervously, Dax gathered in his consciousness and forced it down into his chest and into his lungs. As his lungs strained to exhale his carbon dioxide laden breath, he checked to ensure he hadn't missed anything, and that it was safely sequestered where he wanted it. His lungs burned, but he took one moment to ensure he affixed a tether to himself so he could find his way back. Everything felt right. At least he hoped it did.

Finally, he let his lungs expunge the breath, his chest squeezing until everything was expelled into the cabin of Tomi's car. His body slumped and fell across the center console, stopping when his head landed on Tomi's shoulder.

"What the fuck, man?" Tomi shoved his boss's body off himself.

Dax's body tumbled the other way, his head hitting the passenger side window with a light thud. Focusing in, the interior of the car and its two inhabitants looked desaturated and slightly fuzzy. He checked one more time to ensure the tether was properly affixed. He tried to nod to himself then realized he had nothing to nod, so he pushed himself toward the several inch open gap in the window and out into the night. He could sense the chill rain's existence and could even almost feel it passing through his essence. It felt like the slightest of tugs followed by a light stretching as the drop fell out of him on its journey to the ground until his essence disconnected from the drop, snapping back to rejoin the main body of his being.

He was so focused on the drops falling through him that he barely noticed Tomi pull back into the road and drive away. Forcing himself to ignore the rain, he flowed toward the biker bar, homing in on the glow of its neon sign. As he neared it, he realized the anticipation he'd felt in the car was gone, left behind with his body. Without the organs and glands to pump the various chemicals a human body was awash in, he felt almost clean, but also disturbingly empty.

Over the last few years, he'd grown used to living in a human shell, its natural processes regulating his life and existence. Now he'd cast off the fleshy prison he'd been sentenced to. In a moment of concern, he touched the tether, plucking it to ensure it was still firmly attached. Once the subtle vibration returned to him, he pushed on.

The Harleys and custom choppers filled the pothole and gravel filled parking lot. Every minute or so, a noisy bike would pull into the lot and post up alongside the rest, disgorging a beefy biker who joined his brethren inside. Dax waited for the next one, then followed him in when the gigantic mound of body hair and muscle working the door waved him in. Hard rock music blared as bikers moved about the bar, getting more drinks or finding places to sit.

There were two differences that separated this crowd from any other bar. There were no women. And everyone was heavily armed. The bikers were here for business, and that business was Dax.

Dax hovered in the corner, watching. Every time the door opened, the crowd inside paused, their eyes drifting toward the door to see who was entering, their hands drifting toward weapons. When they saw that it was just one of their fellows, they'd relax imperceptibly and go about their business milling about and waiting.

As he watched, he noticed one biker who others moved out of the way of, giving him respectful nods as he passed. The man was tall and muscular with long brown hair on top and the sides and back shaved. The Norse white supremacist themed tattoos his ilk preferred covered his arms and probably the rest of his body under the T-shirt, jeans, and black leather vest.

Drifting toward him, Dax paused when he opened a door leading into a back room. There. Two people were tied to chairs. Jamie and an older woman with similar features. Another chair with a man tied to it was tipped onto its back, its inhabitant motionless. She was here.

A quick glimpse revealed high, short windows with the glint of iron bars blocking the outside. There would be no easy ingress into that room. Satisfied with the scene, he pushed his awareness back toward the exit, slipping out when someone else entered.

With a quick thought, he yanked the tether and zipped along it, across the street, into the neighborhood, and a couple more streets back. As he slammed back into his body, he jolted up straight and inhaled noisily.

"Holy fuck," Tomi gasped out, covering his heart with his hand. "You scared the shit out of me."

"Sorry. I've never tried that before." Dax coughed lightly, trying to get his breathing to steady.

"Did it work? Whatever the fuck it was?"

"Yeah. It's like we expected."

"Packed full of muscle-bound, racist assholes?"

Dax chuckled mirthlessly. "And heavily armed, but I found the kid and her parents."

"You don't have to go in there. This is the girl's business, not yours." Tomi narrowed his eyes and raised his eyebrows.

"Those bikers made it my business when they put those bullets in me. They may not have pulled the trigger, but they sent them on their way."

"So, what are we going to do? Boudreaux's on his way with a couple buddies and some equipment, but that's not going to be enough to take out what looks like a fortified bunker."

"I'm going to walk in and fetch them."

Tomi's eyes opened wide. "By yourself?"

An evil grin spread across Dax's narrow face. "Yeah."

Tomi shook his head. "You're a fool."

"No, I'm pissed off. I don't think they know who they messed with. It's time they learn."

"I want to back you. You're my friend and I owe you—"

Dax held up a hand to interrupt Tomi. "You don't owe me anything. The time when there was any debt between us is long past. You can drop me off and go back to the bar. I can't ask you to die for me."

"Shut your dumb ass up. I'm not going back to the bar. What do you want me and Boudreaux to do, then?" His eyes flicked up to the mirror as a vehicle pulled up behind them. "That's Boudreaux now."

Dax nodded and stepped out of Tomi's car, Tomi following him. Boudreaux jumped out of the driver's side of the black Sprinter van and walked up to Tomi. They clasped hands and pulled into each other, bumping chests as they patted each other on the back in a hug.

"What's up, brother?" Boudreaux said.

"Just trying to keep a scrawny white guy alive."

Boudreaux laughed. "Same shit."

"Different day," Tomi finished.

Boudreaux ducked back into the van as three more men exited it. He tossed something rigid and black to Tomi. "This ought to help."

Tomi chuckled, turning to Dax. "Put this on under your clothes."

Dax caught the bulletproof jacket and looked it over. It appeared to be about the right size for him. Setting it on the trunk of Tomi's car, he removed his leather jacket then pulled his black T-shirt over his head.

"Damn, you ain't kidding, Tomi. He is scrawny." Boudreaux laughed, though to Dax's ears it didn't sound like a mocking laugh.

Dax wasn't muscular. The body he'd taken hadn't been muscular nor had he done anything in the intervening years to change that fact. With a shrug and a smirk, he pulled on the vest and tightened the Velcro straps so it was as snug as it could be. "That'll hopefully keep any special bullets from finding purchase."

Tomi nodded, looking him up and down.

"Unless they shoot you in the face or the balls," Boudreaux said.

"Then you're fucked," Tomi added.

The five Black men laughed as Dax tugged the T-shirt over the vest and followed it with the leather jacket. Looking down at himself, he did look bulkier and maybe slightly more intimidating. Though muscles had never been his strength. He had other tools in his arsenal.

"Thanks for the vest and for the assistance." Dax dipped his head to Boudreaux respectfully.

"Tomi vouches for you, but more importantly, the manbo says to keep an eye on you and lend a hand if needed. So, I'm here with my friends to lend a friendly hand. What's the plan, skinny man?"

"I want you five to move the vehicles up closer, then protect my exit. I'm going to be coming out with up to three people."

"You're going to walk in there by yourself. Into a bar full of bikers, and walk out with the hostages?" Boudreaux asked, his face incredulous.

One of the men he'd brought with him started laughing. "You got a second vest for him, Dreaux? 'Cause with the big balls he's swinging, he's gonna need extra protection."

The rest of the guys cracked up.

"Sorry. Didn't think to bring an iron jockstrap," Boudreaux said before turning back to Dax. "So that's the plan? Wait for you. Watch the front door and protect the hostages?"

"Pretty much."

Boudreaux looked at Tomi. "He's scrawny, but he's gutsy. It'll be a glorious funeral. He'll just need to find one more pallbearer. We're one short. He want a traditional brass band?"

"Sounds fine to me." Dax popped his collar up and adjusted his shoulder length hair so it lay outside the jacket. "See you in a bit, gentlemen. I'll walk from here."

THIRTY-FOUR

DAX

Dax strolled confidently across the street and through the gap between the bikes. The burly doorman stepped out from his nook under the porch lights.

"Who the fuck are you?"

Dax pushed a bit of the flames into his eyes and let his voice partially drop into the hollow airy register his other form used. "I'm the guest of honor. This is your one warning. Walk away and live for another day." He let the flames burn brighter.

The doorman backed up and slid out of the way, pulling the door open. The man shook as a fine sheen of sweat broke out on his bald head. When Dax cleared the threshold, every eye in the place turned to him, the loud conversation stopping. Only the occasional noise of a glass on wood could be heard along with an occasional stray cough and the blaring strains of some shitty southern-fried rock.

Dax extended an open hand toward the jukebox, letting a bit of his essence intermingle with the electricity flowing through the machine, then gripped and tugged back hard. The jukebox crackled and stopped, the speaker squealing shrilly until it petered out. Sparks flashed as smoke and the scent of burnt electronics wafted into the air. Chairs scraped against the floor as some of the more timid bikers pushed away from him.

A heavy man with a balding gray ponytail stepped out of a door on the back left side of the room. "Who the fuck ruined my jukebox? I'll take my money for it from their hide."

Several hands pointed toward the door and Dax.

"W-who the fuck are you?"

"I'm here to collect my people. You have taken them, and I want them back." His raspy, airy voice carried throughout the silent bar, sending goosebumps and shivers through several of the burly men.

The man with the ponytail took a second before stiffening his spine. "Wanting isn't getting." He laughed, though it sounded empty and forced and ended after a few chuckles. "They've served their purpose."

Dax raised an eyebrow. "And that is?"

"Bait," he replied, pulling a gun from the inside of his black leather vest. He pulled the hammer back and pulled the trigger.

Air whooshed from Dax's lungs as he slammed into the door frame, pain exploding in his chest and back. A second shot punched into the other side of his chest, compounding the pain. As his knees buckled, a third shot smacked into the center of his chest over his heart. It stuttered and skipped several beats. His butt hit the floor, and he slumped against the door frame, his head lolling forward.

Silence reigned, the acrid scent of gunpowder spreading through the room.

"Is...is he dead?" someone asked.

Dax started laughing, at first quietly then he let it grow. As the volume grew, he pulled the last of his humanity from his voice and rolled to the side, pushing his way to standing but keeping his head down. He forced the fires of hell and a burning star into his eyes and let his skull peek through his facial skin. Raising his head, he cut his laugh abruptly short.

"This is your last warning. Flee or perish."

To emphasize it, he shucked the remainder of his human façade and let his robes flow. Raising his right arm, he gripped his fist and brought it down. A long-handled scythe filled his grip. The wooden shaft curved to the ground, a couple grip handles stuck out midway and near the bottom. The huge, curved bill of the blade jutted from the top of the weapon—two feet of gleaming, razor-sharp steel. The whole thing glowed with dark malevolence.

He raised his left hand, pointing toward the man who'd just shot him. "Except for you. You. Belong. To me."

Taking one step forward, he waited for their reaction.

"Shoot him! Now!" the boss screamed.

Reaching out with his left hand open, he clenched it, yanking back, and simultaneously extinguishing the light of his eyes. The bar's lights exploded into darkness, sparks flitting from some of the fixtures. Only an exit sign and the neon bleeding in through the small front windows illuminated the room.

The sound of cocking guns augmented the fitful sparks hissing into the air. Drifting on silent currents, Dax reappeared in the back of the room as a cacophony of gun fire erupted, shattering the silence and blasting the darkness with muzzle flare.

"Where is he? Did anyone hit him?" someone asked as the gunfire slowed to a trickle.

The light of his eyes exploded, the flames flickering hatefully across the room. He swung his scythe in a broad chest-high sweep, harvesting blood and screams. Stepping forward, he reversed directions and brought the scythe through for another pass. A hollow laugh seeped from his mouth, eerie, discordant minor harmonics coloring it.

"Fuck this…" someone mumbled and took off.

Fist on flesh resounded followed by curses and a couple more gunshots. A body hit the ground, its owner groaning piteously. The delicate bouquet of impending death filled Dax's senses and redoubled his laughter. Thus far, he'd only let the blade sing, its edge rending death from life. But if he reached out… If he grasped the frayed thread of the biker's life, he could snap it and draw his soul forth from his body to do with it as he willed.

Letting go of one of the scythe's handles, he brought his hand up briefly before stopping himself. With a frustrated growl, he grabbed the handle and waded into the middle of the room. There were too many targets, too many chances to draw attention. The blade would serve well enough. It could end life like any mundane blade, and it would do the job just as well without involving him in their souls.

Bullets and screams ricocheted around the room, drawing blood and fear from their allies more than causing him any pain. Occasionally, one would whiz through what would have been his human flesh…an odd sensation as it tugged through what wasn't there.

One of the faster bikers made it to the door and barreled out of it, letting a column of light brighten an angular swatch on the floor at the front of the bar. Dax was about to bring his scythe around for another pass when someone switched the lights on, though only about half of them flashed to life.

Dax hesitated for a split second as the change of light flared in his enhanced night vision and was rewarded with a couple rounds in his bulletproof vest covered chest and back, knocking him about. Shifting his grip to the shaft of his scythe, he yanked his hands away from each other as if he were extending the weapon. But instead, the scythe handle transformed into a short shaft about two feet long with a chain at the end that ran fourteen feet, ending in a weighted iron ball shaped like a skull.

Crouching in a fighter's stance, he kept the short-handled scythe low in his right hand as he let the chain run loose in his left hand, the weighted ball thunking ominously onto the hard wooden floor. He surveyed around him as bikers flipped tables and made impromptu barriers to hide behind, leaving him standing in the middle of the room. As he pivoted, looking for the ponytail who'd been giving orders, he brought the chain up and into a slow rotation, speeding it up until it flew above his head, the air whistling eerily through the chain links and the nooks of the skull.

The glint of metal in the dim light drew his eye, and he unleashed the skull, the chain clacking over the bones of his hand as it rattled through. Wood splintered explosively, spraying anyone nearby in slivers. He chuckled maliciously when he felt the shiver of the skull mashing into flesh run up the chain. A pained scream turned the chuckle into a laugh. With a step and a yank, he brought the skull back, cinching up on the chain and sending it back into its deadly rotation.

The only warning he received of the impending attack was a guttural growl and a flash of gray fur leaping at him. Ducking, he pivoted around while maintaining the flight of the skull and brought the scythe blade up. The growl ended in a piteous yelp of pain as he opened up the wolf shifter's stomach mid-flight, spilling his intestines and blood onto the floor as the shifter continued its leap. With a sad thud, the wolf landed in a heap and twitched, letting out an occasional whimper.

He had to remind himself it wasn't a wolf, but a man who was trying to end his existence. But the animalistic noises of pain spiked his anger, his eyes flaring brighter as he lashed out with the skull. Another table disintegrated under the force of his attack, though this time those hiding behind it escaped the retribution of the iron skull.

As he wondered why the bikers' response wasn't more bellicose, the glint of metal peeking over the bar top drew his attention. Pivoting, he unleashed a hasty attack with the skull toward the bar. Instead, muzzle flare ignited his vision and pain blossomed across his chest as he stumbled backwards. Something large caliber had blasted him in the chest, something bigger than the vest had absorbed so far.

Dax cracked into the wall but caught himself before he slid to the ground. At the lull in the action, the less brave of the bikers popped up from their hastily constructed defensive works, the airspace above their heads now clear as his chain lay strung out on the floor, the skull gleaming in the middle of the floor where he'd been standing moments ago.

The bikers opened fire. More rounds pounded into his chest. Though one hit lower, searing pain across the outside of his left ilium. He'd have screamed if he had air in his lungs…or lungs. His knees lost the capacity to hold him upright, and he slid to the bar's dirty floor for the second time that evening. After a few moments, he lost track of the specifics of what was happening, everything blurring into a cacophony of muzzle flashes, exploding gunpowder, and a pummeling of shots hitting his chest.

With each hit, the flames in his eyes grew dimmer until his head flopped forward and all he saw was his tattered robe-covered lap. Even that was fading away… A line of scorching hot pain exploded across the right side of the crown of his skull, and his vision ignited, not into flames, but into some deep, darker place.

THIRTY-FIVE

DAX

Aplace devoid of light.

The tightly controlled explosions stopped. The impacts vanished. The muzzle flashes disappeared.

With no air around him, he felt weightless as he existed without a body in a perfect vacuum. Time ceased to exist, because it had yet to exist… A single point of light flickered into his awareness, drawing him toward it, ever expanding. He flew faster as it pulled him in with ever-increasing force.

Soon, the point of light encompassed all in front of him. He tried to shift his awareness and found what felt like the place from where he'd started. In reverse, he now stared at a single tiny point of darkness, until it blinked away and he was surrounded completely by the point of light.

Without control, he felt like he should be screaming. He'd been screaming… That was something he remembered somehow. But how could he scream when there was only his incorporeal awareness and the point of light, which completely encased him?

Around him, the light contracted and expanded, pulsing at first slowly but then with ever-increasing speed. The pressure pulled and pushed on him until it finally compressed so tightly that it seemed it would never expand again, crushing and constricting tighter and tighter until he was completely enveloped within the singularity.

When he thought that would be his eternity, everything exploded, disgorging light and matter and time in all directions, expanding brutally beyond his comprehension and understanding.

All at once, he was everything and everywhere and in all time and he was nothing…

Then it happened. Where there had only been the awareness and the beginning, an ending occurred. Something exploded and collapsed, destroying all its own possibilities. But from it, the ending of possibilities was birthed.

THIRTY-SIX

JAMIE

"Is...is he dead?" someone whispered.

"Go check him," someone else replied.

"Fuck you, you go do it."

Jamie, body tensed, breathed harshly. Once Dax showed up and the lights went out, she could only see flashes of gunfire. The constant screams and gunshots sent adrenaline screaming through her veins. Her only hope as she tried and failed to wiggle free from her restraints was Dax's victory. If he was dead...

So were they.

There would be no way the bikers would let them live after she'd created so much death and mayhem by ratting them out to the man she was supposed to kill. Biker gangs weren't known for being the forgiving types, and this one even less so.

"What the fuck..." a man said in a barely audible gasp.

The screams started again. After the intense silent interlude, the sudden return to mayhem caused another burst of adrenaline. Though there was the impact of weapons on flesh, the guns stayed still for the moment. Futilely, she tried to break or slip out of the ropes, but they refused to give any ground.

"Don't just stand there. Shoot him!" It sounded like the man with the ponytail—the head biker. "Put one in his fucking head!"

"Fuck that, we filled him full of lead and he's coming for us…" someone replied. Outside, motorcycles fired up and rumbled away at high speeds.

After a brief delay, the gunfire resumed, and the pitch of the screams intensified. Then something smashed a bunch of glass. A hollow, raspy, terrifying laugh filled her ears and sent uncontrollable shivers through her body. She wished he'd stop laughing. It turned her bones to jelly. But as long as he kept laughing, her chances of getting out of here alive remained a possibility. Though she couldn't ignore the laughter, she tried to push aside the sound of bodies being violently destroyed. But that was easier said than done. Those sounds would haunt her for a long time.

Her mom squealed when someone burst through the doors into the backroom. The big, bald man with the ponytail—the one who'd started this all when she'd walked in on him beating her father—looked around frantically.

"Ivar? Ivar?" ponytail yelled from the back room. "Where is he? I'm going to kill that coward."

With the doors open, the carnage outside in the main bar grew even louder. She couldn't avoid the sounds now, not that she really could earlier.

Looking back over his shoulder into the bar, the biker boss stepped deeper into the room, his eyes finally settling on Jamie. A nasty grin spread over his face. He crossed the room and grabbed her by the hair. Pulling out a knife, he sawed it across the ropes tying her to the chair. As he freed her, she struggled, but he stopped her by the expedient of yanking harder on her hair. She screamed in pain.

Once the last length of rope around her ankles snapped, he dragged her up from the chair and pulled her along with him toward the bar.

"You're finally going to be of some use to me," he mumbled as they crossed the back room.

She tried to keep her balance while avoiding more tugs on her hair. Once they cleared the door, he yanked her in front of him and wrapped one of his meaty arms around her while pressing a gun to her head.

"Drop the weapon!" he shouted. "Or I paint the walls with her brains."

A terrified whimper fell from her lips. She wasn't sure who to be more afraid of. Dax wasn't Dax right now. The Grim Reaper stood in the middle of the room, surrounded by the gory bodies of his victims. In his hands, he held a short-handled scythe attached to a long chain with a big metal ball on it. Blood and viscera covered the ball. She'd seen weapons like this in the martial arts movies Cory liked to watch. He had a scythe attached to a meteor hammer.

Her stomach gave a nauseous gurgle and a small lurch. Instead of looking at the blood and guts, she focused on the burning eyes and let them fill her vision. They still scared the shit out of her, but at least they kept her from throwing up all over herself.

When Dax hesitated, ponytail pressed the gun into her head harder. "I'm ready for the Valkyries to take me to Valhalla. Are you two ready for a trip to hell?"

She had to do something. She growled through the gag and tried to lurch forward and break his grip. But he squeezed tight and pressed the gun into her head even harder. He shifted along with her, keeping his control of her.

"Drop it!" He pulled back the hammer on the gun.

Jamie's eyes widened. She breathed raggedly, her body trembling, and her attention focused entirely on the feel of metal pressed into her temple. He dragged her closer to the wall, glass crunching under his feet. Though she went along with him, she stayed alert for any chance.

When he stumbled on something and more glass cracked, she lifted her foot, stomped down with all her might, and lunged for the gun. She twisted, trying to break his grip, then turned her back to him and drew forward her leg. With a muffled scream of effort, she unleashed a mule kick into his knee. He grunted, and they tumbled to the ground.

As they struggled for control of the gun, it went off, filling her nose with exploded gunpowder and unleashing a nasty squeal in her ears. She ignored them as she wrestled with the bigger man. She was faster than him, but she couldn't break out of his grip, and no matter how hard she hit him, he seemed to shrug it off as he tried to regain his control over her. She wished she didn't have a gag, because she had no qualms about fair fights and biting if it meant her life.

Stars exploded and her world grayed out for a moment as an elbow slammed into her head. She tumbled away from him. But as she fell, she wrenched the gun from his hands, landing in a heap with the gun under her.

Nearby, the big biker dove to the ground, then rose onto his knees, the glint of steel reflecting from something he held—someone's discarded gun. A vile grin on his face, he swept the gun over to point it at Jamie then back to Dax.

She coughed, smoke assaulting her lungs. As her ears cleared, the crackling of flames told her from where it was coming. Flames nearly engulfed the back bar, and an occasional bottle exploded into shards. Soon, the whole bar would be consumed.

The man with the ponytail forced his way to his feet, coughing against the smoke. "Hem. I guess you don't need lungs, do you?" His self-amused chuckle ended in another cough. "I guess there's no point in talking more." He pulled back the hammer and aimed it toward Dax's head.

Dax took a step back, raising his hands, though she couldn't tell if he was asking for mercy or about to launch another attack.

"No…" Jamie whispered, rolling to her knees and pushing her way to standing.

She cocked the gun and squeezed the trigger before she had more time to think about it. The shot vibrated up her arms, and a waft of spent gunpowder joined the stench of burning wood and plastic. She stared at the biker, her eyes wide and unblinking.

Blood dribbled down his ponytail from the hole in the back of his head. He thudded to his knees, his body upright for a moment before he collapsed, falling on his face. Dead.

As she stared at the man she'd just shot, something heavy and metal thudded to the floor. A whimper rose from her throat. She'd killed a man. Shot him in the back of the head. He was dead.

She inhaled sharply and looked down at her gun-filled hands. She'd used that gun to kill a man. A small stream of smoke rose from the barrel. Her body trembled, and she forced the gun away from her. It tumbled from her fingers and fell to the floor with a thud heavier than a lead brick.

THIRTY-SEVEN

DAX

The smoke spread throughout the bar, and the flames became more indiscriminate as they fed their appetite. Dax heard muffled screams from the back room. He stepped forward and peered through the door. The woman, her chair still standing, caught sight of him and screamed louder. Moving back out of her line of sight, he pulled his chain in and returned it to its place in the aether where he kept his scythe.

"Jamie," he rasped out. "Go free your parents." When she didn't move, he added some extra weight to his voice. "Jamie. Go."

She shook her head and scrambled to her feet. He knew he needed to put his human façade back on, but he loathed the thought of what his shoulder would feel like once it was encased in flesh. That last bullet had been one of the rune covered ones. He didn't fancy finding out how the other nicks and cracks would feel once he was wearing muscle and flesh again.

Taking a deep breath, though it was more symbolic than real, he pulled his body around his bones. A thousand points of pain radiated from every corner of his being, but the shoulder burned with an immediate fiery agony.

Behind him, the door burst open. He spun, reaching for his scythe again.

"Dude, what the fuck did you do in here?" Tomi asked as he looked around, his jaw hanging open.

Boudreaux and his friends shoved their way in behind him. "Shit. Let's strip the place down before there's nothing left. Start with the guns."

Tomi shook his head. "I'll hit the office."

"Help!" Jamie yelled from the back room.

Wondering what new trouble she'd found, he jogged around the bar, crouching low to keep under the billowing smoke. She had the gag out of her mother's mouth but couldn't remove her bindings.

He bent over and ran his hands over the rope. If her mom was a wolf shifter like her, and why wouldn't she be, she should have been able to pull the rope apart. But underneath the outer coils, something strong and powerful ran through its core.

"Stand back." Dax waited until Jamie scrambled out of the way to finish pulling his scythe back into this plane.

Careful to keep the long, curved blade in check, he slid it along the rope between her hands, then pulled. When his blade met the magical thread running through it, he felt a zing of familiarity run up his arm just before his blade broke its power and severed the rest of the rope. Stepping around front, he severed the cords keeping her feet tied to the legs of the chair.

Jamie now squatted next to a man who was probably her father. He was coming to and starting to struggle. She shoved him from his back onto his side none too gently, then stepped out of the way, making room for Dax to free the man.

"Hurry the fuck up, Dax. This place is about to fall around our ears," Tomi yelled.

Looking up, he saw that Tomi was right. The bit of divider running along the doorway from this room to the main room had protected them from the earlier smoke, but now it was so thick it was falling into the room, turning into a stinky haze. Jamie held her shirt over her nose but still coughed as she helped her mother up.

Her father grunted as Dax slammed the backside of his scythe's blade along his back before yanking it free and slicing through the ropes holding his hands. Flipping the blade, he swung it between the man's legs and severed the rope. Now freed, her father jumped up to flee but immediately fell on his face.

Jamie's mother was smarter and took her time to rub some feeling into her ankles. Threading an arm under her mother's shoulders, Jamie got them moving toward the exit. Her father, not able to stand or unwilling at this point, crawled after them, mewling and coughing.

"Come on, Dax!"

He nodded to Tomi and strode out. When he passed Jamie's father, the man lurched to his feet and caught himself against the nearest wall then threw himself forward, barely maintaining verticality as he tumbled out the front exit. Tomi peeked in one last time and held the door open for Dax as he strode out.

Off in the distance, they heard the sound of sirens.

"Cops or fire, either way, we don't want to be here when they arrive," Boudreaux said, waving his buddies into the van they'd arrived in as they loaded guns and other stuff they'd purloined. "Tomi, if you ever need someone to run the streets with, let me know. You know how to put some money in a brother's pocket."

"You got it!" Tomi waved as Boudreaux jumped into the van.

"Where'd all these vans and trucks come from?" Dax asked, noticing several vehicles that hadn't been there when he entered the bar earlier.

"We called some friends. Figured there'd be some good scavenging." Tomi grinned wickedly. "Lot of the boys got themselves some nice bikes. Now let's go!"

Tomi jogged off toward his car. Jamie and her family stood around, looking confused and scared.

"Shit. Follow us." Dax waved them after him as he followed Tomi.

Dax held the front seat forward as they squeezed into the back seat of Tomi's car, squishing together. He threw the seat back, eliciting a pained male grunt from the back. Dax took one last look at the bike bar, his eyes narrowing. Something powerful approached.

A being stepped out of the flames, the souls of the dead bikers in tow. She stood tall, with a bit of droop in her face and shoulders. The light cast shadows over half of her, but the shadow covered area appeared darker than any shadow should have been while the other half looked like the normal skin of a fair white woman.

Dax chuckled to himself. The Norse had come to collect the souls of the bikers, but she was no Valkyrie and they weren't going to join the honored dead.

Hel made eye contact with him and gave him a single nod before raising her hand and opening a pit beneath her. She violently shoved the souls into it and sealed it after them. With a quirk of her lip, she faded into nothing. As if her presence had restrained the fire, the roof collapsed, sending sparks and flames belching into the night.

"Dude, come one, we got to go!" Tomi yelled, revving the engine.

With nothing left to see, Dax jumped in. Before the door was even closed, Tomi lurched forward. Dax yanked his hand back, letting momentum close the door for him, then buckled himself in.

Behind him, he could see the distant flashes of red and blue lights as Red City Fire and Rescue showed up too late to stop the fire or rescue anyone. As soon as Tomi found a turn, he took it, weaving through the neighborhood.

"Where do you want me to drop them off?" Tomi asked.

Jamie's mother spoke up. "I don't care where you drop him off, but he won't be going home with us."

"Honey…"

"No. No more. I don't want to see anything from you but divorce papers."

Dax pulled down the passenger side shade and opened the mirror. Jamie's dad slumped into the tiny space, pouting, his eyes darting around as if he was working on his next scheme. Jamie did her best to try to push closer to her mother, but there was no room for separation in the tiny back seat.

Tomi, doing his best to hold in his snicker, cleared his throat. "I don't think we should take them back to the girl's place. A lot of those bikers managed to get on their bikes and ride."

Dax rotated his shot shoulder, wincing. "I didn't go to all that trouble to free her to just turn her back over to them." He sighed. "The boy is probably still waiting in the tearoom. I guess that's the best place to start for now. Let's give the bikers some time to clear out and regroup. Once word gets out, they'll probably go underground as soon as possible."

"Right," Tomi replied, reaching down to turn on the radio so he could drown out the bitter silence coming from the backseat.

THIRTY-EIGHT

DAX

Tomi turned the music up, singing and banging his head along with the beat. Dax, tired of watching the cold stares, pouting, and scowls, flipped the shade up. Every bump they hit, and there were plenty in a city where corruption left no potholes filled, sent jolts of pain through his body, but at least it distracted him from the backseat.

When they arrived at the bar, he held the seat to let Jamie and her family out. Tomi disappeared inside.

Jamie's mom whirled on her husband. "Get your stuff and get out of the apartment. If you take anything that isn't yours, I swear I'll call those bikers myself and tell them where to find you."

"We live on the other side of town and the buses stopped running for the night," he whined.

She folded her arms across her chest. "You got two feet and a pair of shoes on them. Carry your own pathetic ass out of here."

His shoulders slumped. "What if I get mugged?"

She barked a bitter laugh. "What do you have to take? You've pissed everything away." Then, she turned her back on him.

Mumbling, the man shuffled off, disappearing around a corner. Dax stood silently, trying to mind his own business. He breathed a sigh of relief when the side door opened in the alley, and Tomi poked his head out.

"Hey, Dax, come on." He disappeared back inside, save for his arm, which held the door open.

Checking to make sure he didn't see any cops, Dax ushered Jamie and her mother down the alley and into the door, directing them to head into the tearoom. Tomi lifted his hand and pantomimed a drink.

Dax nodded. "Whiskey." Then he disappeared into the tearoom.

"You smell like smoke," Cory said, his arms wrapped around Jamie as he hugged her tightly. When he pushed back, he had a huge grin plastered across his face.

"Yeah, well, things got messy," Jamie replied.

Dax slid around the counter and filled several glasses of water, setting them on the bar. Jamie's mother took two, handing one to her daughter.

After draining half the water, she set it down, clasping her hands in front of her. "I don't know who you are or why you helped us, but thank you."

He held out a dirty hand. "I'm Dax."

"Sharon." She took his hand and gave it a quick shake.

Jamie stepped up beside her mom and took a glass. "Thank you, Dax, for…"

"I owe you, Jamie. If you hadn't stepped in at the last moment there, he'd have put one of those bullets in my head and I'm not sure I could have shrugged that off." He didn't like owing anyone, especially someone who'd shot him, even if she'd made up for it in the end.

Jamie's eyes flicked to her mother then back to Dax. "Um, after everything, I think we're even."

He nodded, looking at her knowingly. He'd keep her earlier transgression secret. It would only do harm to have it aired now. "Fair enough."

Tomi slid into the room, a bottle in his hands. "I have the cure to what ails you."

Dax pulled out five glasses and placed them on the bar. Before anyone could say anything, Tomi poured a finger in each glass, setting the bottle on the bar where it would be easy to grab for a refill.

Sharon raised her nose in the air. "I'm not sure I'm in the mood for whiskey. And I think the kids are too young for such things."

Dax lifted an eyebrow. The hard eye roll from Jamie nearly made him chuckle. Cory's shoulders sagged, and he gave a half-hearted pout before his ubiquitous, friendly expression returned. Neither of them reached for the glasses.

"Ugh. We need to find a place to stay. Then we have to try to get our stuff from the apartment without being seen by those bikers," Sharon said, pacing away from the bar.

Jamie waited until her mother's back was to her and slugged down the shot of whiskey, wheezing as it burned its way down. She covered it with a faked cough—natural enough after surviving a fire. "Mom, Cory said we can stay with him. There's plenty of spare room."

Chuckling to himself, Tomi filled the glass so it looked untouched. Dax shook his head, a faint smile tugging at his lips.

Dax grabbed a glass of whiskey and leaned up against the bar. "Tonight is probably the safest time to clear out your apartment. I guarantee those bikers are going to be too scared to go looking for vengeance at the moment. They'll be in survival mode until someone shows up to take charge. That's assuming they can pry them out of whatever deep, dark hole they find to hide in."

Sharon turned around, staring at him with narrowed eyes. "Are you sure?"

"Mom," Jamie said, her voice deadly serious. "Trust him when he says they're terrified." She turned to Cory. "Can you help us get our stuff out tonight? We can see about a cheap rental truck to get the furniture in the morning."

"Jamie…" Sharon started, her voice slipping into "mom" mode.

"Look, Mom. It's the best plan we have."

Sharon turned on Cory. "How are you involved in this? Do they know where you live?"

"I don't think so. When they came out and grabbed me, I stashed my ID in the car before they pulled me out. They didn't go looking for it." He shrugged, side-stepping the question of his true involvement..

Jamie stepped up next to Cory, staring her mom in the eyes. "I guess if we go back to the apartment and Cory's car and ID are where he left them, then we'll know we can go there for a little bit."

Sharon clenched her jaw. "I don't know…"

"Mom. Would you trust me for once? We have to get out of that place fast before they do come looking for dad or us. We can move our stuff out fast and go to Cory's for now. Then we can make a real plan."

THIRTY-NINE

DAX

They waited until Jamie and her people left, then slid the door shut, locking it. Tomi took the first undrunk shot and tossed it back, then grabbed the second.

"Good thing you didn't pour doubles." Dax smirked, throwing back the last half of his shot.

Tomi chuckled. "Yeah. I intend to go up front and drink some much better whiskey." He picked up the next shot, but only sipped from the glass. "Now what?"

"What do you mean? We keep our heads down and go about our business." Dax shrugged.

Raising a skeptical eyebrow, Tomi leaned closer, sliding onto a bar stool. "Do you think that's even going to be possible?"

"I just want to run this bar and keep a low profile." He leaned back against the back bar, folding his arm across his chest.

"I get that's what you want, Dax. But really, is that even possible?"

Dax made to speak, but Tomi held up a hand to forestall him.

"Think about it. A lot of bikers ran out of that bar and rode off. Do you think they're going to renounce their beliefs and allegiances? I mean, maybe some will… I'm sure you managed to scare a fair few of them. But do you think those kinds of beliefs just disappear? They're steeped in ignorance and hate. Those kinds of beliefs are hard to wash away. Plus, they didn't just try to kill you, they tried to kill you for someone or some reason."

"Why? Since I landed here, I've minded my own business and kept to myself." He swirled the whiskey as he thought about it, taking a sip.

" 'Since you landed'?" Tomi chuckled, shaking his head. "May I remind you, you 'landed here' and immediately killed a biker? You're currently walking around in his body."

He narrowed his eyes, focusing on Tomi. "I made some modifications…"

"You burned off the tattoos, but that's about it. Also, might I remind you, you took the money that biker had extorted from people like my Mama and used it to buy this bar. Did you think they'd never come looking?"

"It might not be the same gang. I don't remember what their patches were."

Tomi raised an eyebrow. "You really want to stake our lives on that?"

Dax sighed, shaking his head. He lifted his glass and looked at the amber liquid as he swirled it, letting the light play across its surface. "I guess I didn't really think of it much at the time." He threw the shot back, and he exhaled noisily at the burn. "We've gone several years without being noticed."

He looked down at the bar between them, staring at it as he thought over Tomi's words. His friend was probably right. He knew this kind of stuff. But Dax was sincere when he said he wanted to lie low and return to the status quo. He'd dipped his toe into a fair bit of power before he was finally done at the biker bar.

There were those who were supposed to be watching him, making sure he kept his nose clean. He wasn't interested in voiding the deal they'd forced on him, but where was the line? When was he allowed to defend himself? They'd forced him to become a nearly powerless human.

Though, as evidenced by earlier tonight, the walls they'd built between him and his own powers weren't as strong as they'd told him… Or perhaps they weren't as strong as they themselves even thought. He'd attracted the interest of Hel, though she hadn't been in the gang who'd teamed up against him. Or perhaps she had been keeping an eye on the scumbag bikers, waiting to collect them as soon as she was able.

"Yo, you going to just space out forever?" Tomi took the last glass and poured it back into the bottle. "I'm not going to burn my liver up on that stuff when there's better to be had, and I feel like celebrating."

Dax raised an eyebrow. "What are we celebrating?"

A wicked grin spread across Tomi's face as he hitched his eyebrows up once. "Wait here."

Tomi slipped out of the tearoom, then reappeared a couple minutes later. He had two wrinkly brown paper bags in one hand and a briefcase in the other.

"Presents? You shouldn't have…" Dax deadpanned.

Tomi paused for a moment, his head quirked to the side. "Did… did you just make a joke?"

Dax blinked slowly at him, the corner of his mouth twitching. He tried to hold his lips straight, but the quizzical look on Tomi's face coupled with the twitch in his friend's lip became too much. He grinned and chuckled lightly.

Tomi let out a quick laugh and shook his head. "There might be hope for you after all."

"So, what's in those?" Dax causally pointed between the bag and the briefcase, using his fore and middle fingers held together.

"Well, my friend, fortunately our two-wheeled vehicle enthusiasts had business interests other than trying to kill you." He set down the briefcase then dumped the bag onto the bar.

Wads of bills tumbled out into a pile that seemed to keep growing. With a quick snatch of his hand, Dax grabbed one that slid off the pile and fell off the edge. He set down the empty whiskey glass and thumbed through the wad of bills. All hundreds.

He flipped through them again. "Every bundle?"

"All hundies, and there's more in the briefcase."

Shaking his head, he forced himself to look up.

Tomi had a broad and open grin plastered across his face. "Who-ever the boss biker was… Well, when you busted up their bar, he didn't close his safe when he popped out to check on you. I left the drugs." He pulled out the second bag and upended it on the other side of the bar. A bale of plastic wrapped green herb bounced off the bar. "At least most of them. I hope this is good shit."

"It's legal here, Tomi. Why would they have bales of pot?"

"I don't think they're only a local club. They're probably running it to states where it's not legal. We're not that far from several. Besides. Free weed tastes better than weed you have to buy." He pulled out a knife and cut a small slit into the plastic wrap. Lifting it to his nose, he took a deep inhalation, a smile spreading across his lips. "This'll do."

"I'm glad you're satisfied with your purloined pot."

" 'Purloined pot,' that's good." Tomi chuckled. "Not right now, but soon, you're going to join me and we're going to fire up some of our ill-gotten gains."

"I've never tried it."

Tomi chuckled. "Then you can check that off your list of human experiences."

"I'll leave it to your discretion. Now, we appear to be out of whiskey…" He left it hanging.

"Help me stash this cash in the safe first. We'll figure out what to do with it later, but the bar top of your tearoom isn't the most secure spot you've got right now." Tomi opened the brown paper sack and used his arm to scoop the pile into the bag. After the bar top was clean, he bent over and picked up the bundles that had fallen to the floor. He stood and was about to crinkle the top closed when Dax stopped him.

He held up the bundle of hundreds. "Don't forget this one."

Tomi held open the bag, tipping the opening toward Dax. "Yeah. Wouldn't want him to get lonely."

Dax tossed the bundle over the bar, and Tomi caught it.

"What about your bale of weed?" Dax asked.

"Stash it behind the bar?"

"Why not? It can hang out with my dried leaf collection." He gestured toward the shelves of loose-leaf tea.

"It'll feel right at home."

Dax tucked the bale out of the way, moving some stuff in front of it to block it, then helped Tomi stash the cash in the safe. Together, they strode into the front of the bar, taking a pair of empty bar stools at the end of the bar.

"Hey, cuz," Tomi said, smiling at his cousin.

"There are my boys!" Little Suzie called. "What'll it be, tonight?" She reached into the undercounter cooler and pulled out a can of Rainier and wiggled it toward Dax. "The usual?"

Dax held up his hand, halting her. "Not tonight. Tomi, it's your call."

"Give him the can, Suz. He'll likely want his beer-flavored water. And a couple good whiskeys. You pick the first round." Tomi took the Rainier from Suzie's hand and opened it, setting it in front of Dax.

A wicked grin spread across her lips. "I know just the thing." She grabbed a bottle of Uncle Nearest 1884 Small Batch from the shelves and filled two of the nice whiskey glasses they kept around for the connoisseurs. "If a Black woman is pouring, she's gonna pour something made by a Black woman."

Dax raised his glass toward Suzie, giving her a nod of acknowledgment before turning to his friend. "Tomi, what should we drink to?"

"Let's drink to the first of more shots…" He hoisted his glass.

"Well, we've already passed the first a few shots ago, but I'll drink to it, anyway." He touched his glass to Tomi's then took a sip. He exhaled, letting the Tennessee whiskey burn before dousing it with a drink from his beer.

It was indeed the first-ish of many more. Too many more. Dax vaguely remembered laughing more in a few hours than he'd laughed in the last year. And when Suzie decided she'd had enough of them, she poured him into a taxi.

FORTY

DAX

As he nearly tumbled out of the elevator, he caught himself on the opposite wall and rallied himself to make the walk down the long hall without falling over. He trailed his fingers along the wall, occasionally relying on its solidity to keep him from finding the floor.

He hummed a tune as he staggered down the hall. He'd never been prone to singing before or at all. But for some reason, he needed to hum a song, though he kept it quiet, he hoped. When he fumbled his keys into the lock, he struggled to bend over and snatch them from cruel gravity and the iron grip of the floor. Eventually, he fished them off the carpet and slid the right one into the lock.

The first thing he noticed when he entered his apartment was the smell of smoke. He lifted his shirt and held it to his nose. It still smelled of fire, but the smoke he smelled was different, more aromatic…

"Byenveni lakay, zanmi m."

Dax whipped his head around toward his couch, stumbling to the side. He caught himself on the back of his recliner. Baron Samedi sat on the couch in his dapper suit and top hat. His feet were resting on the coffee table, his legs crossed. Today, he wore his full human persona—a Black man with dark brown skin, a shaved head, and set of sunglasses with one lens missing. He held a glass of liquor in one hand and a lit cigar in the other. At least he smoked good tobacco, though Dax didn't care for the scent with his human nose. Morty sprawled on his back in the Baron's lap, his front paws sticking up, kneading the air.

"Traitor…" Dax mumbled.

The Baron held his hand holding the drink to his chest and looked affronted. "Mwen? Oswa chat ou?"

Dax nodded his head, figuring it was a relatively neutral greeting. "My pardon—" He belched quietly, covering his mouth. "I would normally show the respect of speaking the Kreyòl, but language access is not as available to me as it used to be. And certainly not in this state."

The Baron laughed. The deep, resonate sound brought a small smile to Dax's lips. "I find the sight of you intoxicated worth the annoyance of speaking English. When you uttered 'traitor,' did you refer to me or to your perfidious four-legged friend here?" He gestured toward the kitten with his glass filled hand.

Dax held his hand and wobbled it side to side.

The Baron laughed again. "Ever honest. What is the name you call yourself in this form?"

"Dax."

"That's succinct enough. I'll be brief, since I'm not sure you can handle a lengthy conversation. Though perhaps we could try sometime while we share as wild a number of drinks as you've consumed this eve." He put the cigar between his teeth, closed his lips, and drew in a puff of smoke, releasing it slowly to haze the air around him.

"What do you want, Baron?"

"Let's just say there are those who are watching you."

"This I know. I've been watched since I was exiled here."

With a chuckle, the Baron raised his glass, tipping it toward Dax, then took a deep drink. "Not everyone watches with their eyes only."

Dax rubbed his temples. He was in no state to untie the word puzzles of trickster gods. "How trustworthy is this information?"

Feigning outrage, the Baron held a hand to his chest. "You wound me, sir."

"I know you."

"Of old, you did, and I'm little changed in the intervening time. My words are honest and offered freely."

Dax swiped a hand over his tired eyes, rubbing them quickly before narrowing them as he evaluated the Baron's words. "Why?"

"Call it a gift of thanks for the kindness you paid Esther." He bowed his neck and lowered his head elegantly. "She was a fine woman and a strong soul, and you gave her a peaceful passing. For that, I am grateful."

Even in his drunken state, the Baron's words rang true and honest. This time. And it didn't mean they wouldn't have a hidden edge later, but in this moment, Dax would have been stupid to ignore the warning in the Baron's words.

"Thank you, Baron. I'd bow in respect, but I'm afraid I'd fall on my face."

The Baron laughed uproariously, throwing his head back. He started to fade away, the laughter the only solid thing left of him in the room. "Bon chans, Misye Lanmò."

As the solid legs disappeared out from under him, Morty fell onto his back and popped up, arching his back and floofing his fur as he looked around, hissing. Dax chuckled at the aggrieved kitten.

Sniffing, he still smelled cigar smoke. The lit cigar floated in the air. The bright cherry at the end flared as if someone were taking a drag. A last puff of smoke filled the air before the cigar dropped from the air, landing on the couch.

Dax's eyes shot open wide as he stared at the lit cigar smoldering away. With a shake of his head to get himself moving, he dashed into the kitchen and came back with a glass of water. He picked up the cigar, pouring the water onto the black spot on the couch the lit cigar had left. When he judged the spot effectively drenched, he dropped the cigar into the glass, letting it hiss as the water put it out.

"Fucking trickster gods…"

He lifted the glass and put it to his lips but caught himself before he did something disastrous. He took it into the kitchen and grabbed a fresh glass of water for himself and flopped into the recliner.

Morty, over the affront the trickster had caused, jumped onto Dax's lap, head butting his empty hand and purring. Absentmindedly, he scratched the kitten's ears and back until the little fluff ball settled down and went to sleep.

Despite the drink, he didn't feel tired thanks to the Baron's warning. Tomi was right. There probably would be no going back, even if there was a "back" to begin with. With a sigh, he rubbed his forehead. The Baron's visit had dampened the…joy—that was the word he settled on, though it took him a bit to find the unfamiliar feeling—of tonight's celebration with Tomi.

He drank the rest of the water and set the glass on the table, being careful not to disturb his kitten. He'd think about the Baron's words later, when he was clear-headed and had time to process them.

For now, he'd focus on his furry little friend, tonight's victory, and the time spent laughing with his friend. Those were good things. Human things. And they'd do for now.

EPILOGUE
DAX

Dax waited outside the building for Tomi. When he saw his friend walk around the corner, he fished the keys from his pocket.

"Catch," Dax said, tossing them to Tomi.

He caught them then held them up. "These my set?"

"Yup." He pulled the door open, holding it for Tomi. "Congratulations. We own the whole building, now."

Tomi got a dopey grin on his face. "This is the first time I've owned something bigger than my car."

"I mean, it needs a lot of work, but it's ours."

"I know. Mama's already making lists of all the equipment she'll need for the restaurant. At least some of the stuff already there is salvageable." Tomi used his keys to open the door leading up to the stairs.

"Having your mama's gumbo around the corner from the bar is going to be too convenient." He followed Tomi upstairs.

They'd decided to sink some of their biker money into buying the building the bar was in. It had a defunct restaurant Adele could run, though it wasn't as big or as fancy as the one she'd worked at in New Orleans. But Mama Adele's, as the working title, would be able to serve home-style New Orleans cooking to the neighborhood, including directly to the bar. They hadn't decided what to do with the apartments on the upper floors. Most of them needed to be gutted entirely before they could be built out properly.

Ahead, Tomi paused, unlocking the door that opened onto the roof. The flat roof was one of their favorite features and promised to be a delightful place to retire to on sunny days such as today.

"Nice, you already set us up," Tomi said, stopping by two patio chairs with a small table sitting between them. A cooler sat on the ground under the table. He set his backpack down and pulled out a six-pack of Rainier tallboys. Pulling two off the ring and throwing the rest into the cooler, he popped the tops and set them on the table. Next he pulled out a pipe and a small bag of their purloined pot. "My friend, we're going to celebrate our new money laundering venture…"

Dax snorted and sank into his chair, grabbing the can for his first cold, spritzy sip.

"I mean, our new restaurant and apartment building purchased with totally legally obtained money…" He winked, loading up the pipe. When it was ready, he took the first puff then passed it to Dax.

Curious, he took his first hit, holding it in like Tomi had, eventually exhaling it with a cough.

Tomi chuckled and took the pipe back, setting it down. With his beer in hand, he raised it toward Dax. "Here's to you. You've always done right by my family since that first night. We appreciate all you've done for us."

Dax lifted his can and tapped it against Tomi's. "Thank you for everything you and your mama have done for me. You're the closest thing I have to friends or family."

Tomi smiled awkwardly, reached into his backpack, and pulled out a small Bluetooth speaker. Soon, they had one of Tomi's old school punk mixes playing in the background of their conversation.

At first, Dax didn't feel anything. But after a while, he noticed his head swirling as he spaced off, a grin playing across his face. Tomi chuckled and handed him a fresh can of beer and another pass at the pipe.

"This isn't bad stuff, certainly not for free." Tomi exhaled.

"Hmm? I wouldn't know."

Tomi took a drink of his beer, then snorted and turned abruptly, spitting his beer out over the roof. Once he got his coughing under control, he turned and laughed. Dax had grabbed the pipe and was taking another puff when he noticed more smoke than there should have been.

"Holy shit, dude, that's a hell of a party trick." Pointing at Dax, Tomi's grin stretched across his entire face.

He looked down and saw what Tomi had pointed out. His human façade had slipped and the smoke he'd inhaled rolled out between his ribs, making him look as if he were on fire. Laughing, he slapped his human skin on and set the pipe down. As he thought about it more, he laughed harder, which resparked Tomi's laughter.

Once the hilarity trickled to a halt, Dax let out a deep sigh and relaxed into his chair. The ridiculous laughter left him feeling lighter and more at peace than he'd felt in ages. He grabbed his beer and enjoyed the cold liquid pouring down his throat.

The sun shone on his face. No one hunted him at the moment, and he was sitting by his friend, having a good time. Today was a good day.

The Red City Reaper rides again in
Death Orders a Double.
Keep reading for a brief preview.

THE RED CITY REAPER RIDES AGAIN IN

DEATH ORDERS A DOUBLE

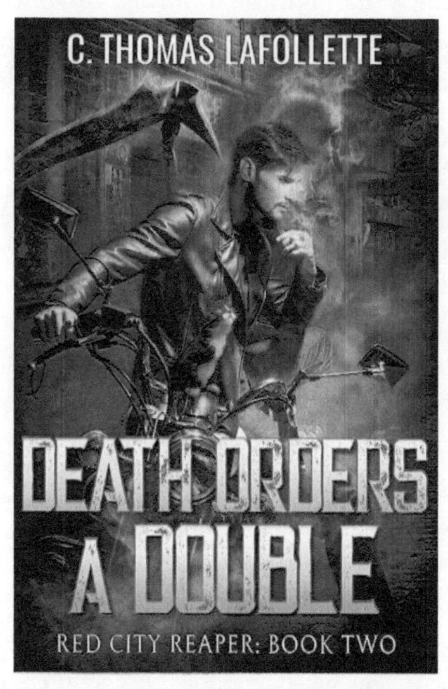

CHAPTER 1 - DAX

Dax peered at his watch surreptitiously for the third time in an hour. Normally, Tomi would be working the night shift with Suzie, but he'd asked for it off. In truth, Dax didn't need to even be there. The rough rain had kept even the regulars home. Usually it didn't rain this hard in the middle of the spring.

"Don't worry about Tomi," Suzie said, stopping to lean up against the bar. "He'll be fine."

Today, the short black woman had her natural hair in two puffs. She wore holey black jeans and a black band T-shirt with the collar cut out and the waist hem removed to reveal her midriff. Her thick-soled Docs elevated her a couple inches, though she was still a few short to reach average.

"I know. It's just been a while since he's had a date." It had been a couple months since the night he'd burned down the biker bar, and he was glad things seemed to be returning to normal. Though, the extra work of getting the restaurant ready for Adele to open filled a lot of the spare time he used to have.

Suzie snorted. "You're not kidding." Tipping her head toward the can of beer in front of him, she asked, "Need another?"

He lifted the can and threw back the last warm swallow. "Gack. Yeah."

Laughing, Suzie cleared the empty and grabbed a full from the undercounter cooler, popping the top and setting it front of him.

A skinny white man in ratty faded black jeans and a matching denim jacket sauntered a bit unsteadily to the bar. "Suzie, my love, when will you agree to go out on a date with me?"

Suzie glanced toward Dax, rolling her eyes. "When you stop being a straight white man, Chet."

"Alas, our love will go unrequited then…"

" 'Our'? You got a mouse in your pocket or something?"

Straightening up on his bar stool, Dax swiveled around and put on his grumpy face, which in all fairness was almost always his normal expression. "Chet. You know you're not supposed to hit on the bartenders. If I have to warn you again, I'll eighty-six you."

Chet leaned toward Dax. "But—"

"Unless the next words out of your mouth are an apology and a promise to remember the rules, I'll add you to the wall of assholes, right now."

Chet, head hanging, turned toward Suzie and mumbled something.

"I'm sorry. I didn't hear you." Suzie leaned closer, her hand cupped around her ear and an eyebrow raised.

"I apologize, Suzie. I won't let it happen again."

Narrowing her eyes, Suzie nodded once, her shoulders relaxing a little. "What can I get you?"

"A shot of whiskey." He set a ten dollar bill on the bar.

Pulling a rocks glass from the stack, she plunked it down on the bar top a bit more forcefully than was necessary and grabbed the well whiskey from the trough where the other well liquors were stored. She kept a careful eye on the pour, making sure Chet didn't get a drop more than what was considered a shot.

Chet almost made like he was going to complain then caught the thunder in Suzie's eyes and thought better of it, slamming the shot back.

Suzie snatched the ten. "Thanks for the tip."

Sighing, Chet wound his way through the bar and left.

"Thanks for having my back, Dax," Suzie said, clearing the glass from the bar.

Dax shrugged. "Everyone deserves a harassment free work environment. If he does it again, take his picture and add it to the wall of assholes."

Tomi had found an old polaroid for the purpose not long after they opened the bar. When it had broken, they replaced it with one of the new versions that were becoming popular. Once a patron made the wall of assholes, they rarely got off of it. It was a far more reliable justice system than the courts of Red City.

"If he argues it or tries to give you shit, bring out the judge." Dax smirked and winked at Suzie before taking a deep drink of the cold, cheap beer.

The judge was two-thirds sized wooden baseball bat they kept behind the bar to handle anyone who decided they had more booze and balls than brains. They'd never had to use it in earnest—usually a mere appearance was enough to get the idea across.

The door to the bar opened, and Dax swiveled on the bar stool, sagging in disappointment when a white man in his last twenties or early thirties wearing a gray suit walked into the bar. The few regulars who had ventured out looked up from their conversations to check out the stranger.

Men in suits, in Dax's experience, meant trouble. But city officials and inspectors rarely were out and about at this time of night. If it was a liquor agent running an ID sting, they typically tried to look appropriate to the venue. Dax narrowed his eyes as the man approached the bar.

The man stepped up to the bar, staring at the wall of liquor bottles on the back bar. Absentmindedly, he hoisted himself up onto a stool. "Damn, you've got a good whiskey selection. I'd like some of the Dickel Bottled in Bond, please."

"I'm going to need to see your ID first," Suzie asked.

She must have been getting the same vibe Dax had. The man raised an eyebrow but grinned politely, pulling his wallet out of the inside breast pocket of his suit jacket, and handed it to Suzie. She looked at it thoroughly under the light of the small lamp they kept behind the bar, even going so far as to take out the UV flashlight they kept for checking seals and larger denomination bills to make sure someone wasn't trying to float a counterfeit by them.

Making a small noise to indicate it surprisingly checked out, she handed the ID back to the man. "Dickel Bottled in Bond it is. Rocks?"

"Neat, please."

She reached for one of the scratched up rocks glasses, like the one she'd just served Chet in. The man winced, his eyes flicking to the nice dram glasses they kept for higher quality whiskeys. She snickered and grabbed a dram glass for him.

He pulled a credit card from his wallet and set it on the bar. "Can you leave it open?"

Suzie nodded and grabbed the card, clipping it up by the register. The man took a sip and sighed happily, going back for another drink.

"Rough day?" Suzie leaned against the bar, propping herself up on one elbow.

"I just finished work for the day."

"Yikes. I'm guessing you weren't working the swing shift at the old suit factory."

The man chuckled. "No. Accounting. Quarterly taxes are due soon. Didn't want to go home to unpacked boxes, so I thought I'd see what this place was about."

Dax eyed the man. He seemed to check out, though he wasn't sure why a man in a suit would pick their dive for his drinking needs. The thought about taking a peak at his life thread to see if he could glean anything from it but decided against it. The man appeared to be just a whiskey lover in a suit looking for a drink. The only suspicious about him was Dax's heightened paranoia after the recent shootings.

"Well, welcome to the House of the Rising Sun Pub and Teahouse. I'm Little Suzie."

He nodded and extended a hand. "I'm Geoffrey." He leaned a little closer after Suzie shook his hand. "Is this really a tearoom?"

Suzie snorted, her eyes flicking toward Dax. "In the back room, though it's not open this time of night."

"Hmm," Geoffrey sat back on his bar stool and contemplated his whiskey, the conversation apparently exhausted.

Everyone was welcome at the Rising Sun, but they didn't often get someone in a suit who chose to stay as a patron. Geoffrey seemed comfortable, ordered a good whiskey, and was polite. They could do far worse than a regular customer of his type.

The sound of the door opening drew Dax's attention away from the new customer, but before he could swivel around to see who it might be, Suzie called out, "Hey, Cuz!"

Dax relaxed. Tomi had arrived—Dax checked his watch—at a time that meant nothing to Dax. He didn't know if this time indicated a good date or a bad date. He'd never even been on one. It seemed a silly human pursuit and meant nothing to him.

"So… How'd it go?" Suzie waggled her eyebrows at her cousin.

Tomi, saying nothing, pulled his large bulk up onto the barstool between Dax and Geoffrey, resting his elbows on the wooden bar top. With a groan, his head sank onto his hands.

"Not well, I take it?" Dax asked quietly.

"I don't know," Tomi replied, leaving his head in his hands.

Suzie reached out and patted his forearm. "Sorry, Cuz. Can I get you a little liquid condolence?"

"Give me a tallboy of Rainier." Tomi lifted his head when the beer was slid in front of him.

Dax spun to face Tomi, resting his elbow on the bar. "What happened?"

"I'm not sure. We seemed to be doing good. The conversation was flowing. I made her laugh a few times. I thought I was a shoo-in for at least a second date. Then…" He huffed and shook his head. "Then she asked me my star sign."

Suzie snorted. "Seriously? 'Hey, baby, what's your sign?'"

Tomi nodded, taking a deep drink from the can. "I didn't think anything of it, so I told her. Then it was like Antarctica in there. I could see her interest waning until she called the date, saying she had a meeting in the morning she needed to get rest for."

"Did she say why?" Suzie asked.

"No. I was so thrown off by the sudden change, I couldn't get my mind working fast enough. All I know is she asked me my sign, then couldn't get out of there fast enough."

"That sucks, Cuz. If that's all it took, then she wasn't a good fit for you." Suzie patted his hand then walked to the end of the bar to help a customer.

"She's right," Dax said. "You're the best guy I know. If she couldn't see that, then she's a fool."

"Thanks, boss."

Dax felt bad for his friend, but at least it had only been a first date. It had been a while, but the last time Tomi had dated anyone, he'd gotten attached after a few dates and had been sad for a while. He'd probably get over this quickly. But what did he know?

Tomi shoved the empty can toward Suzie.

"Want another?" she asked.

"No, I'm going to head out. I have to help mama in the morning." He shoved the heels of his palms into his eyes and sighed.

Dax signaled to put the beer on his tab, not that any of his employees ever paid full price.

Standing up, Tomi waved then headed out the door without saying anything.

"I hope he's not too upset," Dax said.

Suzie shrugged. "He's always been a bit of a romantic, so he can take it a hard when things don't go as well as he wants them to. But he's resilient."

Finishing his beer, Dax threw down a few dollars to cover Suzie's tip. "Since it's not likely to pickup, I'm going to head home and make sure the Morty hasn't burned down the apartment."

"Later, Dax." Suzie turned to Geoffrey. "Another?"

"Sure. Uh, who's Morty?"

Suzie laughed. "His kitten."

The Red City Reaper rides again in
Death Orders a Double.

CONTENTS

GLOSSARY

Adyeu - Goodbye

Bon chans - Good luck

Bonswa - Good afternoon/evening

Bourré - A popular card game played in the New Orleans region of Louisiana

Byenveni lakay, zanmi m - Welcome home, my friend

Cher - dear (a term of endearment)

Lwas - spirit, god, saints

Manbo - female voodoo priest

Manman - mother (a term of respect)

Misye Lanmò - Mr. Death

Mwen, oswa chat ou? - Me or your cat?

NEWSLETTER

The Centurion Immortal is a Luke Irontree prequel novella and is exclusive to the Dispatches from C. Thomas Lafollette news-letter. Please sign up for your free copy and you'll also receive a twice-monthly news-letter with news, book updates, recipes, drinks tips, and other fun stuff. Your email will never be given out, rented, or sold.

CThomasLafollette.com/newsletter/

ACKNOWLEDGMENTS

Thanks to my talented partner Amy Cissell, my ARC team, and all those who helped make this book come alive.

ABOUT THE AUTHOR

C. Thomas Lafollette is a student of history and a world traveler. He's dined with a Prime Minister, read poetry with Yevgeny Yevtushenko, and drank beer with monks. He's the author of the action-adventure urban fantasy series Luke Irontree & The Last Vampire War and the forthcoming Red City Reaper series. Besides reading and writing, he loves a good action movie, be it a Hollywood blockbuster or a classic Samurai flick, as well as the occasional rom-com. He lives in Portland with his partner – the devastatingly talented author Amy Cissell – his stepdaughter, and their two jerk-face cats.

facebook.com/CThomasLafollette

bookbub.com/authors/c-thomas-lafollette

amazon.com/C-Thomas-Lafollette/e/B09JMTR7W7

goodreads.com/cthomaslafollette

threads.net/@cthomaslafollette

instagram.com/CThomasLafollette

tiktok.com/@cthomaslafollette

ALSO BY C. THOMAS LAFOLLETTE

Luke Irontree & The Last Vampire War

Book 0 - The Centurion Immortal

Book 1 - Dark Fangs Rising - March 22, 2022

Book 2 - Dark Fangs Raging - April 19, 2022

Book 3 - Dark Fangs Descending - May 17, 2022

Book 4 - Blood Empire Reborn - August 23, 2022

Book 5 - Blood Empire Avenged - September 20, 2022

Book 6 - Blood Empire Infiltrated - October 18, 2022

Book 7 - Blood Empire Burning - November 15, 2022

Book 8 - Ancient Sword Falling - March 21, 2023

Book 9 - Ancient Sword Unyielding - August 22, 2023

Book 10 - Ancient Sword Shattering - January 4, 2023

The Luke Irontree Historical Adventures

Rise of the Centurio Immortalis - April 5, 2022

Fall of the Centurio Immortalis - May 31, 2022

The Moonlight Centurion*

The Highway Centurion*

Red City Reaper - A Dark Urban Fantasy Adventure

Book 0 - Dead in Red City*

Book 1 - A Shot For Death - March 26, 2024

Book 1.5 - Death Uncaged - March 21, 2024

Book 2 - Death Orders a Double* - June 25, 2024

Book 3 - Death on the Rocks*

Book 4 - Death with a Twist*

*Forthcoming

Titles and release dates may be subject to change.

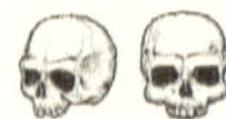